MOOKIN THE MOOK
BOOK 1

MOOKINATION

Brian J. Page

PICCOLO PRESS

MOOKINATION

THE POWER OF THE BLUE

My sincere and heartfelt thanks to all those who helped through numerous rewrites, edits and changes. I would not have reached this point without you.
Particular people need special mention:

The long-suffering Mrs Tina Page,
Paulus Tapender,
Georgina,
Autumn,
And, of course,
Maya.

Edited by The Incredible
Jenny Papworth.

Mookination.com

mookination2020@gmail.com

mookinthemook@gmail.com

Facebook, search: Mookination – The Power Of The Blue

Twitter – Mookination @Mookination

CONTENTS

PROLOGUE

1: OF SECRETS BIG AND SMALL

2: THE ROOT OF ALL LEARNING

EPILOGUE

MAPS

<u>WARNING</u>
THE FOLLOWING MAPS
CONTAIN SPOILERS!

PROLOGUE

1. A Million Years Before Anything

Lush, unchecked growth hid the true nature of the land in every direction as far as the eye could see. The only exceptions were odd up-thrusting plateaux, towering mountain peaks, meandering rivers or plunging gorges; largely it was unbroken and satisfied every shade of green it was possible to perceive.

This gave the landscape a rolling, gentle look, like soft felt, that belied its true nature. Every square centimetre was a battlefield of roots, seeds, fungal growth and creeping, crawling things. Every vertical metre was a triumph in the race for the canopy and life-sustaining sunlight. The battle had raged for millions of years and would doubtless continue for many more.

Above the canopy, the air split apart with a sound like the ripping of stout cloth. A small black circle hovered there, wavering slightly in dawn's early light. Air rushed into the blackness as dozens of small metallic spheres rushed out, silver-grey in appearance and surrounded by a blue haze. They zoomed off, each in a different direction, and were quickly lost to sight. An hour passed, and each returned, disappearing into the blackness whence they came.

The blackness shrank to a mere pinpoint, and the sound of air whistling through the tiny gap could be heard. Another hour passed before the pinpoint irised open once more, drifting upwards until the flow of air was barely noticeable. It hovered there, several kilometres high in the rarefied upper atmosphere. Then it stabilised and winked open in a wide oval shape, a vast black cut-out in the sky.

A lens-shaped disc drifted inexorably from the blackness, barely clearing the hole at its widest point. It was followed by ten more of exactly the same size and by many, many more of varying smaller diameters. Each was the same silver-grey and surrounded by a blue-tinged halo.

The larger craft stayed in rough loose formation as they sank into the atmosphere; the smaller craft zoomed off. Like their even smaller brethren, each chose a different direction and vanished into the distance.

The eleven big ships chose a large lake, one of the planet's largest bodies of fresh water, and settled on the surface, within reach of the shore, with barely a splash or ripple.

The parts of the craft nearest the water's edge wavered and flowed, as if melting, but instead unfolded and reformed into ramps leading down to the moist sand. Moments later, figures walked cautiously down the ramps from each ship and on to the shore; the first few fanned out, forming a perimeter, weapons held at the ready.

All were similarly dressed in form-fitting clothing with integral boots and gloves and a transparent dome helmet that joined at the neck and shoulders. The only discernible difference between them were coloured, diagonal stripes on the left shoulder denoting rank and discipline. The suits were proof against moderate impacts and penetration, tough and resilient and able to provide basic medical care to the wearer. They processed body waste and perspiration and were impervious to gas and liquids. If immersed in water, they could provide air for up to an hour. As much as they protected the wearer, they protected the outside environment from the occupant too.

'Lance Corporal Firestarta Spekalmook! Here! Now!' said an authoritative voice over the open comms link.

'Sir. Yes, sir!' replied Lance Corporal Spekalmook.

A group of a hundred had disembarked from the lead craft, perhaps half that from each of the ten others, and were performing routine tasks all along the beach.

'Lance Corporal, do you think your colleagues in Life Support are a bunch of idiots or perhaps that I issue directives just to fill my spare time? Hmm?' said the commander, speaking directly to Spekal, their clear dome helmets touching.

'Uh, no, sir,' replied Spekal.

'Which?'

'Neither, sir,' said Spekal, spotting a no-win question when he heard one.

'Then why, oh why, were you about to take off your helmet? Hmm?'

'I, um, thought it was safe, sir. My HUD* is showing all green, sir.'

'All green, is it? A bit like all the plant life here about?'

'Uh, yes, sir,' said Spekal, not sure where this was heading.

'*Green* is how we would like it to remain Lance Corporal, and while *you* are safe and snug in your suit, we can at least ensure that you are not responsible for any contamination that might occur to the local flora and fauna. Understand?'

'Sir. Yes, sir!' replied Spekal sharply. He had remained at attention throughout, but pulled himself even straighter and more rigid, staring into the middle distance.

'Carry on, Lance Corporal.'

'Thank you, Commander,' Spekal replied smartly, saluting in traditional Navy style, left fist clutched to the chest. He trotted back to his squad, which was trying desperately to appear busy setting up tables and equipment for the science team. Curiously, no one was looking in Spekal's direction. He deliberately barged into one of his friends, who dropped the plastic box he was carrying.

'That was your fault!' he said.

---

*Heads-up display. Displays information on to the inside of the helmet, visible only to the wearer.

'Me?' said Lance Corporal Morningsidemook, Spekal's squad leader and closest friend. Although of equal rank, Tinka was presently squad leader, with one 'pip' on his lance corporal stripe, and therefore slightly senior. 'I only *suggested* it would be okay to remove your helmet. It wasn't exactly an order.'

'You wait, I'll get you back. You know I will,' said Spekal, only half joking.

'Ha! Not on your best day and my worst day. Now grab some boxes and look busy, or they'll find us some proper work to do.'

Commander Fastheart Freddimook turned to his young assistant, shaking his head. 'Always skating on thin ice that boy,' he said, half to himself.

'Yes sir,' agreed Sergeant Mobiusmook. 'He does show enormous promise though, sir. One of the best recruits we've ever seen.'

'Hmm. Promise is not always enough, Mo. We just have to hope he doesn't blow us all up in the meantime. Are we ready to proceed?'

Sergeant Mobiusmook consulted her own HUD, her eyes defocusing slightly and flicking across the information projecting on to the inside of her helmet.

'Drones are starting to report in now, sir. Plasmic energy levels are abundant, off the chart in some places.'

'Good. Well, we expected that from our long-range scans, but good to have it confirmed in the field, as it were. So, the Great Experiment begins.'

'A proud moment, sir.'

'Indeed. Perhaps you would give my compliments to Professor Derr? She may commence operations in her own time.'

'My pleasure, sir.' Sergeant Mobiusmook switched to the secure comms link and spoke briefly.

Moments later, hatches on top of the large craft irised open,

4

releasing wave after wave of metallic spheres. Each the size of a large beach ball, they reached a designated altitude, carried aloft by the blue-tinged haze surrounding them, and sped off to a predetermined location. There were 250,000 in the first batch, each containing many billions of medical-grade derbots. Many more would follow over the coming millennia, while the Mooks underwent the Big Sleep. Once released, the derbots would insinuate themselves into every living organism on the planet, making a snip here, an adjustment there, until every part of the insanely complicated jigsaw fit together. It would not be a perfect fit. There would be gaps, dead ends, a few glaring holes, but this planet was about to get a makeover in order to give the Mooks' precious cargo a home.

This was not the first time the Mooks had assisted an emergent species, but it was the first time they had ever transplanted one without their knowledge or consent. The trick now was to allow them room to grow, to nurture them without them suspecting they were not native to this world, this system or even this part of the Million Keyways.

This planet had been chosen. Its past had seen major catastrophic impact events and destruction on a planet-wide level that eliminated vast amounts of native species. At present, there were no emergent life forms capable of evolving into sapient species, nor were there ever likely to be. Not quite a blank canvas, but enough of one for their purpose. One day, many, many years hence, their charges would be introduced to plasmagication and all the wonders it offered.

If they survived.

B.J. PAGE

A Little Over One Million Years Later

2. 1794 – Pacific Ocean

Little four-year-old legs raced along the well-trodden path, grass stalks whipping across his bare skin. He was naked apart from a loincloth and tanned a deep golden brown. The course grass left marks which would itch and irritate later. He barely noticed, though, as he was on an important errand. Mamma had told him not to stop until he passed on the message, but his heart felt fit to burst, his legs were hurting and his breath was becoming ragged. Luckily it was mostly downhill.

The little path joined the big path which followed the tiny stream back to the village. He paused where the water bubbled out of the bare rock and formed a small crystal-clear pool, cupping mouthfuls of water and splashing his face and head as he had seen others do. He set off again at a fast walk until his breath returned somewhere close to normal, then began trotting until the knots in his legs eased. His bare feet made little slapping noises as they connected with the packed earth of the path. The soles were as tough as leather but he'd picked up a cut on his big toe on the rocks somewhere above, leaving spots of blood whenever his right foot touched down.

There were few trees, but the grass and undergrowth was twice as high as him and he was glad when he finally burst out into sunshine at the edge of the upper field. The L-shaped field had been cleared and tilled, the edges marked out with stones of all shapes and sizes. The soil was rich, dark and fertile, and rows of bright green stems were pushing through again. Thurs had no idea what was growing there but would help his parents as much as he could come harvest time. The field was uneven and ran over the crest of a shallow hill. In the inside corner of the L shape sat a big black rock jutting out of the soil. It was as big as their house and he'd sat in its shade many times when his parents had been working the field. He knew it wasn't far now and this spurred him on a little. Cresting the hill, he could see down to the village which was little more than a cluster of crude huts made from rough timber, mud and stones with roofs covered in large, broad leaves.

He skirted the lower field, bare of crops but neatly furrowed ready for planting. Past the pig pen and round to the front of his house, the largest, apart from where the other mums lived. He pushed open the recently installed wooden door made from precious planks salvaged from the ship, some of them showing scorch marks at the edges. It was dark inside, but he knew his father was resting on his straw mattress, his shoulder bandaged where he had been stabbed with a pointed stick. There had been a big argument and some fighting a few weeks ago amongst the men and afterwards his dadda had been covered in blood and three of the men went away and never came back. It had been happier since but there was more work to do and dadda was still poorly.

He went straight to his father's side and shook him awake. 'Dadda, Dadda!'

'What? Thurs? What is it, son? What's wrong?'

'It... it's... Mamma. She...' His breath was coming in gasps, his little face bright red and his coal black hair plastered to his head. His father grabbed him by the shoulders, wincing at the pain in his own shoulder, now mostly healed but still stiff and sore. The stick had gone right through his upper right shoulder just below the collarbone. His wife, Mai, had cleaned and dressed it with a poultice but even so, it had become infected. She had cleaned it again with the last of the ship's rum and packed it with honey gathered from the island. The fever had lasted for several days, but now he was on the mend.

'Take it slowly, son. Breathe deeply. Mamma sent you?'
Nod.
'Is she hurt? Is the baby coming?'
Shake of the head.
His father gave him a drink of tepid water from the jug beside the bed as his heart slowed and his breathing eased.
'Okay? Slowly now.'
'Mamma said to tell you there is a ship coming.'
'A ship? Are you sure, lad?'
'Yes, Dadda. A big black ship with white sails.'
'Where were you?'
'On the cliff. Mamma was picking berries.'
'Stay here, son. I will be back soon.'
'Is there trouble, Dadda?'
He ruffled his son's hair and smiled at him. 'Trouble? Of course not, Thursday October Christian. Just Dadda being careful.'
Also barefooted and naked from the waist up, Fletcher snatched up a well-worn leather satchel and slipped it over his shoulder. He ran from the ramshackle house, retracing his son's footsteps almost exactly, even stopping at the same pool for a refreshing drink. Fletcher kept his hands high to avoid the grass, his legs protected by a faded, worn and tattered pair of blue breeches which stopped mid-calf in jagged frays bleached almost white by salt water and sun. The path, little more than a game trail, led upwards between jagged volcanic rocks that would slice open the careless or unwary. The way levelled out on to a flat, grassy cliff, bushes and shrubs growing some yards back, native to the island and covered in small clusters of dark purple berries.
The berries were bitter until almost spoiled but could be eaten with a little honey or else the juice fermented into a strong brew.
He found Mai, his Otaheiten wife who was far along in pregnancy, seated on a smooth white boulder which formed a

natural seat against which she reclined, feet dangling over the edge. She was in shade and sheltered from the wind, which crashed waves against the cliff a hundred feet below. She had her eyes closed and appeared to be asleep, but she stirred when she heard him approach. She was wearing a grass skirt and one of his old white shirts stretched tightly over her bulging belly. Her waist-length black hair draped over her left shoulder in a single braid.

'A ship, beloved,' she said, pointing off to the west, where Fletcher could see a black speck and a white sail. From his satchel he removed his brass telescope, extended the four sections to its full length and put it to his right eye. He tracked along the horizon, overshot and moved back, twisted to focus, and she leapt into clarity. She was sailing roughly south, but even as he watched, he caught the glint of sun on glass and a few minutes later she turned to port and was bow on. Fletcher rested the brass tube against the white rock to steady his focus and rest his right shoulder.

'She's seen us,' he said, as much to himself as to his wife. 'She'll be here in two hours. Damnation!'

He angrily snapped shut the telescope and stowed it back in the satchel.

'What will you do, my husband?' asked Mai.

'I have a plan, my angel. It's not much, but to the British, I am a dead man. They must not find me alive.'

Fletcher had known this day would come, but he hadn't planned for it to end this way. He hadn't really planned at all. After spotting the ship, he'd made his way down to the tiny beach, dragged his dugout into the surf and paddled out and around to the east of the island as the ship circled about and dropped anchor in Bounty Bay. Fletcher had water and provisions, bread, fruit and sun-dried meat and fish, enough to last five or six days. He had a straw hat and a parasol fashioned from scraps of sailcloth to keep off the sun. He planned to stay out here for as long as he could, pretending to fish, but the damnable current kept catching him. Three times now he had been caught up and only luck and exhaustive paddling had kept the nub of land in sight. His injured shoulder could not take much more and there were specks of blood on the bandage.

On the fifth morning, the ship had hoisted sail and moved out into the wind, cutting in front of Fletcher about half a mile away. A whaler from the Americas by the look of her. He could go home, home to everything he held dear.

The whaler sailed east at first, until she had set her sails, then turned south and was soon once more a mere speck on the great blue. There were no safe landings on the eastern side of Pitcairn, and, as Fletcher paddled back around to Bounty Bay, back towards his beloved family, a stiff easterly breeze blew up, increasing the swell and pushing him further out. After an hour or more of frantic paddling, he realised he wasn't going to make it.

He and his friends had been out here a thousand times in little boats just like this one: a dugout fashioned from a hollowed-out tree trunk with an out-rigger. The fish they had caught had become an important part of their diet, but the current had always been tricky. Their island was one of the most remote on the planet and, thanks to luck or fate, Fletcher knew it had been incorrectly charted on Admiralty maps. There had been little chance that the Navy would ever find them, but it seemed that day had finally come. One ship had found them, and others would follow now that their location had been more accurately mapped.

The great Pacific Ocean swirled around their spit of volcanic rock, creating eddies and whirlpools on its leeward side which could have you spinning like a top. Venture a little further and there was the chance of being swept away as the current re-converged. Normally, there would be two or even three in the narrow boat, enough to overcome the current and get back to the island. Fletcher, alone and in his weakened state, never really stood a chance. No one from Pitcairn would come for him; he was too far away. He drifted and wept and shouted at the moon and the stars and waited to die.

His supplies ran out after nine days, even though he stretched them out as far as he could. He ate the last of the fish and drank the last of the water from its pig's bladder. He knew he had perhaps three to five days without water before raging thirst would drive him to drink from the ocean and that, of course, would kill him. By that time his lips would be cracked and split, his tongue a swollen black lump in his mouth and he would be too far gone to care. He resigned himself to his end and said his goodbyes while he still could, asking whatever gods held his fate for forgiveness for the bad things he had done.

He was not sure if he was awake or dreaming after that. He stopped adding notches to his paddle, marking the days, and drifted in and out of consciousness, from dream state to living nightmare.

At some point he was awakened by soft gentle rain on his face, filling his upturned mouth but nearly choking him when he tried to swallow into his parched throat. The rain was his saviour and he praised the Lord, the gods of the sea, the gods of the weather and all gods everywhere. He drank his fill from the water in the bottom of his little dugout canoe and refilled his pig's bladder, drank and refilled it again. He was intoxicated for days on sweet nectar, the happiest man alive.

A second miracle occurred on a sea as flat and calm as a millpond. The area around his boat became wildly agitated, boiling up as if some monster of the deep was about to engulf him whole, boat and all. Then, for fifty yards on all sides the water filled with fish. A great heaving, flopping, leaping, writhing mass of silver and black iridescence. More fish than was ever seen by one man; he feared they would swamp his boat when they started leaping into it of their own will. He was overjoyed, scared and elated at the same time. He wept and then sat in shocked silence as the sea beside him bulged upwards, fish and all, as a true giant, a leviathan of the deep, rose up, close enough to touch, its massive jaws gaping wide and then snapping shut on tons of fish before crashing back to the ocean. Then a second to his right, a third to the front and a fourth behind sent his bobbing cork of a boat rocking so that he had to cling on for dear life.

As quickly as it began, it was gone. The fish, the whales, all gone. The sea became calm once more and except for the flopping fish in the bottom of his canoe, he would have thought it all a waking dream. Far off, he caught a glimpse of sleek black shapes gliding in and out of the water blowing great geysers skywards. He stood on shaking legs and shouted after them, 'Thank you! Thank you, O Lords of the Deep!' He ate until he was ill, then ate again with deliberate slowness, and this time kept it down.

Over the next week his strength slowly returned, and with it, his mind. He gutted and dried the fish as best he could, fighting a daily battle with squawking gulls, attracted by the scraps, until he caught one bare handed and killed it. He couldn't face it raw, though, and cooked it after a fashion by slicing it thinly and using the large lens from his telescope to focus the sun's rays. The wings and carcass he fixed to the prow of his little boat, and the other birds seemed to leave him alone after that. Several times his boat was nudged by dark shapes in the water, black triangular dorsal fins cutting through the waves like knives through butter, but they didn't bother him beyond that.

There were fifty notches on his paddle now. He had started adding them again when he regained his senses and he estimated he had lost about ten days or so to delirium. His food would run out again soon, but he had enough water for perhaps a week. His body was caked in salt and covered in sores caused by his poor diet.

On the sixty-third day, a storm blew in not long after dawn, the sky growing dark again with frightening speed. Lightning flashed and struck so close there was no gap between eye-searing flash and bone-rattling bang. His boat was picked up, swirled and tossed about by twenty-foot high waves and the howling wind threatened to blow him into the sea. The rain struck his ravaged body with the force of buckshot, chilling him to the bone. He lashed himself to the boat and lay there shivering uncontrollably, powerless in the face of the ocean's wrath. It could have been hours, it could have been days; in the dark of the storm, he had nothing against which to measure time.

When he next woke, the great blue had regained much of its previous calm. Huge gentle swells lifted and lowered him, and he managed to stand up and look around. The boat was awash, and he spent some time bailing with cupped hands, then emptied his satchel and used that as a makeshift bucket. Everything else was gone. Food, water, hat and parasol, even his paddle. The only things left were his satchel, his telescope and his knife.

He was a dead man. After so much, he wouldn't last forty-eight hours.

Shortly after noon, the sun still directly overhead, as a wave lifted him above the surrounding ocean, he thought he glimpsed a thin black line on the horizon. On the next swell it was confirmed. A black line. Land! On the next swell, the black line again and below that, a white line. Clouds or fog, he assumed. The black line grew higher: he was moving closer. His chest heaved and swelled. Dare he hope? Out here, with no paddle or sail, a miss of a hundred yards was as good as a hundred miles.

The line grew higher, the whiteness expanding too until it stretched before him in a great expanse the like of which he had never seen before. A towering mountain of thick fog rolled over and engulfed him. White out. Fletcher could no longer tell where he was heading. He was once more in the lap of the gods.

The mist parted momentarily and there, outlined against the sky, was a huge island: craggy, snow-tipped peaks, lush verdant slopes, palm-lined beaches. He was going to miss it! The mist swirled and closed around him again, but he had seen enough and sprang into action. He was caught in a current like that around Pitcairn, but he had a chance and that was all he needed. He paddled frantically, using his satchel gripped in both hands, but without effect. In a last desperate attempt to steer, he held a death-grip on the strap, his knuckles white with the effort, and trailed the satchel behind the boat. It inflated in the current and was nearly wrenched from his fingers, but he felt the boat turn with the drag – he had a rudder.

A thousand yards out, the mist lifted like a bride's veil but he didn't have time to wonder what could cause the flat vertical wall of fog as dead in front of him, marked only by a line of white foam, was a reef. A coral reef was the dread of all mariners, often unseen, uncharted and deadly. Able to shred the hull of any craft afloat and rip to pieces any survivors. He was committed now, he could only hope his trusty dugout, barely six inches in the water, would skid over the top like skates on ice. He hauled in his satchel, emptied it, repacked his telescope and knife and slipped it over his shoulder one last time. He knelt and gripped both sides of the dugout as tightly as he could and then he was amongst it, the hull scraping, the foam and spray lashing his face. For a tiny fraction of a second, he thought he'd made it, but then the bow caught and plunged downwards, throwing him in a flailing arc into the lagoon beyond the reef.

He had time to wonder at the serenity of the crystal-clear waters, the peace beyond the storm. *Almost Fletch*, he told himself, *almost*. He tried to kick for the surface, but it was a half-hearted attempt. He was a shell of a man now, compared to the one who had climbed into the hollowed-out sliver of wood. *That's what he was*, he thought, as the surface shrank away from him, *I'm a hollowed-out sliver of a man.*

As blackness closed in around him, he thought of his wife, Maimiti, and their beloved children: Thursday October, just four years old, his little brother Charles and a third, yet to be born. He and Mai had hoped for a girl and would name her Mary Ann. As all men do, he hoped he would not be forgotten, hoped he'd left his mark. As his last breath left his mouth in a stream of silver bubbles, he felt movement in the water around him. *Sharks*, he thought, *at least it will be quick,* but instead, he felt hands on him, grasping his legs and arms. Something slid over his face, something warm that covered his eyes and nose, went inside his mouth, down his throat and into his lungs and took away the terrible ache there. He smiled and let the darkness take him.

3. Mookination

Mooks:

Mookons generally occupy the mountainous slopes and coastal areas of Mookination including Snake Pass College. They are also designated mentors to the Merfolk.

Mookins live almost exclusively within the caldera of Mookination. Their primary role is agriculture, but, as they form, by far, the largest population of Mookination, Mookins will often migrate to other areas.

Mookundas are primarily concerned with mining and mineral extraction, spending months at a time below ground, but with one notable exception: they are responsible for the care and incubation of dragon eggs, and, after hatching, their onward transport to Olympus Mons.

Mookouts are specially trained Mooks, tasked with entering the Bigfolk world. They are assigned missions that require intervention from Mooks of a plasmagical nature. Mookouts are trained at the Learning Tree. Many Mookouts remain in the Bigfolk world for many years at a time, and there are presently over 6,000 on long-term infiltration. Not all Mookouts are, or need to be, combat trained.

Mookipedia

To: Mook High Council
From: Chargrilled Spannamook, Mookon Security
Subject: Recent security breach

Sirs and ladies, we have determined that the subject was a lone human male (Bigfolk), of English descent, formerly a British naval officer. He passed through our outer sensors in a small wooden boat (dugout type, Polynesian design) which was thought to be a drifting log. He passed into the Sunset Beach Lagoon and would have died but was rescued by the resident Merfolk.

Subject was in poor physical health and in need of urgent medical treatment. A D-way was opened between Sunset Beach and the Learning Tree where he was transferred to the hospital wing and released to the care of Dr Finestra and her team.

We have upgraded our sensors as a result of the breach and modified the deep ocean current to form a ring flowing outward from Mookination which should prevent any and all shipping from entering the area. It should be noted that the Merfolk have lodged an official complaint, and we must view this as merely an interim solution.

We recommend a complete review of all defences over the next 50 to 100 years. We are seeing a large increase in ocean-going vessels in the Pacific as Europe goes through its present expansion. No doubt this will increase sharply as technology improves, possibly steam-powered vessels will be next. Certainly, if the Bigfolk follow the model, we are projecting lighter-than-air flight within the next century, and powered flight in less than three. It may therefore be time to consider going to a full state of masque sooner rather than later. The plasmic designated for the task is at optimum and ready to go.

Kindest regards
Director Spannamook

To: *Mook High Council*
From: *Dr Finestra Moorishmook, LT Medical Centre*
Subject: *Type 1 human Bigfolk male, answering to the name of 'Fletcherchristian'*

Male Fletcherchristian was in the extreme stages of malnutrition and dehydration, suffering from heatstroke and severe sunburn. Most of his body was covered in sores associated with his poor diet. We estimate he had been adrift for between 75 and 100 days on the open ocean with little or no protection. It was necessary to induce a coma for the first week while rehydrating and administering derbots. It also gave us the opportunity to remove a small leather bag which Fletcherchristian refused, even while unconscious, to relinquish. Such tenacity is to be admired.

During treatment, one thing occurred that we did not anticipate: Fletcherchristian had been extensively tattooed on most parts of his body including back and front torso, arms, legs and buttocks. I'm afraid to report that the derbots removed most of the tattooing before we had chance to intervene, the only exception is a sunburst or star design on the left breast which seemed to be of older origin. As a result, it may be difficult for him to convince his Bigfolk friends of his identity, if that was their purpose. It may be possible to recreate the tattooing if he can recall the designs.

Fletcherchristian should reach optimal health in another four or five days. He may require extensive counselling or memory modification before he can be reintroduced into Bigfolk society. He is now conscious but sedated; he has no idea of his present whereabouts.

Regards
Finestra Moorishmook

To: Mook High Council
From: Clearwater Mobiusmook, Director of Security,
           LT Mookouts

Subject: *Human Bigfolk male Fletcherchristian*
Human Bigfolk male Fletcherchristian has been signed off as A1 by LT Medical Centre, although he is still sedated. All derbots in male subject will deactivate after mission completion and will dissolve without trace. It was decided to leave in place all scar tissue including a large recent injury to the upper right shoulder, but it should be noted that internal damage was repaired; all visible scars are now cosmetic.

Subject may be concerned over loss of tattooing and regrowth of six previously missing teeth. Subject was questioned while still partially sedated, and when asked 'Where did you sail from?' subject replied with what sounded like 'P-mouth'. According to Mookouts in place, this is likely to be Plymouth where there is a large wet-navy dockyard. The leather bag in Fletcher's possession was imprinted with his name and the words 'HMAV Bounty', a designation of a warship from this approximate location, now listed as missing.

We respectfully suggest and request permission to transport Fletcher via D-way to town Plymouth located British Isles, northern hemisphere. Subject will remain sedated throughout and all normal security protocols will be implemented. Subject will be implanted with a tracker and furnished with appropriate clothing and local currency. Commander Firestarta is presently preparing for a mission in the northern part of the British Isles and will observe him covertly for six months post re-insertion to ensure no ill effects are apparent.

Respectfully yours
Director Mobiusmook

To: *Director Mobiusmook, LT Mookouts*
From: *Mook High Council*
Subject: *Human Bigfolk male Fletcherchristian*

Dear Auntie* Mo,

Hope you are fit and well? My love to all the family. Permission granted. Please proceed with caution.

Kindest best wishes
Eldron Kwisby Jaggerimook

PS: Auntie, please warn Firestarta that we would prefer it if there were no 'incidents'. KJ

*It should be noted that use of 'Auntie' or 'Uncle' is a term of endearment used by Mooks to refer to all chronologically older Mooks outside immediate family. As Mooks are extremely long-lived, there are no rules regarding marriage, which can last only until children reach maturity. Every Mook is closely related to every other Mook. They see themselves as one, large extended family. This also leads to many extended families, polygamous and   same-sex groups.

B.J. PAGE

4. Plymouth Who?

Fletcher awoke to sunlight through curtains. He lay there for several minutes, at peace, calm, serene. He did not know where he was. He sat up and found he was fully dressed in smart gentleman's clothing. Tunic, crisp white shirt, breeches and hose. Shiny black boots beside the bed and a hat, gloves and cane on the dresser. An overcoat hung from a hook on the back of the door, also new.

He rushed to the window and drew back the drapes. Plymouth! He was in Plymouth, he'd recognise it from any angle; he had a view of the harbour and of the bustling market. He couldn't be, it wasn't possible. The last he remembered was, was... he wasn't at all certain. He sat down on the bed again and caught a glimpse of himself in the mirror on the dresser.

What? What was this? He grabbed the mirror in both hands, examined the back for some form of trickery. He examined the reflection of his own face again. The years were gone. It was the face of his youth. His hair, of late receding, was now full, black and wavy. His skin was lighter, teeth whiter. Teeth! His tongue probed the inside of his mouth; he had all of his teeth, even though he remembered – vividly – every extraction. But the most staggering of all, his tattoos, lovingly, if painfully, applied by his wife, Mai, over several years were gone.

He had a wife! And two sons! And another on the way. What trickery, what witchcraft was at work here? He remembered, he remembered... but there were gaps.

His head swam, and memory flooded back. *The ship!* The voyage that seemed doomed almost from the off, the foul weather beating them and driving them back from the Horn. Back across the Atlantic to Tasmania and then on to Otaheiti. Five months of paradise. The mutiny and flight to freedom

23

across the seas. The searching across two thousand miles of ocean and a dozen islands for sanctuary. And then finally Pitcairn. Their new home.

He remembered. It all came back in a rush, swamping him with sights and sounds and feelings, the thirst and the hunger, the near death, new hope and... the reef. He remembered the reef, remembered death enfolding him and then hands lifting him up, saving him once more.

Afterwards, there was only vagueness. Shapes, sounds, warmth and safety. Questions from... someone, a woman. He could recall a woman. Endless questions when all he wanted to do was sleep. Her hair. He remembered something about her hair. Stripes. Her hair was striped, like a zebra or a tiger. He'd reached out to touch it and she'd stuck a needle in his arm and ice had rushed into his veins.

And now this. He must learn more.

He donned boots, hat and gloves, picked up the cane and walked to the door. He picked up the overcoat and found it absurdly heavy but draped it over his arm. There on the hook, his old satchel. Scuffed and worn, salt-stained and faded, but his. Inside the flap, once embossed in gold but now just a dent in the leather, his name: Fletcher Christian, HMAV Bounty. It was too much. He snatched it up and ran from the room, along a landing with other doors leading off and down a dog-leg staircase. He pushed open the door at the bottom and found himself in a large hallway with more doors leading off and a hatch with an office beyond.

'Ah, good morning, sir. I trust you slept well?' A man had appeared behind the counter, seemingly from nowhere, startling Fletcher. He was short with a large hooked nose and receding grey hair. He was wearing a white shirt and an apron. Fletcher did not know him, had never seen him before.

'You startled me. Who the devil are you?' Fletcher demanded.

'Why, I am the landlord, sir. Your host and humble servant,

Cornelius Scrum. Hotelier and purveyor of fine ales.'

'What day is it, Mr Scrum?'

'Why, it's Saturday, sir. Best day of the week, don't you think?'

'No, the date, man, what is the date?'

'Oh, I see, sir. The date.' He flicked pages in a book in front of him on the counter. 'Why, it's the twenty-second of February already, hard to believe. Another month flown by.'

'And the year?'

'The year? Why, everyone knows the year, sir.'

'Well, I forget. Indulge me if you would be so kind.'

'Of course. It is the year of our Lord 1794. Will that be all, sir?'

'Uh, yes. Thank you,' said Fletcher.

'Would sir like a tonic? Or a hair of the dog perhaps? Your friend said you might be a little woozy, begging your pardon, after a night's heavy libation. He specifically asked me to see that you were all right.'

'Friend? What friend?'

'Your friend said you might be a little confused. Short, stout gentleman, sir, not one to upset, if you understand me.'

'I don't.'

'Well, he was very generous, paid extra for your room, paid three nights all-in and more on top, he did. But he had *the look*, sir.'

'Describe him. Please?' said Fletcher, not at all sure what the fellow meant by 'the look'.

'Well, as I said, not tall like yourself, about shoulder height to you. But very broad. Huge in fact. Massive hands. And the eyes, sir, dark green, stare right through you and take the varnish off the wall. Red hair. Big moustache, this wide, sir.' The landlord held his hands out either side of his head, at least a foot apart. 'Most striking, sir.'

'I don't recall...'

'And Scottish too.'

'Scottish, you say?'

'Yes, sir, the accent. Edinburgh I would say. And of course, he was wearing the kilt. That was a giveaway before he opened his mouth.'

'I need some air,' gasped Fletcher.

'Will sir be back for dinner?' But he was talking to Fletcher's fleeing back. 'Damn and sugar,' said the landlord.

Fletcher wandered the streets in a state of utter confusion. He put on the overcoat against the February chill and hung the satchel around his neck. He didn't know why, but he couldn't bear the thought of parting with it. Inside he found a battered telescope and a rusty knife, both of which he recognised as his, together with a heavy drawstring purse, which definitely was not. He peeked inside without removing it from the satchel and was shocked to see gold coins. Newly minted guineas, with the face of George the Third. At least a thousand pounds. In both pockets of the coat he found the same: a leather purse, each containing, he again estimated, a thousand guineas – a small fortune. This only added to his confusion. He had never been poor; indeed, his family had once been rich, but after the death of his father, and his mother's loss of the family fortune, they had survived on an annuity of forty pounds. Not quite poverty, but this was wealth such as he had never dreamt of.

As the day wore on, he grew more and more confused. He was unable to figure it out. He roamed the streets of Plymouth, stumbling, muttering, barging into people and through the crowds. He found himself drawn back to the docks, to the ships tied there, to the goods being loaded and unloaded, to the seafarers, the crews and officers of ocean-going ships. He had some vague idea of buying passage back to Pitcairn, but all those he approached were merchantmen bound for Europe, Africa, India or the Far East.

He would find a ship, he would buy one if he had to, and

he would find himself a crew and sail her back to his beloved wife and children.

'Fletcher!' A shout from behind. He quickened his pace – he was still a wanted man and would be tried for mutiny and hang if caught. *And now someone had recognised him.* He kept his head down and slipped around the corner into Fore Street, but the footsteps persisted.

'You, sir! I say, hold up!'

He ignored the man, pulled his hat down to cover his eyes, and pushed through a knot of men outside a tavern. Someone in the crowd grabbed at him, tearing buttons from his shirt. Fletcher turned to strike, and the assailant saw the mad look in his eyes and released him. He hurried on, fearful of being re-cognised.

'Fletcher, stop!' *Damn, the fellow was persistent.* Another hand grabbed him, spinning him about, tearing his shirt even more. He looked straight into a face from another life. In the mad dash, Fletcher's coat had come undone, his shirt buttons ripped off so that his chest was exposed. The man's eyes were drawn to the sun-burst tattoo on Fletcher's left breast.

'Fletcher. Fletcher Christian, it is you. What are you doing here?' the man said in a hoarse whisper. 'Where on earth have you been?'

'Peter? Peter Heywood? Is it you?' said Fletcher. The last he had seen of Peter was waving from the beach at Otaheiti. Peter had elected to remain behind. Unknown to Fletcher, Heywood had been captured and court-martialled for mutiny. He had been found guilty, but pardoned by King George.

The man smiled. 'Yes Fletch, it is I.'

Fletcher at first felt relief, followed closely by blind panic rising in his chest and he pushed Heywood away, hard, with both hands. Heywood stumbled and fell. Fletcher ran, ran for all he was worth. Ran down alleyways, twists and turns, jumping walls and gates in his effort to get away. He heard feet running after him, but lost them in the labyrinth of Plymouth's back streets and alleyways.

When at last he paused for breath, he had no idea where he was: a darkened alley piled with rubbish and dark doorways leading, he assumed, into the backs of taverns, shops and warehouses. Somewhere, he had lost the cane.

'Hello, dearie, bit lost, are we?' A heavily made-up woman, old enough to be his mother, had appeared in the doorway opposite, just a few paces away. Fletcher was leaning against the wall, gasping for breath.

'Uh, no, madam, I am fine. Thank you.'

'Spoil your nice clothes, resting there, you will. Come inside, why don't you? Make you a cup o' tea. Or something stronger, perhaps?' She winked at him. He noticed her clothes: lace-up boots, calf-length skirts in green velvet, patched in several places. Black lace bustier revealing far too much bosom, painted lips and rouged cheeks, chalk-white powdered face and breasts. She sported a blonde shoulder-length wig which was slightly askew, as if she'd donned it in a hurry.

Fletcher, familiar with the workings of the seedier side of old port towns, felt his hackles rise. He was about to be separated from his money, his clothes and perhaps even his life.

'Most kind, madam,' he said breathing hard, 'but I must be on my way. Another time, perhaps?' He turned to walk away, but found the alley blocked by a mountain of a man. Over six feet and nearly as wide it seemed.

'Ev'ry fing all right, Ma?' said the mountain.

'Reggie. This is my boy – Reggie,' she said to Fletcher. 'Gent wuz turnin' down me 'ospitality, 'e was.'

'Wuz 'e now?' asked Reggie. Fletcher backed up, slow steps, and turned about, but was brought up short by another ominous figure blocking the other way. He was trapped. 'And that's Harold. Me other boy. 'E don't talk much, Harold. More of a do-er, our Harold. Likes ripping arms off, don't you, son?'

Harold's shoulders shook in obvious glee at the prospect, a

curiously girlish titter escaping his lips. Harold was short, five foot three at best, but his massive girth seemed to almost fill the alleyway.

Both boys were dressed in a mishmash of clothing: expensive looking boots that had seen better days, dark breeches that were shiny with grime and of indeterminate colour. Reggie wore a grey fisherman's jumper with several large holes revealing a grubby under-shirt.

Harold was wearing clothes that had been altered to accommodate his large girth, a triangular wedge of leather on each side of his breeches and an extra piece sewn on his coat so that it could be buttoned up. He wore a shirt that had once, in a previous life, been white, with a woollen hat pulled down over his ears giving his podgy face a grubby, cherubic appearance.

They both grimaced rather than smiled, revealing tobacco-stained chipped teeth.

'Yes, 'e wuz, son. Most upset, I am.'

Reggie produced a leather blackjack – a cosh filled with lead shot – from his right coat pocket, smacking it noisily into his left palm.

'Can't 'ave me ma gettin' upset,' said Reggie through his matted, food-stained moustache and beard. Harold, by contrast, was reasonably clean shaven, but with several scabbed cuts. Either he wasn't very good at it, or his razor was blunt.

Fletcher glanced from one to the other, both still a dozen paces away, and backed into the wall again opposite Ma. Harold continued his tittering, his eyes gleaming.

'Ah... um, no need for this, lads. I... I will gladly pay for the good lady's time.'

'Pay?' said Reggie. 'Oh, yu'll pay all right. No one upsets me ma. No one.'

As he took a step closer, Fletcher grabbed his knife from his satchel and held it in front of him for both to see. It was a brass and hardwood handle with a four-inch blade, now rusty and dull, hardly describable as a weapon.

Harold drew a short sword from inside his coat. The blade was eighteen inches long and slightly curved, wickedly pointed.

'Threat'nin' us now, are ya?' said Reggie.

'He he he. Ow!' said Harold, letting out a sudden yelp as a short man with a huge chest and arms appeared behind him.

'Ah, there ye are,' said the man. Not much taller than Harold, the index finger of one of his enormous hands had poked hard into the pudgy flesh of Harold's right shoulder. He was dressed in a green and black kilt and sported an enormous red moustache, waxed into sharp points. He had long red hair tied back in a ponytail beneath a green and black tartan bonnet to match his kilt. He folded his massive arms across his chest, straining the seams of his white cotton shirt.

Harold was staring at his limp right arm, which was refusing to do his bidding. The pain of shattered bones had not yet reached his brain but would do so any moment now. Firestarta was standing between Ma and Fletcher, having walked around Harold, the better to keep an eye on Reggie.   'Madam, go about your business,' he said.

'Who the 'ell are you, to be orderin' me about?' she said with venom, also folding her arms.

'Owww!' said Harold, his blade clattering to the floor.

Firestarta turned his head and looked straight into Ma's eyes. Her mouth dropped open at what she saw in the dark green depths, and she stepped backwards clutching her chest and slammed the door. A strangled scream came from inside.

'Oh, great. That's all I need,' said Firestarta.

Reggie needed no more prompting. His ma was screaming and that rarely happened unless the law was on to her. He bellowed and charged, raising the blackjack over his head. Doors opened on either side of Ma's and an assortment of men rushed out brandishing makeshift weapons. Fletcher saw movement. The red-headed chap moved, but so quickly he was a blur. Air exploded from Reggie's mouth as he came to an abrupt stop and with Firestarta's right fist buried into his solar plexus. Reggie collapsed to the cobbles, concentrating on making his lungs function again.

Firestarta turned back to Fletcher to find the alley filled with angry-looking men bearing down on him. 'I dinee have time for this,' he muttered to himself. 'And you,' he said, pointing at Fletcher, 'ye didne see this.'

Fletcher gaped, eyes bulging incredulously as a ball of blue light appeared in the Scotsman's left hand. He saw him push his arm forward and the blue ball expanded and rushed from his hand into the group of men who were scattered and dashed against the walls of the alley like ninepins. Each fell to the floor amidst the muck and the filth in a tangle of arms and legs. All were unconscious. Harold was still standing, looking down at his useless right arm, flopping against his side like a dead fish. Firestarta picked up Reggie's blackjack, walked up to him and said, 'Nighty night,' and cracked him under his left ear. He turned back to Fletcher before Harold hit the floor.

'Who? What?' said Fletcher.

'Let's get a wee dram,' said Firestarta, leading him away by the elbow.

'Cheers,' said Firestarta, sinking his scotch in one. 'Och, leave the bottle, son.' The landlord nodded, wiped the bar and swept the small gold coin Firestarta had placed on the dark wood, all in one deft motion. Firestarta picked up the bottle and joined Fletcher at the table, polished smooth by generations of drinkers' elbows. He placed two shot glasses down and poured Fletcher's first and his second drink – his first was a test that the liquid was genuine and unadulterated. Apparently satisfied, he sat opposite Fletcher and sipped from his glass.

They were alone in the snug of a popular tavern called 'The Gamecock', and although the main bar was quite busy, the snug was quiet. At best, it would seat only eight people;

for the time being they were alone.

'Who the hell are you? What the hell are you?' snapped Fletcher. Firestarta put down his glass mid-sip, placed his hands flat on the table and regarded Fletcher. He saw fear and confusion there. The man was ready to crack.

'This is not your home, laddie, is it?'

'No. No longer. My home is on the other side of the world. I don't belong here. Not anymore. How did I get here? I just don't understand. The last thing I remember is... is...'

'Ye were in a wee boat, son. Ye nearly died. We, my people, we rescued you from certain death. When we asked you where ye were from, ye answered, 'Plymouth', so that's where we brought ye.'

'You're not... are you really Scottish?'

'Babysitting, believe it or not, is not my main job. After you, I have other things to attend to. In Scotland. Accent slipping a wee bit, is it?' said Firestarta, in flawless English.

'A bit. And that thing you did, in the alley? What are you, a warlock?'

Firestarta chuckled. 'Not the way you mean, son. We prefer the terms 'users' or 'wielders'. Witchcraft has too many bad connotations these days, thanks to the Dark Ages.'

'My tattoos, my teeth, my hair? I don't understand any of it.'

'You were pretty far gone, son. We fixed you up a wee bit.'

'A bit? I'm ten years younger, man!'

'Are you complaining?'

'Well, no, but it was quite a shock, to say the least.'

'There, um, may be some more, uh, shocks in the future.'

'Like what, may I ask?'

'Well, you won't get sick again, ever. And, providing you are careful, you will live a long time. At least a hundred years, and not age much until the last ten years or so.'

'Really?'

'Really. If you get injured, you will heal, quite quickly. But not your heart or your brain. Only one each of those. So look after them. You'll be a bit stronger too, maybe a bit quicker.'

'I can't believe this. It's not possible,' said Fletcher incredulously.

'I'm afraid it is. Which you shall find out in time. Now, Fletcher, it's time for me to listen to your story. The truth of it, son, I'll know if you are lying.' Firestarta fixed his dark green eyes on Fletcher and continued sipping his whiskey.

Fletcher took a gulp of his drink, followed by a great, calming breath, and began relating his tale to Firestarta. He told of his chosen career as a British naval officer and his friendship with William Bligh. About the voyage of the Bounty, the hardships and trials before even reaching Tenerife and the bad luck and foul weather that seemed to haunt them. He told of the changes that his friend and mentor Captain Bligh underwent during the voyage, their attempts to round Cape Horn and being driven back by fearful seas. What should have been an easy run for Bligh's first command was dogged by bad seas and misfortune. Eventually, unable and unwilling to gain the Pacific Ocean by their chosen route, they re-crossed the Atlantic to Van Diemen's Land and onward to their destination, Otaheite. There, everything changed. Even Bligh seemed calm and relaxed, arranging the collection of breadfruits for transport to the West Indies.

Fletcher went on, telling how he met and fell in love with his beloved wife in a virtual paradise-on-earth. It lasted five months, then Bligh and the Bounty set sail for the West Indies, their destination before returning to England. Fletcher, having married in secret, had to leave behind a pregnant wife. Many of the men had talked about staying, having enjoyed the freedom and hospitality of Otaheiti and its people. Twenty-four days later and over one thousand three hundred miles from paradise, mutiny.

He told of his shame at leading the mutiny against Bligh, but of not having any choice. Bligh had become surly, morose and bitter, dealing out harsh punishments for small transgressions. The crew were plotting to take over. He was a torn man. The crew would have slaughtered Bligh and all who opposed them if he had not taken charge. At the least, he gave his former friend a chance, placing him and the others in the longboat, complete with supplies and a sextant, setting them adrift thirty miles from the island of Tofua. They sailed the Bounty back to Otaheite and the men kidnapped eleven women (his wife amongst them) and six men from the island. Sixteen of the crew, some of whom took no part in the mutiny, including Peter Heywood, elected to remain behind. With only eight crew plus Fletcher, they needed the six Otaheiten men to help sail the ship. They set sail without warning, stranding the Otaheitens aboard.

He told of the subsequent search for a place to colonise and after many, many disappointments, their eventual landing at Pitcairn Island. Fletcher had known that the tiny island had been wrongly charted by the Navy and hoped there was little chance of them being discovered. After stripping her, they burned the Bounty, stranding themselves.

It had been hard at first; there were problems, arguments and fights amongst the men. The Otaheiten men were almost slaves, but if they were to survive, it was a necessary evil. One which Fletcher promised he would have set right in time. He had never been happier.

Firestarta listened quietly, without interruption or comment. When Fletcher lapsed into silence, he asked, 'Is that where you want to be, laddie?'

'Oh yes. My heart is there,' answered Fletcher.

'Here is the deal. I can take you there, right now, this second. *But* you forget me and everything you've seen or are about to see. Anything I say or do is between us. Deal?'

'Deal. Just one thing, though.'

'Aye?'

'I have a friend, Will Wordsworth. We were at school together. I would very much like to see him, let him know that I am well. He would get word to my family that I am alive and happy.'

'Not the man who chased you today?'

'You saw that? No. Not Peter. Peter was with us on the Bounty, I left him on Otaheite. I don't know how he returned to England or even if we are still friends.'

Firestarta's head came up as he heard raised voices from the main bar. In a speckled mirror behind the bar he could see men in dark hats and coats talking with heated animation to the landlord.

'Time to go,' he said, standing.

That same blue ball of light was in his left hand again, but this time Fletcher saw a beam of light lance out and, in front of the fireplace, it seemed to rip the air open with a sound like splitting canvas. An opening appeared, a rectangular space of blackness, its edges tinged with blue. Firestarta grabbed him by the scruff of his neck, frogmarched him to the black void and said, 'Don't be scared, it's just one step. Just don't look down. Or up. Or sideways,' then shoved him roughly through the opening.

There was only one way into the snug, through the door to the street, and Firestarta could see dark figures through the grime of the adjacent window. He followed Fletcher into the void.

As the door to the snug banged open and the edges of the blackness started to close, a large hand and muscled arm came back from beyond, grabbed the bottle of Scotch from the table and vanished again as the portal shut with a loud snap.

'Blimey. Did you see that Sarge?' said one of the black-coated men.

'No. No, I don't think I did,' said the Sarge, shaking his

head. Ever practical, the Sarge could handle drunken sailors, vagabonds and villains. This was beyond his experience. 'And if you've any sense in that head of yours, you didn't either!'

PART 1
OF SECRETS BIG AND SMALL

(Present day)
1. The Water Garden

<u>**Mookination**</u>:
The home of Mooks on planet Earth, an extinct shield volcano approximately the same size as Hawaii (the Big Island) and midway between Ecuador and Papua New Guinea. Originally formed from six separate eruptions from between one and five million years ago. The last eruption created the impressive caldera (the hollow centre of the island) and probably formed the eastern-most split known as 'Giant's Cleave'. The island has been undetectable to human Bigfolk for over 200 years due to total masque* being in effect. The masque is powered by a single designated plasmic** and extends 300 miles in all directions. It is proof against all forms of Bigfolk observation, including orbital, sonar, radar and photography. To all intents and purposes, it simply is not there

*See 'Masque & Masquerade'
**Mookination has five functioning plasmics, the filaments that concentrate and draw plasmic energy from the planet core and beyond.

Mookipedia

Mookin was nearly out of the school gate, heading for home, her mind occupied with the afternoons lessons, before one of her friends tugged her arm and said, 'Mookin, where are you going? The Water Garden? Remember?'

She stopped, turned on a heel, and sped back into the school grounds. 'Thanks, Sky,' she shouted over her shoulder to her friend. She had almost forgotten.

Feet pounding, heart racing, purple hair streaming behind her, Mookin ran as fast as her long legs could carry her. Earlier, during a class on basic plasmagication glyphs, a message had been passed to her. She had been summoned by the Big G – Grandeldron Fastheart Freddimook – to meet in the Water Garden after school. He was the most senior of all Mooks, last survivor of the original Mook High Council, the first eleven. In his 'day job', he was mayor of the Three Mookins (Mookinsouth, Mookinorth and Mookinwest) and most knew him as Big Mook or, more affectionately, as Uncle Big Mook or UBM.

Past the great hall, past the library, into the orangery, through the big greenhouse and down the path to the towering outer wall. No time to stop to sniff the flowers or admire the blossom, she sped along the path at the base of the outer wall to where, behind a privet hedge clipped in the shape of a grumpalump, a hidden archway held a wooden door. It creaked and groaned through lack of use as she pushed it open, flakes of peeling paint coming away on her fingers as she shoved it closed behind her. This was a short cut which she hoped would make her not *too* late for UBM.

She hurried along well-worn twisting paths of random stone, brick and tile, relishing the moist air of the garden, heading down its many terraces towards the central sound of splashing water. The Water Garden was attached to the school in Mookinsouth and was a wonderful place to spend peaceful afternoons, with its many strange and exotic plants from all around Mookination's jungle regions, its hidden areas with seats and swings, and its hundreds of tinkling streams and splashing waterfalls cascading into deep pools where rainbow slivers of fish could be glimpsed darting between plants.

As she dashed between flowers as big as dustbin lids, sending clouds of sweet-scented pollen into the air, Mookin was at last able to see the top of the tower at the very heart of the garden. Styled after a Chinese pagoda, the six-tiered structure was all roofs; they surrounded the red-brick tower on all sides, each smaller than the roof below and comprised of green tile. The top-most roof was made of verdigris copper, a bright green that almost matched the tile. Water, pumped up from the pond, cascaded down over each successive roof until, at ground level, it created a curtain of shimmering water, which obscured the lower level from the outside. It was set alone in the centre of the large pond.

Mookin slowed to a walk as she wanted to appear calm and composed for her meeting. A broad path ran around the edge of the pond, and Mookin stopped when she reached a moss-covered stone lantern and then stepped straight out into the water. It looked, to a casual observer, like magic at work, and the first time she had seen it, she too thought it was magic, but the explanation was much simpler. Just millimetres below the surface of the pond there was a glass-bricked path running out to the tower. You just had to know it was there.

As she approached the water curtain, the last slab in the sunken path moved very slightly, causing a wooden beam to slide out of the roof and into the stream of water creating a gap through which she could walk without getting wet. She stepped through. As soon as she had passed, the curtain once again closed behind her. She looked around, as always, pleased to be here.

It was surprisingly warm, dry and quiet inside the cascade. The gurgle of water was barely noticeable, and all other sounds were muffled. A dappled light came from the Dragon Tongues, four perpetual flames springing from metal grilles in the tiled floor causing the shadows to dance and flicker. The base of the tower was open on each side, its weight supported on large arching pillars, the Dragon Tongues set in the centre of each arch, two blue and two red on opposite sides. In the middle, big squishy sofas formed a square.

Uncle Big Mook was standing with his back to Mookin and appeared to be warming his backside on one of the blue flames. He had obviously not heard her enter, so, in as deep a voice as she could manage, she gave a loud 'hurrumph!'

UBM jumped slightly and stepped back so that the blue flame touched his jacket. There was a little 'whoomph' noise as the fluff of his jacket ignited and a band of orange fire rushed up his back, but it vanished as quickly as it came. He spun about quickly, patting with both hands and checking that his striped grey hair, ear tufts, eyebrow and moustache tips were all intact, before looking at Mookin over the top of his glasses.

'Apologies, Grandeldron Freddimook,' she said. She bowed from the waist in formal greeting. 'Did I startle you, sir?'

'Mookin Bettymook. You know very well that you did,' he replied. 'My fault though. My fault. I was miles away. Miles away.' He gathered himself up before continuing. 'Anyway, now that you are here' – he checked his pocket watch hung on a gold chain across his ample belly – 'how are you, my dear?'

She approached him slowly, until they were within arm's reach. It had been quite a while since she had seen him, and then only at formal occasions, with his full entourage in tow. *He looks tired*, she thought. He looked old, of course, he always had, but always full of vigour, always with a spring in his step. She wanted to throw her arms around his neck, hug him as she had as a child, when he would spin her around until she squealed. Now, she towered a full head over him and could probably spin *him* around. 'I've missed my favourite uncle,' she replied. Do they keep you too busy to visit?'

He smiled up at her, their eyes locking in shared memories of parties and picnics and happy days. 'Actually, Betty, they do,' he said, 'and I'm rather fed up with it.'

Mookin opened her arms. 'May I?' she asked.

'What? Yes, of course, my dear. Of course.' She leaned down to hug him, kissing both cheeks. UBM gestured towards the sofas and they both sat down, Mookin kicking off her shoes and tucking her legs up.

'Am I in trouble, Uncle Freddi?' she asked.

'Trouble, Betty? No, not in trouble. Well, no more than usual I expect. Why?'

'Why did you ask to see me? What's wrong?'

'Nothing's wrong, dear. But I am afraid I must ask a favour of you. How old are you now, Betty? Sixteen?'

'Seventeen, Uncle. Eighteen in seven months.' Mookin's curiosity stirred. She had no idea where this was headed.

'Really? I think I missed a birthday or two, somewhere. Please forgive me.' He was quiet for some time, gathering his thoughts, before continuing. 'Ordinarily, what I am about to suggest would not occur until after you graduate in four or five years' time, and even then, probably not for a further five or six years into your chosen profession. Have you given any thought to your future, Betty?'

He looked into her brown, gold-flecked eyes, framed by her purple, non-striped hair. So rare amongst Mooks. So special. Soon, she would need to know what she was. But first, she required training.

'Well, if I'm not in trouble, and as it's Choosday, I was hoping to get home for my Peking duck pizza. It's my favourite,' she explained, a mischievous grin tugging at the corners of her mouth.

'What? No, no, I meant... Oh Mookin Bettymook, you're just teasing your old uncle! Shall we have a cup of tea?'

'Yes please,' smiled Mookin, 'but can I have cocamint?'

'Cocamint? Yes, of course. Anything for my special niece.'

Uncle Big Mook, Grandeldron of the Mook High Council, raised his left hand, thumb and little finger pressed tightly together, a slightly dreamy look in his eyes. Then, as he drew them apart, a spiderweb-thin strand of bright blue light flowed between them. In the centre of the strand, a small white ball appeared and grew to the size of a ping-pong ball. Inside the ball seemed to be a tiny ornate table. A small flash of intense light came from Uncle Big Mook's hand and the tiny table grew rapidly to life size, depositing itself on the floor in front of them, complete with two steaming mugs and a plate of Mayacookies.

There was a faint tinge of ozone in the air, which was soon overpowered by the wonderful aroma of steaming 'coffee'*, which Mookin thought strange, seeing as neither of them had wanted coffee. She leaned forward, picked up her cup and said, 'The cookies are a nice touch, but the table is just showing off. And, um, I think...' taking a sip from her cup, '... mmm, yes. I seem to have mint tea, and you have' – leaning over to peek into the other cup – 'ahh yes, a mochaccino with extra cream and chocolate sprinkles.'

UBM spluttered and went red again. 'Would you rather have the mint tea, Uncle?' said Mookin, just about managing to keep from laughing.

'Erm, yes please, Mookin,' replied Uncle Big Mook, cheeks glowing. 'I should have concentrated more on the drinks and a bit less on the table. Pretty table, though, don't you think?'

Mookin knew her uncle was probably the most powerful and accomplished wielder in the world, and also that what he'd just done was not a conjuring trick. The table, drinks and cookies had to be transported from the school kitchens through what was called a D-way, a doorway, a type of portal.

Moving inanimate objects required only the simplest type of D-way; very little plasmic energy (PE) was necessary, and not much concentration. If Uncle Big Mook was making simple mistakes, he was distracted. He had something on his mind, and it wasn't tables or cookies. Mookin swapped the mugs over, and holding hers in two hands, resumed her position.'Right. To business,' said UBM, picking up his mug and spilling a little on his jacket. Hepulled out his hanky with the other hand and dabbed at the spots on his jacket, all in one

*Coffee is actually a drink called **'kawfee'** by the Mooks. It bears no relation to Bigfolk coffee and has many therapeutic properties in addition to its wonderful aroma. The pronunciation is similar, and it fulfils the same role in social situations and so to avoid confusion, the spelling has been changed.

fluid motion. It was a familiar movement, as if he'd done it many times before and which Mookin was fairly sure he had.

'Your future, besides pizza. What plans do you have?'

'We-e-ll,' she replied, thinking hard. 'I suppose I could join the family, helping Mum and Dad and Djinny run the farm – there is always a lot to do. Dad keeps charming new varieties, and they're always so popular. But then, the last time Mikki was home for a visit, she made dragon mining sound fascinating. The liberation of dragons is such a worthwhile cause and she hasn't looked back since joining the Mookundas.'

'Both noble professions, farming and mining,' said UBM. 'Or you could, of course, join your eldest sister. Being a Mookon has its own rewards too: diving, surfing, rock climbing, the croakanut harvest. Why, the pearl beds and dolphin school are enough for most people, but I hear young Jaci has become quite an accomplished weaver too?'

'Yes, we're very proud of her. She has another exhibition next month.'

A rug by Jacaranda Jacimook, Mookin's eldest sister, takes pride of place in many Mook homes. The fantastically detailed patterns are woven from thread created by Merfolk, who live in and around the reefs of Mookination. Little is known of how they create their fibres, which they turn into thread using a process known only to them. Apart from seafood, it is their only exportable product, which they trade with Mooks in return for metal tools and protection from the large predators of the deep ocean. Mooks do not require payment for that protection, but the Merfolk insist. The thread is much stronger than any other type available and almost indestructible. Mookin had acquired a spool from Jaci on her last visit home, a new type of merthread, even stronger, which she planned to put to an entirely different use than weaving.

'Betty, it is at this point that I must interject. I must ask this favour of you. A situation is developing, out there, in the

Bigfolk world. Would you consider starting training for the Mookouts?'

Mookin choked, spraying coffee everywhere. 'What?' she exclaimed. 'Are you serious, Uncle?'

UBM passed over his handkerchief, and Mookin wiped her chin and the bottom of her cup.

'Yes. Entirely serious, Betty. I only wish it were otherwise, but we have a mission that requires a young female, and I have no one to fit the bill. No one upcoming in training. We have a little time, just enough to bring you up to speed, as it were, but that is it.'

'Do Mum and Dad know? Have you spoken with them?'

'Not yet. I wanted to discuss it with you first.'

'Why? Why me?' Mookin's heart felt as if it would crash through her ribcage, and her pulse was racing. There didn't seem to be enough air to breath properly as her head filled with a thousand questions, but that was the only one she trusted herself to utter.

'Have you ever wondered about your hair, Betty?' UBM asked.

'My hair? What does that have to do with anything?'

'How many of your friends, your family, have your hair?'

'None, Uncle. Is it significant?'

'The purple hair has great significance among the Mooks, my dear. It is more than rare; it is exceptional, and usually so are the Mooks who have it.'

'Well, if you are trying to make me feel weird, Uncle, I have to tell you, you're succeeding.' Mookin knew that she was a little different, she always had. She was the only Mook she knew of without the striped hair. She had never been treated any differently because of it. No one had ever made fun of her, or even questioned why her hair was that way. There were other things, though. Little things that she hadn't mentioned to anyone.

'That was not my intention, Betty; I mention it only in

passing. Each of us has unique attributes. One of yours is your hair. I am sure we will find many more in the months ahead. Now, what is your answer?'

'I... I'm too young, surely?'

'Not for what we have in mind. You will be amongst Bigfolk girls, a little younger than you, fifteen or sixteen, but you will fit in perfectly. There should be no danger of any kind.'

'Can I think about it? Can I tell Mum and Dad?'

'Hmm. Yes. Yes, I think so, it's not exactly a secret. They will have to know where you are going. I would, of course, have discussed this with them, and I will, but I wanted to get your feelings on the matter first. I think, for the meantime, if you agree, we will start you off with two days a week. Let's say every Thawtsday and Fryday until further notice. Report to Commander Spekalmook, at the Learning Tree, bright and early, later this week. He will be expecting you.'

'Commander *Spekalmook? The* Commander Spekalmook? *Firestarta* Spekalmook?'

Firestarta was nothing less than a legend amongst Mooks. The stories about his exploits in the Bigfolk world went back centuries. Mookin was trembling now, a little scared, yes, but also excited. As UBM had said, she had never heard of anyone so young being selected for Mookouts. They were the best: specially selected, specially trained. The Mookouts went out into the Bigfolk world in total secrecy, they spoke to Bigfolk, helped them, protected them from the accidental effects of magic, interacted with them. They intervened, they rescued magical creatures and objects from harm or misuse. They actually got to *use* magic. Every Mook used magic, of course, but not the way Mookouts did. In Mookination, there was a tendency *not* to use it, unless absolutely necessary, the thought being that it made you a little bit lazy and dependent. It was never forbidden, that would be foolish, like telling you not to breathe. No, for mundane, everyday life, you just didn't. It was one of those unspoken rules. Of course, UBM was an Eldron, so you kind of expected him to use magic. But for making your bed or harvesting crops or travelling, it was a big fat no.

They talked for perhaps another hour, UBM reassuring Mookin that she was more than up to the task ahead, that this wasn't the first time that a Mook so young had been selected for a mission, it did happen from time to time, and that she would have all the help, training and support that she would require. Mookin was not convinced. Her legs were trembling as she stood to leave.

Fastheart Freddimook, Mayor of the Three Mookins (Bigmook), former commander of Mook Fleet #991 and senior Eldron of the Mook High Council (Very Bigmook or Grandeldron), watched Mookin disappear as the water curtain dropped behind her and she walked away across the pond, not noticing the water splashing her legs. He loved her deeply, as he did all his descendants, his family. He paused for a moment, gathering his strength about him like a warm blanket on a chill night. He took a deep breath, stood a little straighter, and some of the persona of Uncle Big Mook left him. He turned around and walked through the archway into the tower proper. His casting hand flashed blue and the staircase leading to the tower's upper levels rose upwards with barely a sound, revealing another exit from the tower. This was a spiral ramp that led down into the depths below the Water Garden. Only UBM, the other Eldron and '*the 33*' knew of this place. Freddi himself had overseen its construction long, long ago. The Water Garden had been placed above as means of concealment; the flames, the Dragon's Tongues, were used to burn off dangerous fumes that seeped from the volcano below.

This was Hub, the nerve centre of Mookination, where ultimately all information ended up. Here, it was processed and distilled, helping formulate plans and decisions. Plans and decisions that affected the whole planet, not just Mooks, but Bigfolk too. Three floors, each as large as a football pitch. On the first, Freddi entered the area known affectionately as the Hive, where eleven of the thirty-three Eldrex (one step down from Eldron) reclined in well-padded chairs. They were seemingly asleep but, in reality, were hooked up to the Hub system by Mindlynk (a mental connection similar to the MuRM used by Mookouts). The range of the Mindlynk was deliberately limited, not reaching beyond these walls. Flat-screen displays played in front of them, the visual part of their data stream. The Eldrex, Mindlynked, absorbed, analysed and sifted information from across the globe and shaped it into packets to feed to the Eldron, like chocolates from a bottomless box.

Nowadays, the flow never stopped, and Freddi was quite sick of it. *I'm quite sick of it,* he thought. *What's wrong with these flupping humans? The conflicts and deceits, corruption and exploitation, it just goes on and on and on. Governments and religions? Don't get me started.* He undid his bow tie and let it dangle, unbuttoned his waistcoat and removed his jacket, hanging it carefully on a wooden hanger. He dropped into his chair which swivelled to face his bank of screens as they flickered to life in front of him. The chair grabbed hold of him and filaments snaked into sockets at the base of his skull, hidden by his hairline and so small as to be almost invisible.

The Eldrex on shift acknowledged him as he came online and requested permission to transmit packets to him. He asked them to please hold for a moment. Time in Mindlynk was greatly extended or even suspended; what seemed like a day here could be merely minutes outside. Time here had little meaning. Mentally, it could be exhausting work.

Instead of getting started with the mundane, UBM probed downwards, to the third floor, a part of which was given over to storage. Storage of a very special type.

Freddimook was the last of his kind. He'd commanded the

Fleet, but his fellow Eldron had been the real leaders and decision-makers. He had been almost a token, an honorary appointment to make up the eleven. All gone now.

Dead, technically. Not totally gone, though. Stored. Frozen.

Frozen, but still accessible. He woke them with a single directed thought. Images flickered into being before his mind's eye. They spoke as one now, having been interconnected for so long they were a single entity.

'It is done then?' they intoned. The voice that reached him did not exist in the real world, only in his head. It had a strange, echoing quality, as if spoken through a long narrow pipe. He didn't know if they supplied the voice, or if his brain provided it based on what he expected to hear.

'The first step? Yes. Done.' *Good*, he thought, *they didn't waffle on, at least. That was a blessing.* 'It's up to Firestarta now.'

'Firestarta? Yes. We... recall... him.'

'She is the one, you think?' he asked.

'She is of the correct lineage. The purple is the indicator.'

'We've waited so long. Her great grandmother...'

'An unfortunate incident. The loss, tremendous.'

Their mortal remains were kept at an extreme low temperature, never rising above -150°C, where magical things happened to electrical resistance, the spinal cord and cerebral cortex pumped with fluid to prevent further ice damage. It was the fluid, rich in derbots, that had initially enabled the Mindlynk.

The damage had started slowly: some stuttering, a little loss of balance, some minor memory loss or lack of concentration. It was subtle, not easily noticed. These ten though, who comprised the Hub, had made too many trips in and out of hibernation. While most Mooks had remained in a constant state of induced slumber, to emerge unscathed, those of the Hub had awoken and returned hundreds, thousands of times from the Big Sleep. The effects were, unfortunately, cumulative and irreversible. The repeated in-and-out over thousands of years had done its damage. At the time, derbots had not existed that could affect repairs on damaged brain tissue, so the ten elected to be stored before they deteriorated further. At the extreme low temperature at which they were kept, and with the addition of the derbot-rich spinal nano-soup, an unexpected phenomenon manifested itself. Their minds were set free by the super-conducting super-cold. They began to talk to each other. Tendrils and whispers of thought went one to the other, back and forth over months, years, decades, centuries.

Until they found Fastheart Freddimook and scared him witless. He'd only come to pay his respects, not be mentally assaulted from beyond the grave. Talk about ghosts! He'd sought the help of Dr Finestra and it was she who'd figured it out, quickly establishing a two-way communication. It was the cold, she told him later. Just as you cooled a micro-processor on a computer, the extreme cold turned their minds into super-conductors. They were now so interlinked, she doubted they could ever be revived; it would be impossible to separate their consciousness back into ten individuals.

Ten minds. Ten Mook minds. Linked over a vast period of time. They now had at their disposal an organic super-computer of staggering ability. Freddi had built the Water Garden around them, both a tomb and monument to fallen comrades, and as protection, to disguise what had become of them. Freddi was never sure of the ethics of what he had done, but with no precedent in Mook history to guide him, he had consulted Hub, and they had agreed. It was a lucky accident and should be used to benefit Mooks, they told him. Should he have just withdrawn life support and let his colleagues and friends fade away? Let them die? Would that have been a more fitting end for their sacrifice? He could have built a real tomb for them, above ground, where all Mooks could pay their respects. He didn't know the answers then, and he still didn't.

Soon, he would have to train another to take his place, to act as intermediary between Hub and the outside. Perhaps one of the Eldrex. There were thirty-three of them, eleven on shift at any one time plus, usually, an Eldron such as himself to confirm their suggested course of action. He and the other Eldron were nearing the end of their lifespan. They survived on Mookination because of the five overlapping plasmics. On Earth, it was unique. Away from the island, their energy and abilities depleted quickly, and they could not draw sufficient PE from their surroundings to sustain them. Here, they could last many, many years, but it was a sure sign that the end was drawing near. Soon. Not yet, but soon. He could feel it in his bones.

Freddi had another secret. Something was brewing. Something was lurking out there. They had effectively lost contact with the rest of Mook-kind centuries ago. The Million Keyways, the star chamber, had not received a data burst in all that time. Freddi no longer made scheduled visits to the cave. They were cut off. Something had happened. Something bad. Whether old terror or new, he didn't know, but it was out there. He could feel it.

He signalled the Eldrex and packets were shunted to his in-box. He became part of the machine, unzipping packets of hi-speak*, scanning, distilling, sifting. Pushing more and more data through to Hub. It hummed quietly in the deep, dark cold.

*Hi-speak: concentrated form of Mook communication using a carrier-wave and high-pitched warbling.

2. Big Breakfast

Breakfast, on non-schooldays, has always been special with Mookin and her family. It was a time to catch up, impart each other's news, plans and any other general gossip. As farmers, they were always up before dawn and out in the fields by sunburst, tending crops and fruit to help feed Mookination.

Just her mum had been up last night when Mookin arrived home, her older sister Djinny, younger brother Kikkit and her dad had already gone to bed. She had started to tell her mum about the Water Garden and Uncle Big Mook, but Mum had fussed over her, getting pizza from the oven where it had been warming and placing it in front of Mookin on the table. No doubt her mum assumed she had been at Tammy's or Debs' house, which is where she was often to be found when not at home.

'Everything all right, Betty?' she had asked.

'Yes, Mum. I... have some news, but I'd rather you and dad were both here.'

'He's fast asleep, sweetheart. Will it wait until morning?'

'I guess so.' Mookin's mind was in turmoil. She had a thousand questions and as many doubts and no one to question.

Her mum must have caught some tone or hesitation in her voice. 'I could always wake him...?'

'No. No, Mum. It's fine. It will wait until breakfast.'

'Okay, if you're sure. Mind if I turn in, love? I must have picked two cart-loads of grapples today.'

'You go on up, Mum. Love you.'

'Love you too, sweetheart. Left you some coffee in the pot. Night.' Her mum had kissed the top of her head and left the room.

They were all sitting around the large kitchen table in various stages of devouring toasted sandwiches spread with butterberry and filled with friedbacon, scrambled eggs and cheesfruit. Mookin was on her second and Kikkit was trying to persuade Djinny to split a third one with him. Dad was talking chickens with Mum, and Mookin was wondering if now was the right time to tell them. She decided to wait a moment, until she had finished eating. She reached for the coffee pot and refilled her mug, letting the aroma waft over her. She took a deep breath. 'Mum? Dad?'

Mookin related her encounter with Uncle Big Mook in the Water Garden the evening before, trying to recall every detail. The table had fallen into rapt silence as soon as she had mentioned his name. Even Kikkit had stopped eating, his jaw dropping open when she told them of UBM's proposal.

The silence continued long after she had finished. Mum and Dad, Djinny and Kikkit were all exchanging incredulous looks, unspoken questions on their lips.

'But... that's tomorrow, Betty,' said Mookin's dad, at last.

'I know, Dad. UBM said he was going to speak to you and Mum. I assume he means sometime today.'

'Sweetheart,' said her mum, 'are you sure he said "Mookout", not something else?' She looked imploringly at her husband, as if Mookin had been given a death sentence.

'Betty, this is, uh, unusual, to say the least. I will call in to the town hall this morning, after I've done my chores, and get to the bottom of this. Uncle Freddi has some explaining to do.'

Kikkit, fit to burst, managed to ask, 'I don't get it. What's wrong with Mooky being a Mookout and going to the Learning Tree?'

'Nothing Kik,' Djinny answered for everyone. 'It's a huge honour. Only fifty-five or so Mooks a year get to go to the Learning Tree and fewer still go on to be Mookouts.'

'How do you feel about it, Betty?' asked her mum.

Mookin's mind had been reeling, her thoughts going round and round. Her life on Mookination was perfect. Her family, her friends. Mookination was a paradise, of that there was no doubt: every day was perfection, free from worries, hunger, illness and threat. Then why did it leave her wanting?

Mikki, her oldest sister, now a Mookunda, had been training Mookin from the age of six in the art of climbing and caving. She was accomplished in her own right now and was passing the skills on to her friends. She enjoyed the unknown, the darkness and freshness of previously unexplored caves. The not knowing, the trepidation. That tingle in her belly when she stepped off a rock face in a harness. The danger. She liked the danger, she realised.

She was at the end of her childhood. Tammy and Debs, her closest friends, whom she was meeting later today, had been talking about it lately. Things were going to change anyway. Everything would soon get a bit more grown up and serious as they passed their eighteenth birthdays.

'I'm scared, Mum,' she answered, looking from face-to-face, noting the concern in her parents' eyes, Djinny giving her a barely perceptible nod of encouragement, Kikkit being all twelve-year-old boy and ready to burst. 'But I want this, I think.'

3. The Plunge at Wysend

Food:

Mookination is self-sufficient in the production of foodstuffs. Although not strictly vegetarian, most food is plant-grown and not animal-based, with the exception of fish. Nearly all meat: beef, pork, chicken, lamb and mutton are now produced on specially charmed plants and are indistinguishable from the original animal both in texture and taste. Friedbacon is a recent innovation from the Rosadale-Dell Farm, as are butterberries and cheesfruit.

Plant-derived meat products are normally referred to by their lavour rather than animal type. 'Roastbeef', 'lambstew' or 'friedbacon' indicates the taste and texture, NOT the cooking method. See also section on 'grapples' and 'kawfee'

Mookipedia

Spydasylk Debboramook had a rude awakening. It came in the form of her younger sister, Mirranda Mabelmook, landing squarely astride her and pinning her arms under the duvet with one leg expertly placed alongside each of Debs' arms.

'Ooomph!' exploded Debs, as most of the air was forced from her mouth by the weight of Mabe. It was several bleary, befuddled seconds before Debs realised what was happening. At first, the situation insinuated itself into her dreams, and she was quite convinced she was trapped in a giant sandwich between two massive slices of bread. 'No! No! I'm not friedbacon!' she cried out.

'Ha, ha, ha,' screeched Mabe, as she leant forward until she was nearly nose to nose with Debs and switched on the light. Debs, still befuddled and sleepy, her blue and green striped hair plastered to her face, her dark green sleep-dusted eyes blinking rapidly in the harshness of the reading light, tried very hard to force her head backwards into the pillow in an effort to focus on the blob in front of her face.

'Mabe? Mabel? Is that you? What the flup are you doing? Get off me this second!'

'Uh, nope.'

'Listen, bug-eater, get off me now, and I promise I'll let you off with just a head-rub. Okay?'

'Uh, we-ell. The thing is... Nope.'

Debs gave a tentative wiggle, testing the extent of her captivity. Damn. She was pinned. It was her own fault, she'd taught her sister too well. Usually, it was Debs on top. She struggled some more. Debs was quite stocky for a Mook. She still carried some puppy fat that most Mooks of her build and age had lost, but in fact, she was mostly muscle. 'You'll... regret... this... you little...' She bucked and rocked even more, to little effect.

Mabe laughed harder and leaned forward again, her face a hand's breadth from her sister's.

'What are you doing?' said Debs, a note of panic creeping into her voice. 'You wouldn't dare?'

Mabe's grey-green eyes flashed with wicked glee. She made a hawking noise at the back of her throat, more for effect than anything, just as Debs would do if the roles were reversed, which they very often were. She sucked all the saliva in her mouth into a ball and pushed it forward with her tongue until it dangled from her lips.

'Lizard spit! No! Don't! You wouldn't... No! Wait! I'm sorry. You would, you would.' Debs wriggled and twisted her head away from the trajectory of the spit ball. The spit hung by a slim strand and Mabe sucked it back into her mouth with a slurp.

'Oh, sorry now, are you? Sorry enough to do my chores for a week, eh?'

'What? No chance. I'd rather...' The spit dangled again, and Debs watched in fascinated horror as it glistened. 'Wait, wait.'

Slurp. 'Yes, sister dear?'

'I will...' Debs' eyes bulged and her faced reddened even more. A vein pulsed in her neck.

'...pulverise you, you maggot!' With a concerted effort, Debs managed to slip her hands down the sides of the mattress and push upwards with all her might. Mabe's eyes went wide in surprise as her head crashed into the wooden slats of her own bunk bed above. She hardly paused. Long association with Debs told her it was time to exit the scene. Debs was free. She ran.

Debs rolled from under the duvet onto the floor and was up and running as Mabe disappeared through the door. She launched herself up from the floor and leapt after her, straight into her father's stomach.

'Ooomph! Debs? What on Mookination is going on?'

'Ah. Um. Nothing, Dad. Just playing. With Sis. Sorry, did we wake you?'

'Wake me? No. I sent Mabel to wake *you,* sleepy-head.'

Mabe appeared at Dad's elbow. She poked her tongue out at Debs, crossed her arms and smiled in the smug, infuriating way that only younger siblings can.

'Why?' asked Debs.

'Have you forgotten? It's Woodsday today. You're going out with your friends, aren't you? And you've overslept.'

'Oh flup!' muttered Debs, as she raced for the bathroom.

Woodsdays were the days Mooks of all ages would spend time in the Ringwood. Younger Mooks supervised by older brothers, sisters or parents would play, climb trees and swing on ropes, finding truffles and strange plants and just about anything a Mook could get up to in the woods and jungles of Mookination. Older Mooks were left to their own devices, exploring further into the jungle regions and the lower slopes of the mountains. They camped out, learned bush-craft and survival skills, hunting game and each other. It was not unheard of for an epic game of hide and seek to take place, sometimes with whole villages taking part, adult Mooks too, and sometimes lasting from sunburst until after deepdark. It was a time of learning and appreciation of nature.

At about the same time as Debs was racing to the bathroom, Tammy was setting out from home. She loved the tranquillity of the pre-dawn darkness. She'd been first up and had left her parents a note on the kitchen worktop saying where she was going today, and with whom, as if there was any doubt of that! She didn't know with any certainty what time they would be home, but had said not much after deepdark at the latest. Her red and gold striped hair was tied back in a short plait to keep it out of the way. Her rucksack was uncomfortably heavy on her shoulders but would lighten as the day wore on. A lot of it was food and water. She ran through Mookin's packing list in her head once more, making sure she had everything, and hoping Debs, for once, had done the same. Mookin was, quite rightly, very strict regarding their adventures and drew up a must-have list before each one. If anything was missing, Mookin was likely to cancel or postpone the trip. Safety was Mookin's main concern, she knew.

Tammy was first to reach the village. Mookinsouth was deserted at this time of day. Steam curled from the roof of the bakery across the street, but the shopfront was still dark. Even so, Tammy caught the delicious whiff of freshly baked bread. She would buy a loaf to share with her friends as soon as the shop opened. She searched her pockets and found a single, crumpled credit. *Just enough.*

Mooks didn't really use money, as such. Instead, they exchanged 'credits', like banknotes, but based on work hours. Anyone could issue credits and many Mook families had their own printed notes. If you helped someone with work, household chores, harvesting, fishing, cutting hair, building, carrying – almost anything – they would give you credits. These could be exchanged for goods in the shops or in return for someone else helping you. Each Mook donated work hours each week solely to the community without receiving credits, but apart from this, all other work received credits as payment for time. One hour's work = one credit. It was simple and it worked because on Mookination no one exploited anyone else. No one was rich; no one was poor. Everyone was equal and everyone, including children (who received credits for attending school), worked their share.

Tammy's stomach gave a lurch at the smell of the bread and she was suddenly ravenous, even though she'd eaten a full breakfast not an hour ago. She knew full well that she was going to be burning extra calories today though.

She patted her belly and said, 'Sorry mate, just going to have to wait for the baker.' She dropped her backpack on the ground and sat on the boardwalk step outside the smithery to wait for her friends. She was early. She heard a noise and looked over her shoulder to see lights appear in the back of Mr Morningside's shop. He was already up and working.

Morningside Tinkamook wiped his oily hands on a square of rag that would never be clean again. Although he boil-washed them in one of his own designed and built washing machines every week, they resisted the strongest detergents and still came out looking stained and grubby. *Hmm. Maybe if I added a few handfuls of gravel? That might work. It would provide a pounding action, maybe loosen the oil,* he thought.

He stood back and admired his stock. Everything gleamed in the overhead lights, the bare metal glinting like chrome. Tinka liked to polish and lacquer bare metal until it glowed. Rows of bikes and trikes stood to attention in racks throughout the large barn. Once it had been retired unicorns, the horses of Mookination, which he'd lovingly cared for, plaiting manes and tails, currycombing to a soft sheen and shoeing hoof after hoof. They required attention above and beyond that of normal horses. They were proud and intelligent

61

creatures. But the population had declined in recent centuries and bikes had been a decent compromise.

Now he lovingly cared for them, too. Not quite the same, but he had a gift with all things mechanical, electrical and technical. In an hour or so, they would all be gone, over two hundred of them, as young Mooks and families set off on their weekly Woodsday adventures.

He had the first three ready right at the front, for Miss Bettymook and her friends. She was always first to set off and he'd greased the chains and adjusted the brakes.

Tinka wondered if they would ever tell her. Secrets didn't sit well with Mooks, they gnawed away at your soul, and she would have to know one day. Despite what they told the kids, what they grew up believing, Mooks did have secrets, though. And they kept them. As an Eldron, he had sworn like the others, but it struck a nerve. It was Mookin who would face the challenges ahead. Perhaps it was for the best that she enjoyed these few brief years of childhood.

Morningside Tinkamook, he scolded himself, *you are getting old and maudlin.* He pulled a large bronze-coloured pocket watch from his waistcoat and flipped the case open. The exposed mechanism was one of his own. *Just enough time before opening,* he thought. Re-pocketing the watch, his fingers absently followed the chain draped across his belly to the other pocket. He pulled out the fob nestled there on the other end of the chain. A large, heart-shaped diamond, multifaceted, sparkled in the palm of his hand. Light bounced, reflected and danced from its facets, and rainbows and stars spun within. This was his. They all had one. All of the Eldron. He was sworn to guard and protect it, with his life if necessary. It was entirely mesmerising, both for its beauty and for its legacy. It was a key to the galaxy, yes, or, if necessary, the power to destroy a quarter of a planet.

Maudlin indeed. This would never do. He packed it away and, from a rack on the wall, lifted down a polished lacquer scabbard embellished in gold with his 'glyph', a flat representation of the three-dimensional glyph in his mind that told everything that was 'Morningside Tinkamook'. He unsheathed the seventy-five centimetres of cutting-edge perfection in one fluid movement and placed the scabbard back in the rack. He spun on the spot and launched himself into a complex series of movements against imaginary foes. His morning combat ritual was different each day. Today it was the Katana, tomorrow would be the Bō staff, the day after that, projectile weapons.

His bare feet seemed almost to float across the practice floor, familiar with every ripple and knot in the varnished timber. In contrast to every other metal surface, the blade was dull grey, its 'hamon' a darker grey, zig-zagging along the length, which denoted the hardened edge. It slashed the air with a high-pitched whistle as the blade tip accelerated past 320kph (200mph) producing the 'TachiKaze', the 'sword wind' which only the finest blades achieved. His arms were a blur, the blade describing near invisible arcs around him. Few could best him and it had been centuries since any had tried; with all sincerity, he hoped none ever would again. Now, he practised only for his own satisfaction. He no longer taught, no longer folded steel into weapons.

A final flick and he returned the blade to its resting place. It was one of his own creations, made here on the island, with skills first developed in sixth-century Japan, from ore he mined, blended, smelted and forged right here. The blades were hollow, the metal far denser than normal steel. Tinkatanium he called it, but only jokingly.

There was nothing like it. Except its brothers. Each was unique, but such was his skill that the blades were indistinguishable by eye from one another. Fifty blades rested in racks along the wall, the pinnacle of his art, all in their wooden sheaths, the handles removed and stored. He drew a sliding panel across in front of the blades, concealing them from curious eyes. He bowed and slipped his feet into black canvas pumps. It was time to open the door. The Terrible Trio would be waiting.

Today, Mookin and her two best friends, Tammy and Debs, had arranged to meet up, as they often did, at the edge of Mookinsouth, the village where they lived.

Tammy, Debs and Mookin were very close friends and always had been. All born on the same birthday, of course, as were all the Mooks in their year at school, but drawn to each other from a very young age. They just seemed to click.

Mookin had left her dad at the edge of the farm, where he gave her a reassuring hug and told her, as he always did, to be extra careful. She had walked past the shops, peeking briefly into darkened windows, then hurried the last hundred metres to the Mooksmithery.

'Blacksmith, Engineer, Inventor & General Tinkerer' the black sign with gold lettering announced outside Mr Morningside's shop, as it swayed gently in the morning breeze.

Debs and Tammy, who were sitting on the boardwalk outside, their bulging backpacks beside them, spotted Mookin as she walked down the centre of the road. They waved and smiled, pleased to be out and about with friends again. Tammy handed her a hunk of freshly baked bread.

The bell tinkled above the door of the shop as Mr Morningside pulled it open. Woodsday was always his busiest day, and he liked to open early, before sunburst, to get ready.

'Ah ha!' he said, 'the Terrible Trio ride again!'

'Morning, Mr Morningside,' the girls said in one voice. *We haven't called ourselves that since we were nine,* thought Debs, but didn't have the heart to mention it. Walking through into the shop, they puzzled over some of the weird and wonderful contraptions that Mr Morningside had on display.

Some whirred away on their own, some had little puffs of smoke or steam coming from them, others just sat there ominously, with polished brass and copper parts, offering no clue as to what they were for. The girls had learned that it was a mistake to take too much interest in the kindly old gentleman's inventions, and even worse to enquire what they did. It could be hours before you escaped, and it could even result in small explosions as he insisted on a quick demonstration.

They walked through into the rear of the shop which led out to the bike stable. Mr Morningside followed them out, saying, 'I have your bikes already oiled and tuned, ladies. All ready for your next adventure.'

The bikes, of course, did not belong to the three girls, they belonged to everyone, but Mr Morningside kept these three bikes apart just for Mookin and her two friends. They were old, some of the first batch he had created, but sturdy and in perfect working order. The girls had been riding these same three bikes, with some minor adjustments for height and reach, since they were nine years old. They were black, with gold pin-striping and larger wheels than later models. A cane basket at the front and a metal rack over the back wheel made them ideal for carrying their equipment and these came with ten gears where most had three or five.

Waving to Mr Morningside, they set off east, following the road along the shore of Starshine Lake. They were fast, wheels and legs a blur, and in an hour were nearly at the river where Mookin called for a break. Skidding to a stop, they left their bikes and walked over to a small mud cliff on the edge of the lake. They sat down and took water and crackers* from their packs, their feet dangling over the edge. They had their backs to Giant's Cleave, the enormous V-shaped gash that ran right through the Crown and the Ringwood, and which legend

*Actually 'Krakas', but pronunciation and item so similar as not to matter. Crisp, dry biscuit for cheese.

said had been made by a giant's axe as he used the island to pull himself from the sea into Mookination, and where he had rested before continuing his journey across the ocean. That was the story, but the girls had never believed it. There weren't any giants. Not anymore. And how big would he have had to be to wield an axe that size?

As they sat there chewing, Mookination was still in twilight, a quiet misty place of soft greyish greens and darker shadows. The night creatures were all quiet now; the day creatures were just stirring. There always seems to be a pause, a great expectation as Mookination holds its breath for a split second, and then silently, sunburst flashes in an instant through Giant's Cleave, across the interior of the island, light bouncing off the far side the Crown, glancing off the lake and seeming to set the land momentarily on fire.

All at once, Mookination is a riot of greens and yellows, reds and oranges, deep purples and the deep blue of the lake from which every wave top reflects a tiny silver sparkle of intense light, like stars in the night sky. The Crown, barely visible by day as its dull greys and browns fade into the pale sky, is suddenly plated in the flaming, glittering gold of the morning sun. In moments, the spectacle is over, but it's always worth the pause, and as the girls climbed back onto their bikes, the day creatures were up and about and Mookination had started another fine day.

The girls were heading for the River Wyse, which runs from the eastern end of the lake in a twisting, winding route where it is joined by many streams, brooks and smaller rivers. For most of its length, the Wyse is broad and gentle, great for swimming, perfect for boating and fishing, but further down, it gets squeezed between high banks and rocky gorges, speeding for its final leap.

Cycling hard, the three friends entered the Ringwood's welcome shade before the day became too hot. They had followed the Wyse but, leaving the road, had cut out many of its meandering loops and bends, sticking instead to a more direct trail, until the banks of the river gorge became too high. Then they cut into the woods, weaving through well-worn paths around rocks and bushes, the ground rising steeply until at last it was too steep and rocky to cycle.

Leaving their bikes at a place they called Rabbit Point, next to a large, vaguely rabbit-shaped boulder, they followed a path down and around through jagged boulders towards the Plunge.

They could hear the waterfalls and see plumes of mist rising while still some distance away. It was a beautiful day, with lots of birds in a huge variety of colours all zipping about the upper branches of the trees. Twice they spotted zebra squirrels on the path munching fallen nuts who quickly scampered out of sight around and up tree trunks, only to re-appear as soon as the girls were nearly out of sight. They passed marvellous blooms and foliage but took only cursory notice as they'd been through here many times.

Their plan today was to explore the area around the Plunge. Over thousands of years, the Wyse had carved out a large U-shaped plateau. At some point in the past the Wysend waterfall was undoubtedly the first step in Giant's Stairway. It had slowly eroded its way backwards into the island and today stood hundreds of metres back from the edge.

Emerging from the forest on to the plateau surrounding the Plunge, they blinked in the sudden sunshine before looking around. To their left was Wysend, the waterfall where the river dropped out of the gorge over a small rocky cliff into a deep pool below. The river became a mass of froth and bubbles before spreading out over the flat ledge it had eroded. The water over the plateau, except for the many little rock pools, was only a few centimetres deep and seemed to be hardly moving until it reached the Plunge, where it became narrower, deeper and faster before it dropped into the abyss.

The Plunge was a gaping crack, a fissure fifty or sixty paces back from the edge of Giant's Stairway, narrow nearest the girls, but deeper and wider as it moved to the far side.

Where once the water had all flowed over the cliff and down Giant's Stairway, now it was swallowed by the Plunge before it re-emerged lower down. The top four steps of the Stairway were dry and grass-covered now, but years ago the river had flowed straight over and cascaded down, all the way to the sea.

The girls moved off in single file towards the rising pillar of mist that marked the Plunge, but after just a few steps Tammy, at the front, stopped, causing her friends to crash into her.

'What's wrong, Tam, problem?' asked Debs, following Tammy's gaze back upstream.

'Mmm. Not sure. Does Wysend look different to you?'

'How do you mean? It's a waterfall. More water, less water, that's all they do,' she said.

'No, Tammy's right,' said Mookin, perking up. 'Something has changed. There were some bushes growing near the edge of the falls. They aren't there anymore, and there's something else about the –'

'Well, I can't see any...' interrupted Debs, not giving Mookin a chance to finish. 'No. Wait a minute, it's the cliff behind the falls. It's fallen away into the pool; look, there are some large rocks poking out.'

'Yes,' said Tammy. 'That's what it is. It looks like there's something behind the waterfall too, a shadow. What would that be, a cave or something?'

'A cave!' said Mookin and Debs as one, suddenly very excited.

'Yeah, but why would the cliff just fall away like that?'

'Lots of waterfalls do that, Tam,' answered Debs. 'If the rock underneath the lip of the falls is softer, like sandstone, the water will gradually wear it away.'

From their vantage point, Mookin could see both the cave behind the Wysend waterfall, and the plume of mist spiralling up from the Plunge. Recently, she had been told by her caving and climbing friends that the area around the Plunge had caved in, leaving a much larger opening, big enough to descend through with the help of a tripod, providing their ropes were long enough to reach the bottom. She speculated there was a cavern or, at the very least, a lava tube below the Plunge, and she wanted to be the first to explore it. It would be a good experience for Tammy and Debs, too, who hadn't done much harness and rope work. She looked from Plunge to Wysend and back again, pondered a moment, then a little switch in her mind went 'click'.

'Girls, I have an idea.'

B.J. PAGE

4. Disappearing Debs

Giant's Cleave:

In truth, Giant's Cleave probably saved Mookination. Most likely caused by a large, final eruption of the volcano, it allowed water to drain from the caldera. Without it, over many thousands of years, water would have filled the island, like a giant bowl under a dripping tap. Eventually, the weight of billions of tonnes of water would have split the island apart, causing a catastrophic failure of the plasmics. The Cleave reaches for over a kilometre into the caldera, and, as the River Wyse tumbles into the gorge forming the Wysend Falls, it has carved out a U-shape from which mist and spray constantly rise. Below this, the torrent spreads out over a plateau, running quite shallow. At the far end of the plateau, the river narrows once more and gathers itself for a leap into the dark; the river disappears into a large fissure called the 'Plunge', which appeared over 1,000 years ago following an earthquake. The Cleave floor, where it slopes down from the caldera to the sea, is aptly named 'Giant's Stairway' and descends in steps of between 10 and 20 metres, with the last step to the shingle beach being a cliff of over 50 metres. The Wyse re-emerges about a quarter of the way down Giant's Stairway, at the Love Pool, where it splits into hundreds of pools, terraces and waterfalls that tumble and cascade their way downwards. It's a favourite spot for Mooks, and come Kiteday, when the wind changes in the afternoon and comes roaring through the gorge towards the sea.*

See entries under 'Kiteday'. Further reading: 100 Designs for Kites *and* Tactics of Non-destructive Kite Combat, *both by Flutterby Soaramook.*

Mookipedia

The noise increased as they got closer, rock-hopping and splashing through the many pools of the plateau, mist from the falls wetting their faces, and they almost had to shout to hear each other by the time they reached the pool. Leaning in, almost touching heads, Mookin said, 'Which side? I can't see anything now.'

The other two shook their heads, puzzled.

'Nor me, I think it was the angle of the light where we were. Now the sun is higher, it just looks normal,' said Debs, Tammy nodding her head in agreement.

'Look,' said Tammy, 'we all saw something. There's a large crack up there. I think it might be a ledge, and it runs right behind the falls.' Pointing up to the left of the waterfall, there was indeed a crack in the rock face running horizontally, narrowing to a hairline, that continued on around before disappearing into the mist and spray.

'Can you reach it, Betty?' asked Tammy, as Mookin was the tallest by a head and also the best climber.

Mookin appraised the crack. 'Yes, I'm pretty sure. Give me a second.'

She passed her rucksack to Tammy and she was off, hopping across boulders and then running the last few metres across the flat area at the base of the cliff, before leaping at the rock face, straight up, reaching, reaching, until she seemed to hang in the air for a split second as the fingers of her left hand groped for the crack. She had one hand in, dangled there for a second, then swung her whole body to the right, back to the left, then, as she swung once more to the right, lifted her right leg up and over onto the narrow ledge. Mookin now had both hands and one foot on and was able to pull herself up. She stood slowly, face and hands pressed against the sun-warmed rock, then turned carefully around to face her friends. Looking left and right, she examined her surroundings. 'Yep! It's a ledge,' she shouted down to Tammy and Debs, their faces turned expectantly up at her. 'Very narrow, but it widens out a bit towards the falls.'

'Wahoo!' shouted Debs. 'Me next,' dumping her rucksack and bounding off towards the cliff. Tammy tutted. She now had three heavy rucksacks to lug to the cliff.

Mookin crept along the ledge until it was wide enough for her to lie face down with her right arm draped over the edge. Debs took a similar running leap and caught Mookin's outstretched arm. Mookin swung her friend left, then right and up onto the ledge where she was able to stand up. Debs then moved along the ledge towards the falls while Mookin caught her bag, thrown up by Tammy. She passed the bags to Debs, one at a time, then Mookin repeated the same manoeuvre with Tammy.

'Phew, thanks Mookin,' said Tammy. 'How high was that? I reckon that must be a record, even for you. Must be over three metres. Where's Debs gone?'

Mookin looked past Tammy but Debs had vanished. 'You know Debs, just like a puppy, always wants to be in front. Come on, catch her up before she hurts herself.'

It had taken Mookin just a few minutes to convince her friends that it was worth checking out the cave behind the waterfall. Her thinking was that it could be a lava tube, just as she suspected that the Plunge was too. Volcanic islands, such as theirs, were often riddled with tubes, like Swiss cheese, and Mookin had explored many kilometres of them. They were formed by rivers of molten lava, boring through beneath the hardened crust of a previous eruption. If the hidden cave was a tube, it was possible it could connect with the Plunge, below ground, perhaps offering them an easier way in, without the need to deploy the tripod borrowed from Mr Morningside.

Tammy and Mookin traversed the ledge, watching every footstep, into the mist from the waterfall. Within seconds they were both covered in droplets. Their hair and shower-proof clothing dripping water, they moved into the gloom behind Wysend Falls.

Once their eyes had adjusted to the lower light, they could see there was indeed a large opening behind the curtain of water. Debs was nowhere to be seen, however, so they went straight into the cave mouth.

'Debs?' whispered Mookin into the dark and reached inside her pack to retrieve her wind-up head torch. She quickly charged the biobattery, winding the handle rapidly, before fitting it to her helmet. Tammy followed her example.

Looking around the entrance to the cave, they could see wet footprints going into the darkness. It was large, with rough walls and an oval cross-section. Tammy was surprised at how dry it was behind the waterfall. No spray was coming in from outside and the falls were at least an arm's length from the cliff face. They followed the footprints.

'At least she didn't fall in the water,' said Tam. Thirty or so paces in from the entrance they came to a chamber where five more smaller tunnels led off in different directions. Debs was leaning against the rock wall, backpack at her feet, eating some of her lunch. She had her torch out, but no helmet on.

'Debs,' said Mookin, 'don't go off like that again please, and put your helmet on.' Debs did as she was instructed, because Mookin was in charge.

'Sorry, Mookin, I was just excited,' said Debs.

'It's okay, but we just need to stay safe, and stay together, right?'

'Yes, Betty,' said Tammy and Debs together. Both of them deferred to Mookin in all decisions regarding safety. She was the team leader and the most experienced climber and caver.

'Brr, it's chilly in here. Shall we go back to the entrance and have an early lunch?' said Mookin. Back at the waterfall, where it was noticeably warmer, they sat down to eat.

Mookin and Tammy were both sitting cross-legged, the open end of their packs in their laps, while Debs was sitting with both feet straight out in front, the contents of her backpack strewn about her. She had a chequered cloth tucked into the neck of her t-shirt. She had finished one sandwich and was starting on the second. She chewed a little noisily and seemed to have aquired a big red splotch on her napkin: her sandwich seemed to be made up of slices of roastbeef with bomato* ketchup. The red splotch was where the ketchup had squirted out. Mookin and Tammy looked at each other and smiled. Debs was the messy one of the three. They loved her dearly, of course, but were always rescuing her in her dizzy moments: getting caught on branches, falling in ponds or tripping into muddy puddles. Just generally being Debs. It was a wonder they had come this far today without Debs crashing her bike into a bush or the river.

Debs noticed them looking at her, and said, around a large mouthful of bread and roastbeef, 'Wha...?'

'Nothing Debs,' said Mookin, who now had her pack open and was tucking into her lunch. Today she had the last of the friedbacon from breakfast, some butterberried crackers and a cheesfruit, which she now cut in half with the knife she carried in a sheath in her right knee-length boot.

She cut it in half, and sliced one half expertly into three equal chunks, passing one each to her two friends. For dessert she had brought a melange.** Taking a big bite of her piece of cheesfruit, she carefully packed the uncut half inleafwrap and put it back in her bag for later.

'Mmm. Wow,' said Tammy. 'This is delicious, Mookin. Your dad certainly knows how to charm a cheesfruit. What flavour is this? It's new isn't it?'

Mookin swallowed before replying. 'Yeah. He calls it "Wilton", says it's a cross between "Wensleydale" and "Stilton", whatever they are.'

'Townsh,' said Debs, now with a mouthful of cheesfruit.

'Pardon?' said Tammy

*Bomatos are similar in every way to tomatoes, except they grow on a tree, and, unless plucked before ripe, will fall to the ground and explode. Only mildly dangerous.

**A cross between an orange and a melon that grows on a vine like a melon but is bright orange on the outside. Sometimes you can get an orange flavoured melon, and sometimes a melon flavoured orange.

'Townsh!' repeated Debs.

'What's a townsh?'

'You know,' said Debs, finally swallowing her cheesfruit, "towns", like big villages. In England, I think. At least Stilton is, Wensleydale might be a county.'

'Ah, *towns*,' said Tammy, giggling. 'I know. I was just teasing you.'

Mookin put her hand over her mouth to stop herself giggling too. Debs stood up suddenly and repacked her backpack.

'Hmph. I was only trying to help,' she said as she walked purposefully off into the dark.

'Debs,' shouted Mookin after her, 'wait for us. And put your helmet on!' She stood up quickly, threw her stuff into her backpack, and headed after Debs. 'Come on, Tam, best not let her get too far ahead. Could be a maze in there.'

Tammy had stood when Mookin did and was right behind her. They couldn't see Debs' light wobbling down the shaft anymore and walked as fast as possible after her. Fortunately, Debs was again waiting in the large chamber with the five smaller tunnels leading off it. She now had her helmet on and was kneeling next to her backpack, from which she was pulling her jacket.

'Getting chilly in here,' she said.

'Debs, it's very important that you don't go off on your own down here. We don't know what's in here do we? There could be hidden dangers underground. I really need you to promise.'

Mookin and Tammy were also putting their jackets on. It was indeed a lot cooler than outside, and they were all a bit damp.

'I promise, Mookin,' said Debs, putting her rucksack back on. 'But I'm not stupid, you know.'

'Um, Debs,' interrupted Tammy.

'No, Tammy, let me finish please. You two are always

interrupting me. It's not –'

'Yeah, but Debs –'

'No, Tammy. I know I'm clumsy and a bit forgetful, I know I trip over things, but I'm not stupid!'

'Er, Debs?'

'Yes, what?'

'Debs, um, you, ahh, erm, might want to take your, you know, you may, just possibly want to, ah, take your, like, backpack off again. Before you, kind of, ah, put your jacket on? If you want, I mean.'

Debs, already with an arm in one sleeve of her jacket, was reaching behind with the other searching for the other sleeve hole. She looked down at her arm in disbelief, as if it was someone else's.

'Oh, flup,' she said. 'I am stupid, aren't I?' Her bottom lip started to quiver and her eyes filled with tears. Mookin and Tammy rushed over and put their arms around her in a big hug.

'You're not stupid, babes,' said Tammy.

'We love you, Debby Webs,' said Mookin.

'You're the best friend in the world,' said Tammy.

'We like you just as you are,' said Mookin.

'Yeah, and you're *our* Debs,' said Tammy.

'Really?' sniffed Debs.

'Course. We wouldn't change a thing about you, would we, Mookin?'

'Not a thing. We love you just the way you are,' said Mookin.

'Well good, 'cos I love you two, too!'

'Yoo tu tu?' said Tammy.

'Us tu tu?' said Mookin.

'Oh, stop it you two,' said Debs.

Debs was pointing at the first tunnel on their right from where they had come into the chamber. After they had stopped giggling like a bunch of first years, Mookin had said she could have the honour of choosing which tunnel they went down.

'Just a second, Debs,' said Mookin, 'I want to put my gloves on. I brought you guys some too. They're new.' Mookin removed three pairs of gloves from the side pocket of her black cargo pants. The gloves looked shiny black, and on the palms was a kind of swirling pattern. Mookin pulled hers on, passed a pair to Tammy and turned back to face Debs. Debs had stepped over the little lip at the entrance to the tunnel she had picked. She turned back to face Mookin and Tammy and had her back to the tunnel. Mookin's eyes went big and round as she looked at Debs.

'Debs, you appear to be shrinking,' she said.

Debs looked around quickly, not understanding. 'What? Shrinking? What do you mean?'

'Debs, don't move a muscle. Freeze!'

'I don't... What?' said Debs, puzzled.

'Okay, Debs, first the good news. You're not shrinking. The bad news is you are standing in very slippery mud and you are very slowly sliding away from us.' Before Mookin could say another word, Debs looked down at her feet and looked back at Mookin and Tammy, an expression of curious panic on her face. Mookin could see what was going to happen before it did, and sure enough, Debs was raising her right foot to take a step forward.

'Debs! N-o-o-o-o!' shouted Mookin, rushing forward to grab her and diving the last few paces. As she dived, Debs' right foot came back down into the thin film of mud and immediately slipped backwards, causing her to try to move her left leg forward. In a split second she was frantically running on the spot making no progress. In fact, she was sliding away from Mookin faster and faster as her legs speeded up. She reached out desperately for something to cling on to, but her fingers just slipped through Mookin's as she fell forward onto her belly and Mookin landed face down in the mud, her ankles still hanging over the lip into the main chamber.

Mookin was still reaching for Debs who was now several metres away and sliding faster and faster down the muddy tube. She looked into Debs' frightened face, her eyes bulging and her mouth opening in a scream, 'M-o-o-o-o-o-k-i-n!' as she slipped away into the darkness. The light on her helmet disappeared as the tunnel dropped suddenly away. Her screams became quieter and quieter and then she was gone. Mookin wasn't quite sure if she had heard a faint thud from the darkness before she said, 'Tam. Can you pull me back, please? I'm too scared to move.'

'What just happened?' asked Tammy.

'It's what we call a marl chute. Marl is quite common in caves. Very slippery. You need spiked boots to walk on it or... well, you just saw what can happen.'

'What do we do?' said Tammy.

B.J. PAGE

5. Monster in the Dark

Merfolk:

ACCESS RESTRICTED – The Thallasians (Sea People), or Merfolk, inhabit only the reefs and shallower waters surrounding Mookination and are a transplanted species from A-519-S4-0072-LS, companion planet to the Bigfolk homeworld. Originally airbreathers/walkers, they are presently undergoing metamorphosis to full aquatic species with the assistance of Mook scientists. This is a personal life choice made by the former inhabitants of A-519-S4-0072-LS whose population had dwindled to less than 500 when rescued by Mooks. Tragically, only 25 adults and six offspring
survived the hibernation process. Full aquatic adaptation will be reached within the next four to six generations, and Derbot support will then be removed. Already amphibious, the Merfolk elected to make the necessary change and to remain on Mookination until such   time as we are able to assist them further with the provision of a suitable planet of their own. The Merfolk are in no way related to the Bigfolk and were not transplanted at the same time. The 120 viable embryos were not decanted until recently (5,000 years approx.) and remained on Zooplex* until fully matured and educated. They remain our dependants for the foreseeable future.

Mookipedia

The Mook maximum security facility for plasmagicated, charmed and enchanted creatures on Earth.

Tammy and Mookin returned to the marl chute after a trip to the waterfall to wash the mud from Mookin's clothes. Her cargo pants, which had nearly dried over lunch, were now wet again. She shivered, not from the cold, but at the thought of poor Debs alone, scared, possibly injured, possibly unconscious. Or worse.

Mookin had deliberately walked away. She didn't want to

rush into a rescue. She needed time to think, to run through their options. She had been tempted to dive after Debs, but where would that have got them? Better to take a few minutes and come up with a sound, safe plan.

'So what's a marl chute exactly?' asked Tammy.

'Well, it's just mud really. There must have been flowing water in here at some time. It dissolves certain minerals and clays from the soil and rock it passes through and makes this really slippery, sticky mud. It forms a crust on top but stays wet underneath. Catches everyone out at some point.'

'And what's the plan now?'

'Well, I'm going after her,' said Mookin.

'And me? What do I do?'

'I need you here, Tammy. Look.' From her pack, Mookin had pulled a reel of thick thread. 'This is made by the Merfolk from seaweed. My sister Jaci had it made for me. It's basically a thin rope but using merthread.'

'Mookin, that's much too thin to climb, you won't be able to grip it. Even if you could, if you slipped, it would cut your fingers off. Why not just use our ropes?'

'Well, we don't know how deep this tunnel goes; there's a kilometre of thread on this reel. The ropes, even joined together, are only a couple of hundred metres, and unfortunately, Debs has one of them. Now, why do you think I brought us new gloves?'

'Gloves? What about them?' asked Tammy, looking at hers.

'They are made from the same material as the merthread and the swirly pattern on the palms has tiny bristles woven into it so it grips the thread. In fact, look.' Mookin laid the thread gently across her hand then asked Tammy to pull the thread away. It stuck. 'See, it's almost like it's sticky. You have to peel your hand off.'

While talking, Mookin and Tammy had been busy looking for some way to tie off one end of the merthread. Luckily, just inside one of the other tunnels was a large boulder, almost blocking its entrance. Without it, Tammy would have had to lower Mookin down the marl chute herself, feet braced against the lip.

Mookin stepped into thin orange waterproofs and then her climbing harness, clipping a loop of merthread into the descent rings that would give her control of her speed. Tammy would hold on to the reel, letting the thread out as required through a second descent ring. There were taped marks on the thread to let you know where the end of the reel was. If Tammy got to the end of the reel, Mookin would be half a kilometre away, the thread in a big loop from the boulder where it was tied off, down to Mookin and then back to Tammy. Tammy would then signal by stopping her and tapping on the taut thread. At this point, Mookin would decide if she should go further. This could only be achieved by Tammy releasing the free end of the thread that she held. Mookin would tap the thread three times if she wanted Tammy to release.

If Mookin reached the end of the thread without finding the bottom of the shaft, she would be a full kilometre away from Tammy and would stop and tap again. Tammy would then have the unenviable task of hauling Mookin back up the chute, hand over hand. Their only resort then would be for one of them to go for help. It wasn't much, but it was the best they could come up with at short notice.

Mookin sat down in the mud at the entrance to the marl chute. 'Wish me luck, Tam.'

'Luck,' said Tammy. She gave her a quick push to get her started, and she was off, slipping and sliding in the marl. She accelerated rapidly and twisted the ring-brake of her harness, slowing the rate at which the thread ran through it. Then she was over the drop where Debs had disappeared as the shaft angled down at forty-five degrees. It levelled out again after about fifty metres, she thought, but it was hard to tell how far she had gone in the nearly featureless tunnel. There was a sudden turn to the right, on quite straight for a short time, then another forty-five degree drop.

Mookin's headlight was illuminating maybe ten metres ahead of her into the shaft and it had just levelled out again when, without warning, the walls vanished from the beam. Realising that the tunnel was ending, she quickly pulled on the ring-break as hard as she could, but too late; she was past the end of the tunnel and falling.

With an 'oomph' she came to a hard stop on the merthread, dangling and spinning in mid-air, her harness cutting into her shoulders and thighs, her headlight making circular patterns in the darkness. When she stopped spinning, she was able to look around and see that she was hanging only a metre from the floor and had dropped only a few metres or so out of the end of the shaft. She lowered herself onto the pile of rubble at the base of the cliff, and looked around to see where she was, hoping to find Debs.

Four steps out from the base of the rubble cone was a large pool of mud, the crusty surface looking like it had been undisturbed for centuries. It was impossible to tell how deep it was; the surface was as smooth as glass, except, Mookin could see, some metres out, near the middle of the pool, a large blemish: a hole in the mud, a large Debs-shaped hole like a giant cookie cutter. In the beam of her headtorch Mookin could clearly see the outline of her head, arms and legs, but the hole was deep enough that she couldn't see any sign of her friend.

'Debs!' she shouted. No reply. 'Spydasylk Debboramook! Wake up this second!' Nothing. Not a sound. Mookin selected a small stone from the rubble pile, walked right up to the edge of the mud pool and pitched the stone into the air. Always a good shot, Mookin aimed for where she thought Debs' stomach would be and was rewarded with a loud 'oomph' followed by Debs' familiar voice, 'Who's throwing flupping stones?' Mookin was overjoyed to have found her friend, and it sounded as if she was probably unharmed.

'It's Mookin, Debs. I'm here to rescue you.'

'Rescue me? Who says I need rescuing? And since when did rescues start with stone-throwing at the rescuee?'

'Okay, so where are you then?'

'Um. I don't know. I seem to be lying in a hole, and it's very muddy...'

'Can you sit up? I think you may have passed out for a few minutes and I want you to try to sit up. But listen, this is important: if you feel the slightest bit dizzy, stop, don't move and we'll try something else. Okay?' Mookin did not really want to try to wade out to Debs unless she had to. There would be no point, not without Tammy here to drag them both back.

Mookin heard squelchy, squishy, sucking sounds coming from the hole, and Debs' head appeared above the surface of the mud pool. Luckily, the hole wasn't too deep and Debs still had her backpack on. If she had lost her backpack, it was possible the suction from the mud may have stopped her from getting out.

'Great, well done. Now stay where you are. I'm just going to talk to Tammy.' Mookin turned around and, pulling the merthread tight with one hand, reached for her knife and began tapping rapidly on the thread with the back of the blade. She was using Mook-kode to tell Tammy that she had found Debs, they were both safe and well, she would get back to her soon and they could decide what to do next.

It took Mookin over half an hour of pulling and tugging before she managed to haul Debs free from the marl pool. Using the normal rope from her bag, she had fashioned a loop using a double figure-of-eight knot so that it wouldn't slip and tighten around Debs' body.

She whirled the loop around her head like a lasso and cast it out to her friend who caught it on the second try. Mookin told her to slip her arms through so the rope was around her chest and not her stomach. She then had Debs turn over so she was kneeling on all fours; it was pointless trying to stand up in the super-slippery mud. Debs then grabbed the rope with both hands above the knot Mookin had tied. This was to stop Debs' muddy hands from slipping and the rope sliding up over her head.

Mookin tied the rope to her harness and walked slowly backwards, pulling Debs out of the marl pool. It was hard work, as the crust kept breaking under Debs and she would sink into the mud again, and Mookin only had a few metres to walk back. She had to re-tie the rope several times, but at least the mud got shallower as Debs reached the edge.

Mookin was breathing hard and sweating by the time Debs managed to crawl out. She was covered from head to toe in clinging, sticky grey mud, even her eyes. Mookin had to scrape away as much as she could with her hands before washing her eyes with water from her flask. Even her headlight was completely clogged. Debs was soon sitting up, however, chewing on a fruit bar. Mookin really wanted to get Debs washed off and in front of a fire with a hot drink and a blanket, but that would have to wait.

'How are you feeling?' she asked her sorry-looking friend.

'Okay. A bit sore. Must have landed bum first, I think.' She took another bite of the fruit bar and washed it down with water from her flask.

'There's just one thing I'm wondering though, Mookin.'

'What's that, petal?' said Mookin, her face full of concern.

'When can I have another go?'

'What?' asked Mookin in utter disbelief.

'Well, I mean, I didn't get hurt, did I? And now I know there's a softish landing and it's not really dangerous or anything I think I'd like to do it again.'

Mookin, like all Mooks, rarely, if ever, became angry. But right this second, she felt overcome by a very strong desire to throw Debs right back into the marl pool. Mook calm won the emotional battle and, instead, she leaned forward until her nose was almost touching the tip of Debs' and said in a quiet, stern voice, 'Do you have any idea of the trouble you have caused today? What if you'd landed face down in that muck, eh? Have you thought of that? What if I hadn't brought my sister's new merthread today? Or the special gloves?'

Mookin took a long, slow breath in, not taking her eyes off Debs, and exhaled before continuing, 'Without the merthread, you'd have been stuck down here, in that mud pool, unable to get out, until Tammy and I returned with help. Alone. In the dark. When we are exploring like this, we are a team! We stay together; we do as we are told. For safety, not because I want to be the boss. And that's not to mention how much worry and stress you caused us. Debs, I am so close to angry, I could cry. And you want to have another flooping go?'

Debs blinked her muddy eyes and a tear rolled down each cheek, carving a lighter grey track through the mud. Her bottom lip quivered, and she said in a tiny voice, 'Flup.'

'What?' said Mookin, not sure she'd heard properly.

'It's flup. Not floop. As in flupping, not flooping.'

Mookin let out a strangled noise from her throat, a sound that Debs had never heard before, and, picking up a large rock, she threw it so hard and far, they barely heard the tiny 'crump' as it landed out of sight in the darkness beyond their torches.

Wow, thought Mookin, *this place is huge.*

'And what' – turning to face Debs again – 'the flup is flup anyway? I thought you made it up?'

Debs shook her head, her headlight flicking back and forth across Mookin's face. 'Do you know Parashoota Dinkamook? Well, he keeps grumpalumps on his farm, and I was down there helping him a few weeks ago, looking after the grumpalumps 'cos I really like them, and we'd fed them and given them a drink and we were just finishing giving them a wash down with a hosepipe, when Mr Parashoota said that next was the most important job of all.' Debs took a breath. Mookin waited patiently. 'He went and fetched two huge brooms and shovels and he said it was flup time. So we swept up all the flup in the grumpalumps' yard into a big wheelbarrow and Mr Parashoota asked me to take it around the back of the barn and tip it on the flup-heap. So I did, and it was the biggest pile of flup you've ever seen.'

'Really?' said Mookin.

'Yes. Apparently he uses it for growing tingleberries. Says grumpalump flup is the only thing that works on tingleberries.'

'Oh. So that's what flup is,' said Mookin. 'Well, my dad calls it –'

'Yeah, there are lots of names for it, Mookin. Lots of names.'

Mookin was thinking hard about what to do next. She really needed Tammy here to talk to face to face. Having made a quick excursion into the vast cavern ahead, she would really like to carry on exploring. She'd asked Debs if she was okay to go on, and she said she felt well enough, although being covered in mud was driving her crazy. She'd also checked her eyes, but there was no sign of concussion and no broken bones either.

Mookin went back to the merthread rope and began a conversation with Tammy in rapid code. Tammy was also keen to carry on, so Mookin explained her plan.

'Weeee-oomph,' said Tammy, announcing her arrival twenty minutes later, as she shot from the marl chute. She came to a jarring halt on the end of the rope, up in the air, also twirling rapidly. Mookin had warned her about the end of the chute, and she had been expecting it. Tammy's reactions were very fast, and she'd stopped a full metre before Mookin had.

Following Mookin's instructions, Tammy had untied her end of the merthread rope from around the boulder – she still had the reel – and Mookin pulled the loose end down to the cavern and secured it to another boulder at her end. Back at the top, Tammy had set four cams in cracks in the five-way chamber, looping the merthread through the carabiners, ensuring that it ran freely without catching or rubbing anything. She clipped the reel of merthread to her harness and ran it around her body, then through the ring-brake at the front of her harness. With her new gloves on, she would run a loop of the thread through her hands and would be able to control her speed down the marl chute.

This now left them a huge loop running from the boulder in this cavern, up through the marl chute to the five-way cave, through the carabiners Tammy had set, and back down to the bottom. Mookin was now confident that they had an exit from this cavern if there were any problems, even if one them was injured or if there was no other way out further into the cave system. She had a pretty good idea about what they might find further on, and for now, she wasn't worried about getting trapped down here.

Tammy lowered herself gently onto the cavern floor, careful not to twist an ankle on the boulder pile below the marl chute opening. She unclipped herself from the merthread, unhooked the reel and left it on the ground.

'Wow,' she said, 'that was cool. When can I have another go?'

Mookin glared at her. She opened her mouth to speak but closed it again. *Better not,* she thought.

'Um, where's Debs, Betty?' asked Tammy, scanning the area with her headtorch.

Mookin spun around but could see nothing. Debs had vanished again. 'I... She was right there! I don't understand.'

'Rrrrr-AAArrgh!' One of the boulders in front of them rose up, grew arms and talons and lurched menacingly towards them. A low moan came from the top of it. 'Br-ai-ns! Hun-gry! Br-ai-ns, mu-st ha-ve br-ains!'

Tammy took a step backwards, clutching Mookin's arm. Mookin raised her knife.

'Gotcha!' said Debs, raising her head up from her chest. She had turned off her headtorch and crouched down in a ball. Covered in grey mud, she had blended right in with her surroundings.

'Flupping, flup flup,' said Mookin.

Tammy sat down, clutching her chest. 'Crick on a stick, Debs. I nearly had a flat-cat.'

'Ha ha ha ha. Classic,' said Debs, pointing. 'You should see your faces! Ha ha ha.'

Tammy and Mookin exchanged looks, and both started giggling. Soon, all three were laughing out loud. 'Crikey,' said Mookin, finally. 'I need a coffee.'

6. A Flute from the Dark

Plasmic:

A plasmic is a functioning filament of the substance **quicktanium.** *Although the formation of a plasmic has been observed and documented many times, it is still unknown what exact circumstances are required to produce one. They form only at the critical point of cool-down in an erupting volcano while the lava tube is still physically connected to the magma chamber* and *the planet's molten core, but while there is insufficient pressure within the magma chamber to cause further eruptions. The plasmic Itself begins deep within the lava tube, the quicktanium filament growing rapidly upwards and downwards in a crystalline formation. It forms a branch structure at the top, growing out into the surrounding rock, and a root-like structure at the base, sending tendrils into the molten core. Plasmics that come into contact with air will oxidise and, if not checked, will shut down, resulting in a non-functioning filament which will degenerate into gold and silver. Plasmics that come into contact with fresh water suffer catastrophic failure of epic proportions (see Krakatau [Krakatoa], Kallistē [Thira], Mount St Helens), although it should be noted that salt water above 3.5% salinity has an insulating effect and can be used as a protective insulating barrier.*

Mookipedia

'What time is it, anyway?' Debs asked, 'I've lost all track in here.'

Tammy thought for a moment before replying. 'It's about lunchtime, actually. I know we've had lunch, but we stopped early, about ten-thirty I think, so, it must be about twelve-thirty now.'

'Is that all? I thought it was much later, getting on for teatime,' said Mookin. She had brewed them all a nice cup of coffee, which they had sat and sipped quietly in the dark.

91

Tammy had checked Debs over from head to foot and declared her 'fit'. They decided to push on and explore further out into the cavern.

Mookin regretted having to leave behind the reel of merthread but had no choice. Instead, she had unwound the remainder of the reel and removed two hundred metres of fibre. She had needed to beat it between two hard rocks for over five minutes before even her exceptionally sharp knife had been able to cut it. She had tried to put an edge back on the blade with her whetstone but the merthread had blunted it badly. She would have to ask Mr Morningside to look at it when they returned to the village.

Mookin rewound the rest of the merthread on to the reel and left it on the boulder pile below the marl chute. The length she had taken she wrapped around her waist, under her jacket. She hoisted her pack back on to her shoulders and rejoined her two friends. They all took a deep breath and headed off into the dark.

The cavern was so large, they couldn't hear any echo from their footsteps from any direction, and their headtorches only showed about twenty paces of dusty floor in front of them. They had set off from the marl chute in a straight line towards what they thought was roughly the centre but had encountered little of interest.

No stalagmites or stalactites, which meant there was no water seeping in from above. There was a faint channel in the floor running roughly straight, which Mookin thought had probably been a small river or stream at some time, and which possibly explained the marl chute. Judging from the boulder pile below the opening, it had probably been blocked for ages, the marl chute full of silt and water, maybe just a trickle getting through. Then, the river had worn through and the rock face collapsed, emptying the chute and creating the mud pool. The source of the river, possibly the Wyse itself, had closed up or become blocked, shutting off the underground water course.

Mookin thought they were now about in the middle of the vast space and felt that the ground had sloped down very slightly all the way. She wasn't sure how she knew it was the centre, but she just felt equal amounts of darkness on every side. She felt certain that if they continued, the now-vanished underground river would, in all likelihood, have carved itself an exit and possibly another way out. She decided they should turn right ninety degrees, then keep going until they arrived at the outer wall, and then follow the wall until they found an exit.

This cavern was much too big to have been made by water erosion; it must have been made by volcanic action at the time Mookination first rose up from the ocean. It was possibly, at one time, a huge bubble of molten rock, formed by the main volcano, the lava emptying away through lava tubes, which is what the marl chute and the five-way cave were. Lava tubes could run for kilometres sometimes, boring their way through still-cooling, slightly softer materials like worms in an apple. Mookin was hoping to find other tubes leading off this huge place and thought the chances were good, otherwise there would be water in here, and it was as dry as a desert.

They reached the outer wall and continued in the same direction as before, away from the marl chute. There were no water marks on the walls, indicating that it had never filled with water at any time in its existence.

After following the outer wall for another fifteen minutes, Mookin reckoned they were nearly opposite the marl chute. She calculated the length of the cavern at about a kilometre and the width about half that. Roughly oval in shape, with a slight dip in the centre. She turned to Debs.

'So, partner, it's time you named these places we've discovered.'

'Me? Why me?' asked Debs, surprised.

'It's traditional. You were first in, you get to name them. You can only use your own name once, though,' she warned. 'No Debs' Cave, Debs' Tunnel and Debs' Cavern.'

Debs thought for a few minutes. 'I would like to call the first place, the one with the five tunnels – six if you count the way we came in – Ladybird Cave. The shape and the six legs remind me of a ladybird.'

'Good choice,' said Tammy. 'What about the marl chute?'

'Mmm. What about the Slipanslide? That's about all I did when I was in there.'

'Hah! Good one, Debs, I like that,' said Mookin. 'And the big cavern?'

'Well, I was thinking, maybe, if you two agree, Mud Monster Cavern?'

'Perfect!' Tammy and Mookin answered together. Mookin thought for a moment. 'Of course, we should call the marl pool Debs' Downfall.'

'Or Spyda Falls,' said Tammy, with a chuckle.

'Actually, I quite like that. Yes, that's what we'll call it: Spyda Falls,' said Debs. Tammy, who had only been joking, was speechless.

Mookin estimated they would soon pass the middle of this end of the cavern and would then be heading back towards Spyda Falls, but just as she was going to tell the others, she thought she heard a faint sound.

'Shh, I think I hear something.'

In the sudden quiet, Mookin could just make out a very faint noise or rumble. She turned her head this way and that, trying to figure out the source of the sound. Now she wasn't even sure she had heard anything at all. The other two, who hadn't heard anything, were watching Mookin as she walked in a slow circle, her hands now cupping her ears. She stopped, looking towards the rock face, and was turning her head left to right. Debs whispered to Tammy, 'What's she doing?'

Tammy shrugged her shoulders, shook her head and mouthed back, 'I don't know.'

'It's coming from here…' said Mookin excitedly, slowly raising her head so her headtorch formed a ring on the cavern wall. About head height from the floor was a crack which widened to about a metre as it got higher and stayed roughly parallel as it rose, disappearing into the arching roof of the cavern. Now with all three headlights pointed upwards, they could see perhaps ten metres or so into a rock chimney, before it faded in the gloom.

'Guys,' said Tammy, 'just turn your lights off for a second. I think I caught something.'

Instinctively, the three reached out to hold each other's hands as they did so and the darkness descended like a solid wall. The girls could see nothing, not even the end of their noses. Although not scared of the dark, they all felt a shiver run down their backs at the sheer weight of the blackness all around. This was not like hiding in a cupboard or under the duvet. This was total, utter blackness. Except...

Tammy, who had shut her eyes before she switched off her light, was the first to adjust to the dark. She was now looking up at where the rock chimney would be, and there, like a whisper of a firefly, she could just make out a glow far above their heads.

'Can you see it?' she asked. Both girls nodded in the dark before realising no one could see them.

'Umm, yes, a faint glow,' said Debs.

'Daylight, do you think, Tam?' said Mookin.

'Not sure,' replied Tammy. 'It's very faint. I only just caught it out of the corner of my eye.'

'How come we couldn't see it before?' asked Debs.

'Well, this chimney goes roughly straight up, and the cavern wall slopes back over our heads to form the roof. The chimney bores into the rock, so the top, if it is the top, would be hidden from anywhere but this spot right underneath.'

'Of course. But why did you stop right here? What did you hear?' asked Debs.

'Ah,' said Mookin, 'that's a surprise. First, we climb!'

They sat at the top of the chimney, feet dangling over the edge, munching on fruit bars and getting their breath back from the climb. Debs leaned forward and dribbled a spit ball down into the depths.

'Debs!' Tammy scolded. Tammy had led the way up, and although there were plenty of hand and foot holds, and the Mooks could easily have climbed it without assistance, they still used their ropes for extra safety. Tammy had used climbing cams, wedged and hammered into cracks, which she carried strapped to her harness and taken from her and Mookin's packs before she started the ascent. Carefully clipping and unclipping the rope as she travelled, she made sure it was always threaded through at least three carabiners, attached to the cams. The first leg had been thirty metres, the extent of one rope, the second about twenty-five, and then she was able to pull herself over the lip of the chimney and into a tunnel bathed in soft light. She could see that it angled gently up away from her and was about two and a half metres high by one and a half wide. It did look like a continuation of the chimney, she thought, following some natural fault in the rock.

It had only taken Mookin and Debs a few minutes to cover the last leg, Mookin carefully retrieving the cams as she passed them, clipping them into her belt in case they were needed later on. If they had to return this way, it would be a free descent, repelling down, feet braced against the rock face, rope wrapped around their bodies and through a ring brake. Now, after stowing their gear and munching their fruit bars, they were ready to go on, heart rates back to normal.

'Go on then, Mookin,' said Debs, 'you first. I did the Slipanslide, Tammy gets the chimney, I reckon this next tunnel is yours.'

'Okay,' said Mookin, standing and stretching. 'Have you thought of a name yet, Tammy?'

'What? For the chimney? No, not really. Can it be anything, not just my name?'

'Yes, anything, but nothing too silly, please. It will go on a map one day.'

'Ooo. It's quite hard, isn't it, Debs? I never realised. What about the Shimney, 'cos that's what we had to do to climb it, didn't we? We shimmied up.'

Tammy had mostly climbed the shaft by bracing herself against opposite sides, walking crab-like using side to side movements, her back against a third side of the almost-square shaft, and the others had copied her style.

'The Shimney it is, then,' said Mookin.

The tunnel had run as straight as a ruler, the sides quite rough, but the floor was surprisingly smooth and sloped gradually upwards. There was a draught blowing on their backs which they first noticed in the Shimny and it was quite strong in the tunnel, blowing towards the light. It was only about two hundred metres long, and Mookin simply named it the Elbow.

She stepped from the end on to a wide rock platform, blinking at the sudden light. The sight before her took her breath away.

Tammy and Debs stepped out beside her.

'Wow,' said Debs.

'Oh my gosh,' said Tammy. 'You knew, Mookin, didn't you?'

'Well, I had a rough idea,' answered Mookin. 'I didn't know what we'd find, but this is nice.'

They stood there for fully five minutes without moving or speaking, almost without breathing. Without a doubt, it was one of the most spectacular and wondrous things they had ever seen.

The little tunnel had led them to the bottom of the Plunge and into another large cavern, cone-shaped, with a circular hole at the apex. A great shaft of sunlight angled down from the hole, far over their heads, the water dropping down, brilliant white, in a single column until, half its drop completed, it exploded into a shimmering veil of mist and spray, almost as big as the cavern itself. They had emerged behind and to the right of the cascade, and as they made their way around to the front, the cavern appeared to grow as it came into view.

The spray, this close to the falls, was pouring from their bright orange waterproofs in seconds. The cavern was shaped like an upside-down funnel, and Mookin thought that if she stood a little further back and squinted a bit, the waterfall would look like an inverted wine glass from down here. The roughly circular opening far above would be the base of the glass, the solid-looking column of water would be the stem and where the mist and spray flared out would be the flute of the glass.

Even though it was mostly spray, over the centuries, the falls had carved out a large oval-shaped pool in the cavern floor. There was a small boulder pile forming behind the cascade, evidence of a recent cave-in from above, and Mookin could see that the falls were now falling on a new part of the cavern floor, moving away from the small boulder pile as the lip of the falls eroded.

The torrent made surprisingly little noise in the actual cavern, and she supposed that the sound she had picked up back in Mud Monster Cavern was somehow amplified by the rock, or the shape of the space they were in.

Moving around to the front of the falls, they could see a much larger boulder pile towering above them, the original cave-in that had diverted the river underground, and which was presently lit up by the shaft of sunlight from above. Mookin was forming a picture in her mind, a sketch map of where their journey had so far taken them. The Slipanslide had taken them away from Wysend, north about half a kilometre and downwards about the same. It had dumped them in Mud Monster Cavern where they had travelled back towards the Plunge through the Shimny and Elbow before emerging here, almost directly beneath the Plunge. The river flowed out to Mookin's right, heading roughly east, where, she hoped, it would continue its interrupted journey, out and down Giant's Stairway.

'Mookin,' said Debs, bringing her out of her reverie of cave formation, 'do you think it would be safe to go in the pool? Be nice to get this mud off, don't you think?'

Mookin inspected the pool and had to admit it was tempting. 'Okay, it looks safe enough, but we'll take it in turns. The water's quite shallow on this side, away from the falls.'

Debs walked around the edge of the pool until she came to a part that looked shallow enough. She removed her waterproofs and washed those first, then simply stepped into the pool and sat down in her muddy apparel. Clouds of grey swirled away in the clear water as Debs scrubbed at her clothes, eventually giving in and realising she would need to take them off. Boots, socks, cargo pants and t-shirt all ended up in a soggy wet pile on the rocks. Tammy came down to help Debs wash her blue and green hair free of mud.

The water was quite warm from its travels down the Wyse and across the plateau above, but Debs was shivering by the time she stepped from the pool. Tammy went next, but like Mookin, it was only the outside of her waterproofs that needed cleaning, so it took only a few minutes. As Mookin took her turn, Tammy helped Debs wring out her wet clothes and spread them out on the large rocks of the big boulder pile. These rocks had been in the sun and were quite warm, and Debs' clothes were soon steaming away as they dried.

Debs put her wet boots on together with her spare sweater

from her pack, which she nearly didn't include until Mookin insisted she bring everything on the pack list or she couldn't come. They sat on the hot rocks, watching the Plunge and absorbing the warmth, sharing and finishing what food they had left in their packs. Mookin brewed coffee on her portable stove and passed out steaming mugs that warmed them through.

The shaft of sunlight moved across the cavern, and they were soon in shade again; the temperature dropped noticeably. It was time to move on. Some of Debs' clothes were still a bit damp when she put them back on but she was soon warm again. Her socks were a bit squishy but, unknown to her, would be completely soaked again in a short time.

They started up the large boulder pile, moving away from the falls, following the flow of the river through the pile, heading, hopefully, out to Giant's Stairway. They climbed carefully up the uneven surface, and Mookin paused at the top, taking a last look into the cavern. She could see the tiny opening and little rock platform where they'd emerged from the Shimny through the perpetual mist from the falls. The utterly fantastic waterfall and the Plunge Pool, as she had decided to call it, was quite large, the actual cave floor nearly twice that. She looked up into the cavern and could see sparkles all around the walls and thought that there were either some sort of crystals in the rock, like pegmatite, or else minerals had been deposited over time by the spray from the falls. She wondered what it would look like in here at sunburst. The shaft of sunlight would be pointing straight at the falls; it would split and refract from the cavern walls like a hall of mirrors. There would be rainbows! It would be full of awesome!

Tammy and Debs had stopped a few metres below the crest and looked back up at Mookin.

'Everything okay?' asked Debs. Mookin smiled and described how she could picture the cave at sunburst.

'Wow. We're gonna have to come back, aren't we?'

'What will you call it, Mookin?' asked Tammy.

'Well, I was thinking maybe Crystal Flute Cave. What do you think?'

'That's nice,' said Tammy.

'Lovely,' agreed Debs.

They turned away from Crystal Flute Cave and continued down the boulder pile.

B.J. PAGE

7. The Heart of the Abyss

Portals:

*ACCESS RESTRICTED – Since early times, Mooks have been blessed with the ability to use plasmic energy (PE). Having evolved in a heavily plasmicated environment, PE has so altered our very essence that the two are almost inseparable. Without a source of PE, we would not be Mooks. It is fortuitous that PE permeates the galaxy in the way that it does. One of the ways in which we use this gift is by the use of portals, which we refer to as 'side-stepping'. We are able to open shortcuts between points in space, moving sideways across the distance by connecting doorways. These fall broadly into three main categories: (**Gaps** are microscopic and are used for data burst transmissions or remote observation).*

Doorways (D-ways) *for Mook-sized openings, for personal movement across planetary distances. The main limitation of a D-way is the amount of rotational energy it can absorb. (A Mook standing still at the equator is moving with the Earth at about 1,600kph [1,000mph]; in Britain, for example, this is reduced to approximately 800kph [500mph]. This difference has to be adjusted to match the destination speed, and that is without taking into account the movement of the sun through interstellar space in its orbit of the galaxy!)*

Gateways (G-ways) *for larger objects and for use across interplanetary distances, say between Earth and the moon or Earth and Mars. G-ways are more complex than D-ways and require more than one Mook to initiate. The huge difference in rotational speed and energy is dumped into or extracted from the 'between'*, the hyper-spatial zone through which side-stepping takes place.*

Keyways (K-ways) *are used only for moving very large objects through interplanetary distances or for interstellar travel between star systems. K-ways, require the presence of five Mook Eldrons to initiate and are closely guarded. MOOK ELDRON ONLY*

Mookout Handbook

The overspill from the Plunge Pool disappeared into the base of the boulder pile, and as they descended the far side of it, they could hear the Wyse bubbling and churning through the rocks until it emerged in front of them. As the boulder pile petered out, the Wyse snaked away into the darkness once more. At first, it was quite broad and shallow, slow, lazy even, but quickened and deepened slightly as it vanished from sight once again into a wide, low tunnel. The girls had no choice now except to wade into the water, and Debs could be heard muttering away to herself about just getting dry only to immediately get wet all over again.

Mookin had explained that the Wyse exited the mountain on Giant's Stairway, and their best hope of finding another way out now was to follow its course. If they could find an exit, they could bring other groups down here, friends, family. It would be wonderful to show people their little world.

The tunnel's entrance was a gentle curve over the water, about head high above the water in the centre. Along its edge, though, small stalactites had formed, dripping down towards the river. It looked like a great fanged mouth, devouring the river. Tammy gulped. Mookin shivered. Debs did both, then said, 'Do we have to go in there, Mookin? It looks like a big mouth. Like the rock is eating us.'

'I'm sorry, Debs. It does look a bit scary, but it's our best chance of finding an exit.'

They had to crouch down to get under the teeth but inside, the tunnel roof was over a metre above their heads. They were able to walk normally as the water only came up to their knees. Mookin looked up at the roof and saw the familiar ribbed pattern of a lava tube, although underfoot was remarkably smooth, most likely from water scouring, she thought.

It was hard to judge distance, slugging through the water in the dark with little to distinguish one part of the tunnel from another, but Tammy thought they had been in the tunnel for roughly half an hour. It was gradually widening out, the roof getting higher too, the river splitting into channels and cracks, shooting off in many different directions. Shortly, they reached a big cave, nothing to compare with Mud Monster or Crystal Flute, but still quite large. It was shaped like a funnel on its side with the spout being the tunnel they had just left. The sound of dripping and running water was everywhere. In front of them, the cave mouth was blocked by huge house-sized slabs of rock, like a giant drystone wall.

'Switch your lights off a second please, guys,' asked Mookin. Rather than total darkness, as before, there were a dozen or so muted beams of light shining through gaps and tiny openings in the rock face; most were just pinpricks, some as big as saucers, but one or two looked promising as potential ways out on to Giant's Stairway.

'Okay,' said Mookin, 'looks like we're behind a section of Giant's Stairway.' Switching her light back on, she added, 'We just have to find a way out. Simple! Right, ladies. Debs, you check on the right, Tammy, if you could take the left side, and I'll do the middle bit,' she instructed. 'We are searching for an exit. Look around where the light comes in or the water goes out; we may be able to enlarge any hole and crawl through. Don't crawl in anywhere by yourself or move any big rocks, and shout for help. Clear?'

The girls nodded, headtorch beams wavering comically, and set about their tasks, tired now, but with renewed enthusiasm at the chance to get out in the fresh air again. As much fun as caving was, it was always a relief to be back outside in the daylight.

Mookin had finished looking around her section of the base of the rock face, where none of the openings seemed big enough, and she was now climbing up to look at any shafts of light that might indicate a way through. She was pulling pebbles from one promising hole which she had enlarged to nearly big enough to get her head in, helmet and all, and she was pleased to see blue sky through the gap.

From her right came a thunk, followed by Debs' voice, 'Ow!'

'Debs, what's wrong?' Mookin shouted.

'Ow! Flup! Banged my head,' Debs shouted back, her voice muffled with a distinct echo.

'Are you okay, babe?' Mookin climbed down and moved over to the right, where Debs' voice was coming from. 'Where are you? I can't see you.'

'I'm here, Mookin. Ow. I shouldn't have stood up in the passage.'

'Passage? What passage? You weren't supposed to go in anywhere alone.'

'I thought this one would be okay 'cos it has a door,' said Debs, by way of explanation.

'A door? What do you mean, a door? Like a wooden door?'

'Well, yes. But this one's made of metal. With writing on it.'

'Stay there. We'll find you,' said Mookin, shouting for Tammy to join her. She quickly explained what Debs had said, and they went in search of her. They had only gone a few metres when they saw Debs' light bobbing about. Their view had been obstructed by a large boulder, and where Debs was standing, the cave opened out again into a smaller chamber. There, behind her now, recessed into the side of the cave wall, was, indeed, a metal door, looking as out of place as a tutu on a crocovator.

It was a dull silver grey in colour, studded with brass rivets around the edges with crossways dividing the door into sections. Etched into the metal at head height was a rough heart shape as big as a hand, and underneath that were three rows of letters forming four words, but not in any language Mookin was familiar with, and she spoke several. Tammy even more. Mookin was drawn straight to the door. She ran her gloved fingers across its surface and the raised letters.

They seemed to be part of the door, not stuck on; she couldn't see a join between letters and door, and it looked as though they were a part of the door, cast in liquid metal.

Tammy was examining Debs' head and could see that she had hit it so hard she had dented her helmet. She gently removed it from Debs' head and checked her over for bumps or blood, but there was no damage.

'What do you think, Tammy?' asked Mookin.

'Oh, she'll be fine. The helmet took the brunt.' Tammy shone her light into Debs' eyes. 'No concussion either.'

'No, not Debs, the door.'

'The door? Umm. Nice. Shouldn't be here though, should it?'

'No, not really. Don't usually see doors in your average cave,' Mookin replied. 'What about the writing, Tammy, seen anything like it before? Debs? What about you?'

Tammy thought a second. 'Looks a bit like runes, possibly Viking or Scandinavian. But that was in the eighth and twelfth centuries. This looks much, much more complex and older too. Shades of Babylonian maybe. Not sure, Mookin. Just how old is that door?'

Debs too was thinking hard. 'It kind of reminds me of Merfolk,' she said, 'but Merfolk don't have writing, do they Tam?'

'No, they don't. No need for it, they have exceptional memories, far better even than Mooks. They speak to us in Old Mook of course, not English, but they also speak Merrine, their own language, impossible for us to speak, of course, no gills. Lot of gill sounds in Merrine. And Cetacean of course, they speak that, taught it to the dolphins who taught it to the orcas. Now even the whales speak it, but their voices are so deep, no one knows what they are saying.' Tammy's eyes glazed over with that far-away look in her large blue orbs, her head slowly tilting to the side as she stared at the writing on the door.

Mookin gave her a few moments. 'Anything, Tammy?'

'Um, not sure. Merfolk... something. Not getting it, though. Need to check my books, I think.' Tammy's family had the largest library on Mookination, so big that nearly every room in their house had floor-to-ceiling bookshelves and a steady stream of visitors come to borrow or research thousands of topics.

'Later then. Don't try to force it. Debs, where did you hit your head exactly?'

'Right in the middle. It really hurt. I saw stars and everything. If I hadn't been wearing my...' She stopped as she saw the look on Mookin's face.

'No, Debs. Whereabouts? What did you hit it on?'

'Oh, I see what you mean. In the tunnel or corridor, whatever it is.'

'Uh, what tunnel?'

'The one behind the door, of course.'

Tammy looked at Mookin, and Mookin looked at Tammy. 'You mean it's *open*?' said Mookin, not quite believing what she was hearing.

'Uh, yes. I wouldn't have banged my head otherwise, would I? I was looking at the floor because it was tiled and I didn't notice the roof had got lower, so be careful, all right?' Tammy and Mookin exchanged another look of disbelief, then Mookin turned back to the door, removed her right-hand glove and touched the door with bare skin.

It was old. Very old. Just the look and feel said ancient. The surface wasn't exactly rough, it was as if it had been etched by time itself. Age had soaked into the surface and left its mark. It still felt smooth under Mookin's fingers, but, like old glass, you wanted to show it respect. Pity Debs had kicked it open. Mookin could clearly see her wet boot print halfway up the door. She turned to face Debs and, pointing at the boot mark, raised her eyebrows. Debs managed to look guilty, grin, shrug her shoulders and mouth the word 'sorry'.

Mookin turned back to the door, smiling to herself, before pushing it with her right hand. It was fat and heavy but opened easily. It was hinged on the left, the hinges concealed by the bulk of the door. Open, the corners of the door were rounded, and there was a black mark running all the way around the edge about two centimetres in. Mookin examined the frame and could see a rubbery seal set into it. Closed and locked, it would probably be water and airtight. If there was a lock, she couldn't see any sign of one, and, after all, the door *was* open.

With deliberate slowness, she stepped over the threshold on to what, at first, she took to be a tiled floor, but on closer inspection she could see was actually an unbroken surface. The grout lines that could be seen were fine silver lines in a regular grid pattern across the whole of the floor. Whether etched or painted on to the surface was unclear, but Mookin could feel no raised or indented marks. The floor was as smooth as the door. There was a kind of pattern on the tiles too: simple five-pointed star shapes of varying sizes, randomly scattered across the floor on a dark blue background.

Mookin looked around. She was in a small hallway, a three-metre cube, from which a corridor led off directly opposite the entrance door. The walls and ceiling, she realised, also had the same dark blue background and star-shaped pattern with silver grid lines. Soft light filled the corridor from an unseen source.

She returned her attention to the floor, and noticed that near the centre of the hall, three stars lay *beneath* where the silver grid lines crossed, like targets in a gun-sight, and were connected in a triangle by a separate line, not part of the grid. Mookin had an inkling of an idea, gears were slotting into place in her head. It was a map. A special kind of map, but still a map.

The door was fully open now, and before stepping from the

hallway into the corridor, Mookin asked Tammy to find a large rock and place it inside the doorway, in case the door swung shut. They didn't want to risk getting trapped in here. The corridor was square and wide, with plenty of room for a Mook. Mookin stepped forward, Tammy and Debs close behind.

The star-dusted floor continued unbroken into the corridor, the walls and ceiling. Mookin could see, just ahead, that the ceiling was lower, and thought this must be where Debs had hit her head so hard.

As they got closer, she could see that a section of the ceiling had dropped down along a short length of the corridor. It was half a metre lower than it should be. The floor was unchanged, but the walls, where they joined the floor, were cracked and damaged with vertical cracks running from floor to ceiling under the dropped section. She asked Debs if this was where she had hit her head.

'Yes,' she replied. 'I was following the line on the floor, and I stood up because my back was aching from bending over, when *pow*!'

'Line?' said Mookin. 'What line?' They all looked down at the floor where Debs was pointing, and sure enough, one of the grid lines was twice as thick as the others. It wasn't in the centre of the corridor, but nearer to the right-hand wall by at least half a step. Mookin followed it back to the hallway and confirmed that it was joined to the three stars in the triangle, the base of the triangle nearest the door, and the point facing down the corridor. Mookin didn't know how she had missed it before. It seemed so obvious now.

She quizzed Debs about it, who replied, 'Well, when I first kic... opened the door, there weren't any lines on the floor, but then I took my hat off to clean my light and the lines just appeared when my foot touched the floor. They were glowing at first, then they faded to what they are now, and this line was glowing more brightly. I followed it. But it's faded now, too.'

Mookin thought hard for a few seconds. 'Uh-oh, trouble,' she said, as pennies dropped and mental gears clicked into place.

'Trouble?' queried Debs and Tammy together.

'Yes. Trouble,' said Mookin. 'We shouldn't be here.'

'I don't understand,' said Debs, forehead screwed up in a frown.

'Me neither,' said Tammy.

'This is a star map,' said Mookin, looking around. 'This is a flupping keyway.'

Tammy was still bemused, Debs too, by the curious look on her face. 'What sort of star map, Mookin? We've all studied astronomy and I don't see any constellations. And what's a keyway?'

'Do you remember the day Uncle Big Mook came to school? What were we? Six? Seven?'

Mookin's mind flashed back to a time ten years ago, to a day she'd almost forgotten. She never really wondered why UBM was at the school. Later, she found out he came every four years when the new season's Mooks reached seven and gave his talk. He called it the 'Big Secret'. He told them a story, and that's what they'd all thought it was. A story. An amusing tale. She remembered the doors of the great hall slamming shut with a bang, the blinds snapping closed, plunging them into darkness. She'd liked the thrill of being a little bit scared. A bright light from the stage at the front and Uncle Big Mook appearing in the brightness. He was there in his finest clothes, smiling face, white moustache and tufted ears. She remembered him checking his pocket watch. He told them many things that day, told them about plasmics and how they formed. He showed them galaxies being made from nothing more than dust, suns igniting, worlds taking shape and stars collapsing to form black holes. He spoke of a place called Homestar, how it was in danger from the maelstrom at the heart of the galaxy, of the need to leave and be safe. And

Mooks. He told them of Mooks. Mooks gathering up all the peoples of the Fringe and moving them to safety too. In great ships, not the long way round through space but via keyways. Mooks built the Million Keyways and saved the Fringe. The Scattering. The Diaspora. Out into the galaxy, taming new worlds. Enough room for everyone. But shh. The Million Keyways, the ultimate weapon, the ultimate defence. The Mook's Big Secret.

'Big secret,' said Tammy, 'I remember. Woah. Hadn't thought about that in years. That was a story though, right?'

'I'm beginning to think otherwise, Tam. You remember the bit about Mooks saving, what was it called, the Fringe? What if that were real? What if you needed to get lots of people from one place to another all at once?'

'I guess you'd open a D-way like the Eldron do. A big D-way, what do they call it? A G-way.'

'And if you wanted to go from one planet to another, one star system to another?'

'Really big G-way?' suggested Debs.

'You mean the Million Keyways is real?' said Tammy. 'I thought it was just part of the story.'

'Maybe not,' said Mookin. 'Look, if you wanted to side-step across the stars, you would probably need a...?' Mookin let that sink in a moment, then saw the look on the girls' faces change as they got it. They looked at Mookin, down at the floor, back to Mookin. Their eyes went wide.

'A map!' they both said at once.

'That's right. A galactic route planner. An interstellar A to Z. This corridor is a map of a keyway. These three stars in the triangle, most likely our starting point, one of these three is Homestar.'

'But what's it doing here, Mookin?' asked Tammy.

'I really have no idea. And that's what scares me. I've never heard of anything like this before.'

'So what's at the end of the corridor?' asked Debs.

'I'm not sure, and I'm not sure I want to find out either. Maybe we should just ask the adults to take a look,' Mookin said.

'What?' said Debs, 'and miss all the fun? Come on Mookin, we've had a really hard day. This is our reward. We've earned this.' She looked at Tammy who was nodding her agreement.

'Okay, but this is trouble. Don't say I didn't warn you.'

'Is the roof safe, Mookin?' asked Debs.

'I should think so. It's been like this a long time. Whoever built this didn't plan for the ceiling to drop like that. It was probably a small tremor or earthquake, maybe some erosion under the corridor they didn't know about when they built it. Maybe when the Plunge fell through. Whatever happened, it let the salt water out.'

'Salt water?'

'Yeah. This place was once filled with salt water. That's why there's no lock on the door; the water pressure would have made the door impossible to open.'

'How do you know it was salt water?' asked Tammy.

'If you look at the cracks in the wall, there are salt crystals inside the cracks.'

Debs removed a glove, poked her finger in then licked it. 'Yep. Salt,' she confirmed.

They carried on down the corridor and fifty or so paces in, the line intersected another star, but this time, line and corridor turned ninety degrees to the right. The girls followed eagerly until they could finally see a second room. This one was slightly larger, but still a cube, with a second door opposite the corridor. The line ended in the centre of the room, in the middle of a large star, nearly filling one whole square of the grid design. Mookin pointed at the star and said, 'This has to represent the sun, our star.'

The door was nearly the same as the first one except for two things: the hinges were on the outside, which meant that, like the other door, they both opened *into* the corridor. The salt water was here to protect whatever was beyond this door. Secondly, in the centre of the heart shape, was a smaller heart, but recessed into the metal of the door. Mookin poked her finger into it. It wasn't smooth, but faceted, like a diamond. It rang a bell in Mookin's mind, but she couldn't quite grasp it. Elusive, like Tammy's writing on the first door. She looked at the words on this door, but they were different. Same style but not the same words, and six of them this time, in three lines. Tammy copied the words in her notebook, as she had the words from the first door.

Mookin reached for the edge of the door but knew instinctively that it would be locked. She could feel the rubber seal squashed almost flat, but the door wouldn't budge. In the middle of the left-side wall was a console with a screen and buttons, completely dead. In the top right corner was a hole as wide as Mookin's wrist, but something was missing, removed to stop anyone from using the console. She was not tempted to press any buttons.

'Well girls, that's as far as we go. This door isn't leading anywhere.' They trudged back down the corridor, full of questions. Back in the outer hallway, the door was still wide open, rock still in place. Mookin said, 'I'll get the door, Tam, you get the rock.'

Debs stepped back outside. 'Look at this, Mookin,' she said, pointing at the wall beside the door. There was a lever sticking out of a slot in the wall, and next to it another console, similar to the one inside. 'What do you think that's for?'

Mookin joined her, bending close to examine the lever. It was long and slender and had the appearance of polished chrome. The last part of the handle was knurled to a rough finish and was obviously a hand grip. The slot and console were surrounded by a metal frame with the same chrome look as the lever, and the slot had eleven notches, equally spaced, etched into the metal and coloured black. They were numbered from one to eleven. At least numbers haven't changed, thought Mookin.

'Do you think it opens the other door?' asked Debs.

'No, I don't think so, Debs. This is for something else.' Mookin wiggled the handle experimentally, twisting and pulling. It was moving fractionally and didn't feel jammed.

'Oh Mookin, be careful. I mean, we don't know what it's for, do we?' said Tammy, nervously.

'Only one way to find out. Now you two stand over there and take the rock with you; we don't want the door to jam.'

Debs and Tammy exchanged worried looks, the beams on their headlights flashing across each other's faces, blinding them for a second.

'Are you sure?' asked Debs.

'Yes. I have an idea what's going to happen. Ready, girls?'

They moved off a few steps, peering from around a boulder, and Mookin pulled on the lever, which didn't move. She frowned at it for a moment, twisted it first clockwise, then anti-clockwise. Nothing. Still frowning, she let go of the lever and rubbed her chin, deep in thought. Then, her eyes lit up as she grabbed the lever once more. She pushed hard, the lever moved inwards, then she twisted clockwise and it moved a quarter-turn. There was a 'snick' and the lever slid out from the wall.

Mookin breathed out heavily, not realising she had been holding her breath. 'Safety device,' she shouted over her left shoulder. 'Push *and* twist.' With a silent wish on her lips, she pulled down on the lever. It slid smoothly and quietly down the slot as if Mr Morningside had installed and oiled it yesterday. Mookin stood back and joined her friends.

Nothing happened.

Then, faintly at first, a soft whirring noise like a spinning top rose slowly in pitch, building and building until it was as fast and loud as the circular saw at Mookinsouth lumber mill.

It ran at fever pitch for twenty seconds before slowing down again, then fading almost to nothing. This was followed by a 'thunk' and to everyone's surprise, the lever clicked up a notch, from eleven to ten.

There was a far-off 'ka-thunk' which the girls felt through the floor as much as they heard, followed by another, much closer sound just down the corridor. Then came a rushing, burbling noise from all around them and the lever moved another notch. There was a click in the corridor as a small circular part of the ceiling dropped down and a short pause until a red light came on inside it and started to rotate. Looking down the corridor, Mookin could see red lights turning every five paces or so. Then, in the red strobe effect, from around the corner, came something dark, snaking towards them along the floor. She couldn't make it out at first, then she realised what it was. It could only be one thing. Water.

Salt water.

The lever clicked up again and Mookin went back to the door, put her fingers on it and felt the door quiver under her hand, then slowly, powerfully, it started to close. The lever clicked once more and Mookin needed no more warning. Grabbing her stunned friends, she pulled them out, back into the cave, the smell of brine in her nostrils. As the water sloshed into the vestibule, the door closed against the rubber seal with a soft hiss.

And that was that. Or so they thought. They just stood there staring at the closed door, too stunned to move or speak. After what seemed like ages, Mookin broke the silence by saying, 'Well, I guess we'll never know now. Suppose we better find a way out of here, back to...'

An enormous 'ka-a-bunk' sounded from deep in the rock, seeming to shake the whole cave, sending dust and small pebbles cascading from the roof. The girls staggered, wondering if the whole cave was about to collapse on top of them. There was a deep grinding whirr followed by a screech like fingernails on a blackboard. Mookin saw it first, as she was facing outwards towards Giant's Stairway. Her eyes grew big and round, and the other two could see her lips form the words 'no way' before they realised she was looking past them, over their shoulders.

They both turned with trepidation to see what was going on behind them. Mookin, Debs and Tammy could not believe what they were seeing, it was like something from a dream, a nightmare. A huge, house-sized slab of the outer wall was moving slowly away from them. The screeching, grinding noise was being caused by tiny pebbles being crushed to powder as they were trapped between the huge slab and the sides and floor of the cave. It slid backwards about two metres then the right-hand side stopped moving, the left side continuing until there was a blaze of sunlight, blinding bright after the gloom of the caves. Water was pouring into the gap as the enormous slab swung out away from them on some huge, unseen hinge mechanism.

'Quick,' said Mookin, giving her friends a gentle shove in the back, all three stumbling forward through the water, fumbling into the bright light of Giant's Stairway, eyes blinking rapidly as they adjusted to the light. There was no time to wonder why the big slab of rock had opened when Mookin activated the lever. *Probably just part of a set sequence*, she thought.

They collapsed in a heap, well away from the doorway, on a dry part of the terrace. As it turned out, they needn't have rushed. The massive door stayed open for over ten minutes before there was another, slightly softer 'ka-a-bunk', and it started its slow, grinding return journey. It finished its swing then slid slowly back to its former position. Soon, water was pouring over its face from above, for all the world, just like any other part of Giant's Stairway. Within a few minutes, it was almost impossible to tell where the huge, gaping entrance had been. It blended perfectly with the surrounding steps, terraces, waterfalls and pools.

Mookin thought she would have real trouble finding it again, but then she spotted something through the water and walked over for a closer look. The others tagged along behind, and Mookin showed them what she had seen. On each side of where the door had been, carved into the rock under the water streaming down its face, like the doors in the cave, two distinctive heart shapes as big as a hand. You wouldn't see them unless you knew where to look, especially with the sun glinting off the pouring water.

Mookin knew exactly where they were now. She had always wondered why they called this step of Giant's Stairway the Love Pool. Now she knew.

'Um, Mookin,' said Debs. But Mookin was deep in thought. 'Mookin?' She still didn't answer. 'Earth to Mookin Bettymook,' she said loudly over the sound of rushing water.

'Wha..? Sorry Debs. I was just thinking. Wassup?'

'Well. This might seem silly, but...'

'Go on, spit it out.'

'You promise not to laugh?'

'Course not. What's bugging you?'

'Both of you. Mook's honour?'

'I swear,' said Tammy.

'Me too, I swear,' said Mookin, intrigued now. Debs was rarely this serious.

'Okay, so I was thinking too. Didn't we just come down a tunnel where the river was flowing up to our knees?'

'Yes. Yes, we did.'

'And when we got to this cave, it kind of spread out and disappeared into channels in the floor?'

'Yes, what's your point?' said Tammy.

'My point, Tammy, is how the heck does it get back up there again?' and she pointed to the next terrace up, where the water was cascading over the hidden rock door, a curtain of water through which they'd had to walk when leaving the cave.

'I don't see...' said Tammy.

'Debs! That's brilliant,' said Mookin. 'Don't you see, Tam? The Plunge. Before the hole appeared, the Wyse must have flowed straight over the plateau and down the Stairway and over this door. But when the hole fell through, the river was diverted underground and came out here, and the door was exposed.'

'So someone...'

'Yes! Someone wanted the door to stay hidden, so they pumped the water back up and over the next terrace up so it covers the door.'

'Exactly,' said Debs.

'Wow,' said Tammy. 'They went to a lot of trouble. Must be important.'

'You bet it's important,' said Mookin.

B.J. PAGE

8. The Economical Truth

<u>**Tinkatanium:**</u>
Super-tough metal found and manufactured on Mookination by Morningside Tinkamook. Of extraterrestrial origin, remnant of a meteorite strike on the north side of the island which pulverised to black sand an area of one square kilometre. The resulting fusion of metallic meteor and local minerals created a new alloy which is extremely light, flexible and supremely strong. It is estimated that approximately three to four tonnes remain to be extracted, but the source will then be exhausted.Morningside, a highly respected inventor and skilled sword maker, says the alloy is difficult to mine, smelt and work, requiring temperatures of over 1,750℃, which can only be attained by his furnace twice a year. Construction follows a similar path to that of the Japanese Katana except where the mixing of hard and softer metals for the edge and back of the sword occurs. Mr Morningside will only say that his blades are in fact hollow, that there is no inner core of softer steel and that 'tinkatanium' is the perfect metal for bladed weapons.He no longer folds metal into swords, but if you possess one of his knives, consider yourself most fortunate.

Mookipedia

Mookin did not know how to lie to her parents, and neither did Tammy or Debs, Mooks just didn't tell lies. So they had decided to do the only thing they could: they would be economical with the truth. The girls had decided on the long trek back that now was not the time to tell the whole of their day's adventure. To be sure, they were absolutely bursting to talk about it to anyone who would listen but had grudgingly reached the conclusion that some things were best saved for another day. Tammy was puzzling over the strange writing and Mookin over the heart-shaped indent in the second door.

A little research was in order. A few discreet questions.

This was extremely difficult for the three Mooks, who were entirely open, honest and truthful in everything they did. But this was different. This was a bigger secret even than Uncle Big Mook's. Someone, they were sure, knew about the door they had found and what its purpose was. Someone on Mookination was hiding something. It went against everything that Mooks believed in and were taught.

So, if anyone asked, their journey had stopped at Crystal Flute Cave. They had seen the large boulder pile and thought it blocked the way forward, so they had retraced their steps back down the Shimny. They had not had time to retrieve the merthread reel, so Mookin would tell her sister she had left it in place because she was going back to the cave system for more exploring and to map out where they had been. This was all true of course: they were going back as soon as possible. She also couldn't wait to tell her sister how fantastic the thread was, and how it was going to revolutionise caving and climbing on the island.

They arrived back in Mookinsouth shortly before sundown, which on Mookination was quite early, as they lived inside the volcano's collapsed crater where the sun would disappear behind the Crown at least an hour before the real sunset, which they called deepdark. The time between was twilight, usually a quiet, reflective time for Mooks.

They had dropped off the bikes back at the smithery, where Mr Morningside had taken several minutes to resharpen Mookin's knife, using a special grinding wheel. Puzzling over how she had blunted one of his special blades, he started quizzing Mookin over what had happened to it. Mookin, who had been given the knife as a gift from her dad when she started climbing, hadn't realised Mr Morningside had actually made it.

She always carried a whetstone for sharpening other

knives, her machete and axe, but had never had to sharpen her knife. Until now.

Mookin had been reluctant to show him the merthread at first, as she had promised her sister that she wouldn't show it to anyone else except Tammy and Debs. Not that it was a secret in any way, but there was a limited supply and Mookin was just testing it for the Merfolk. They didn't want people clamouring for it before they could make it in quantity. Although it was similar to the thread Jaci used for weaving, this was a hundred times stronger. In the end, she explained this to Mr Morningside, and he agreed not to tell a soul. He tested it and became very excited, asking Mookin all sorts of questions she couldn't answer. She had to promise him she would ask her sister to get in touch. He said he had all sorts of ideas for how to make use of the incredible material and its exceptionally tough fibres. They thanked him for the use of the bikes and said goodnight. The girls reached the village square (which was, despite its name, more of an oval), hugged and went their separate ways.

Tammy headed west to the Piccolo plantation where her parents grew all sorts of fibrous and woody plants like flax and hemp, bamboo, cotton, reeds from around the lake shore and wool (from real sheep and goats). Her mum and dad had a love for all things paper. They specialised in printing and book binding, producing beautiful paper in their paper mill and printworks as well as manufacturing many natural fibres which went off to be made into twines, ropes and yarns for weaving and knitting.

Their biggest success, though, had been a total fluke. Tammy's dad was the inventor of leafwrap, a clear, thin film derived from the castor oil plant. Mr Moonshaka, an accomplished plant-charmer, had been attempting to produce tracing paper and thought he was perhaps just one or two steps away from success.

Too often, a Mook tried to charm their desired plant in one step and ended up with some truly dreadful specimens. Some with fruits that looked, smelled and tasted delicious, but made you violently sick after swallowing one mouthful. Others that produced incredible fibres that could be woven into silk-like cloth that was completely waterproof, but which was a nasty pinkish colour that couldn't be dyed. Others had a smell that could bring you out in spots in seconds and some were just too horrible to mention, often requiring Eldron magic to eradicate. It was said there were some rather treacherous plants in the jungles and unexplored parts of the island. Not *usually* deadly, but you had to watch where you put your feet.

Mr Moonshaka's third step did not go quite to plan, and the next crop produced leaves that, when picked, turned completely transparent, as clear as glass. Clearly not good for tracing paper. He was about to start over when his wife noticed that the leaves could be peeled apart like layers of tissue paper and were slightly tacky on the inside. Mr Moonshaka had inadvertently created leafwrap, which was now widely used on Mookination for keeping food fresh and tasty. He never did get his tracing paper.

Their home was given over to all things bookish. Every room was crammed with towering bookshelves, stepladders, filing cabinets, maps and all manner of documents. It was a place of comfy chairs, nooks with cushions, reading lamps and window seats all mixed with the smell of fine paper and coffee brewing in the kitchen.

Tammy never knew who she would meet at home. Mooks travelled from all over to make use of her family's extensive library and meticulous record-keeping. It was not unusual for four or five people to be staying with her family, sometimes for weeks or months, whatever their research project required. For this reason, their home was a sprawling affair. It never seemed quite big enough, always on the verge of overflowing or bursting at the seams.

It had started out as quite a normal-sized family home, grown some years ago in blue coral; four rooms downstairs and four up, with a thatched roof. It had been added to so many times that the original house now looked like a porch stuck to the front of the main building – three floors and a basement, not to mention numerous outbuildings stacked to the rafters with storage boxes. The huge basement was given over to the storage of rare maps and important documents from both Mook and Bigfolk sources, some extremely rare; ancient books that needed to be in a temperature-controlled environment, protected from light and air.

Tammy had two brothers: one older, aged fifty-one, Salago Mykamook, who worked with their parents and who was particularly skilled at illustration and design and also liked to restore old books and manuscripts, and her younger brother, aged only four, called Mulberry Kozomook. Already an avid reader, he devoured any book placed in front of him. Tammy adored him, helping him to read and learn. His only fault was that he would sometimes go missing for several hours, which prompted frantic searches, only for him to be found behind a stack of books, asleep with his face stuck to the page he'd been reading.

Tammy stowed her gear in an outbuilding, promising herself she would get up early, unpack and clean everything and put it away in its proper place. She needed a hot shower, food and then an hour or two researching the words on the star chamber doors. She eased open the front door and stepped into the comforting smells of home. 'Mum, Dad, I'm back,' she shouted, peeling clothes off as she made her way to the shower.

Debs plodded off eastwards towards her parents' home, which was a few short kilometres from the village. She followed the East Road as it meandered along, not taking any shortcuts as it was getting dark, even though she knew every millimetre of the fields all around. She soon reached home and turned right on to the gravel drive. Debs liked the crunchy sound her feet made as she walked along and could see the lights of the house at the back of the lumber yard as she walked between tall stacks of timber and logs.

The yard itself was quiet and dark, as was the sawmill off to the left, but during the day, the crane would be in constant motion, feeding logs to the mill to be sawn and cut. Debs' family managed the forest on the eastern slopes of Mookination, harvesting fast-growing softwoods for construction, and wood pulp and hardwoods from the jungle areas which went for furniture-making. Mr Repartee Wendlemook and his wife Mrs Climbshi Brendamook were both lumberjacks and master carpenters and Mr Repartee was also a charm-builder.

Most modern Mook buildings were made using a type of land-based coral and it required skilled charmers to be able to charm the coral into the correct shapes for housing. Usually a timber frame was built and the coral persuaded to grow around the frame. The colour was chosen before work started and the doors and windows were cut afterwards. It could take up to a year to make a new building, and concentration was key, as were frequent site visits of at least once a week, guiding the coral to the proper form. Less skilled charmers ended up with some strange looking buildings, with odd towers and walls in the wrong place, maybe a staircase on the outside or in the wrong colour.

Mostly built of timber, and all on one level, Debs' house had an overhanging wood shingle roof that covered a porch on all four sides, providing lots of cooling shade. There was no chimney breast but the central wall was grown from dark brown coral, Mr Repartee's first coral-charming creation.

Debs had just one younger sister, Mirranda Mabelmook, aged fourteen, and with whom she shared her room. Mabe was a younger version of Debs. There were frequent play fights and chatting into the night. She was attacked as soon as she stepped through the back door and fell to the floor, her sister wrapped around her knees, giggling. Debs reached down and began tickling her sister's ribs. Mabe scrambled away on all fours, now desperate to escape, as Debs pursued her across the floor, a wild look in her eyes and a low growl in her throat.

Twilight was ending, and it was almost deepdark by the time Mookin reached the lane that led to Rosadale-Dell, two valleys folding one into the other, the result of a huge mudslide centuries back, stretching up to and blending into the lower slopes of the Crown, with gently rolling hills of lush green. As she passed beneath it, she looked up at the white curving wooden banner stretched across the entrance to the farm. Red and black letters spelled out *Rosadale* in the centre and underneath the farm name was the family pictoglyph.

Seeing the family glyph, Mookin was filled with everything it meant to her, like seeing a photograph of her whole family. Home, warmth and comfort, food, family and friends. It made her feel proud and good and part of something worthwhile and it gave her a much-needed boost of energy. As deepdark fell across the island, the solberries began popping to life one by one along the drive, giving up the light stored in their silvery globes during the day, illuminating the driveway. The solberry hedge had been planted on both sides of the drive, continuing up to and around the stone courtyard of the main house, along under the windows and in an arch up over the front doorway.

The house was a sprawling affair, two floors with a stone-built front, but extended at both sides and at the back with grey-green coral to match the stone. Open at the front, the courtyard had a large stone barn to the left and coral-charmed stables to the right.

As more and more solberries came on and Mookin reached the courtyard, she was surprised to see a horse and carriage parked at the front of the house. The four-wheeled carriage was gloss black, painted with gold coach lines on the body, fenders, roof and shafts. The doors had a familiar glyph, also rendered in gold, a triangle with an eye shape in the centre. Very posh and only used for one purpose: Uncle Big Mook. It was his glyph, the Mayor of the Three Mookins. *Oh no,* thought Mookin. *Trouble.*

PART 2
THE ROOT OF ALL LEARNING

9. All Aboard the Tigerlily

Big Hiss:

Mookination, situated on the equator, is fortunate enough not to require vast amounts of energy. However, as Mooks are fond of their home comforts, a solution was found for our growing energy needs in the shape of Big Hiss. The geothermal system of heavily-insulated pipes was installed over five centuries ago and carries steam to almost every part of the island. It provides power to drive steam turbines in most households so that electricity can be generated on site and on demand without the need to string cables across the landscape. Complemented by solar arrays, wind generators and biobatteries, we enjoy a surplus of free energy.
Big Hiss is located just outside Mookinwest and is largely maintenance free.

Mookipedia

Mookin could hardly see her hand in front of her face, and she was walking with her hands stretched out in front of her, so she knew that this was true. She was groping, almost blind, wet hair hanging in her face, through the dense mist, reaching out for the cord she knew was there, but which just kept slipping from her grasp. Finally, her fingers found the dangling, elusive thing and closed tightly around it. She tugged sharply downwards and was rewarded with a definite click.

With a brief buzzing hum and a whirr, the ceiling extractor fan sprang into life and began to clear the dense cloud of steam from Mookin's bathroom. In a few moments, all traces of the foggy substance were gone, except where it had condensed on almost every surface and was now running down the walls to form puddles on the tiled floor.

Mookin sighed heavily as she wiped a section of the mirror above the basin with her hand. Looking back at her from slightly distorted eyes, her reflection said, *Note to self, Betty, turn on extractor fan before turning on shower.*

She had awoken far too early and had been luxuriating in the hot water for much too long. Her fingers and toes were now all wrinkly and soft. She wrapped herself in a big, fluffy white towel from the towel rail where it had been warming, and a second, slightly smaller one from the rail above went around her long purple hair with a quick twist and a flick.

Whilst in the dreamy world of the shower, she had decided she was going to have her hair cut. Not just shorter, but very short. Very short indeed. She would ask her mum about it first, but the decision was made as far as Mookin was concerned. After last night's meeting with Uncle Big Mook, she didn't think long hair was an option anymore.

Mookin had eyed the carriage suspiciously, and walking around to the front, she stroked the horse, whose name she knew was Fleet. He in turn, nuzzled her neck and sniffed at her hand expectantly, hoping for a mint, which he loved, or perhaps a carrot. 'I'm sorry Fleet, I don't have any food left.' Fleet was not convinced and started to sniff her pockets, so Mookin walked over to her mother's flower beds and pulled a handful of tulip-like blooms from the ground. She offered them to Fleet who sniffed then munched his way through them in a few seconds. Mum wouldn't notice a few missing; she had hundreds.

'See you, Fleet. Better go see what Uncle Big Mook wants. He's not visited in over two years, so this can't be good.'

Fleet tossed his head and swished his tail. 'Tanx,' he answered in his horsey voice. 'See-eeee yooo.' Not all horses were polite like Fleet, some hardly ever spoke, and when they did it was often nothing to do with what you were talking about anyway. One of Mookin's little things, things besides her purple, non-striped hair, was her ability to talk to – and be answered by – animals. She stopped talking about it when she realised no one else could do it. She never mentioned it to anyone, not even Tammy and Debs. When she was little, she thought it was quite normal, but it turns out Mum and Dad were just humouring her when she said things like 'The baby goat wants her mother,' 'The horse has a stone in his hoof,' or 'The dog wants you to go with him, he's found a hurt lamb.'

Mookin took a deep breath, turned the big brass doorknob and stepped into the hall. Any thought she had of accidentally overhearing snippets of conversation quickly vanished when her brother came rushing down the stairs, jumping the last three steps, socks skidding on the polished wood floor as he made a sharp turn through the lounge, into the dining room, and on into the kitchen, all the while shouting, 'She's here! She's here!' at the top of his voice.

Mookin turned the other way towards the back of the house and into the scullery. Here, she began stripping off her filthy, smelly clothes and throwing them straight into the laundry hamper next to the washing machine. She grabbed an old patched dressing gown of her mum's which was hanging on the back of the door before cramming her feet into her old fluffy slippers. Her boots she wiped carefully with a damp cloth before polishing to a soft gleam with the brushes and polish from under the stone sink. She realised she was just stalling, postponing the inevitable.

She unpacked her rucksack and cleaned it as best she could, her waterproofs she hung outside; the rain would clean them. Her hair was a tangled mud-matted mess that she would have to sort out before bed. Her climbing gear went into the cupboard under the back stairs. She ran up the stairs three at a time and into her bedroom where she splashed water on her face, quickly patted it dry and looked in the mirror. It was worse than she thought. She brushed a few strands of hair back and attempted to pull some clumps of mud out, but it was stuck fast. It would have to do.

She slipped into an old sweater the same colour as her hair and a pair of lilac PJ bottoms with purple polka dots, back into her slippers and back down the same stairs. She paused at the kitchen door, hand on the knob, trying to see through the clear parts of the stained glass. Taking a deep breath, she turned the knob and stepped into the kitchen, straight into one of those awkward silences where everyone stops talking to look at you. Mookin was convinced, as she closed the door behind her and leaned up against it, that her hopes of being a Mookout were fading fast. She smiled at her family, all sitting around the long, scrubbed kitchen table. In Dad's normal seat was Uncle Big Mook.

'Mookin, Mooky, Betty, Bettymook, sweetheart,' they all said at once.

'Mum, Dad, Uncle, Sis, Kik,' Mookin replied.

'You're a little late, dear,' said Mum. 'We were starting to worry.'

'Did you have a good Woodsday?' asked Dad.

'Sorry, Mum. Yes Dad, we did. We found a new cave behind –'

'Well as long as you're back safe and sound, poppet,' interrupted Dad, something he rarely did.

'Hurrumph.' Everyone turned to Uncle Big Mook. 'Erm, perhaps Mookin would like to sit down, she is probably tired and, I'm guessing, a little bit hungry?'

Mookin hadn't realised. Her knees were trembling a bit, her legs suddenly too heavy to hold her up, and her stomach gave a low growl, which she was sure everyone in the room had heard. She sank into the other captain's chair opposite Uncle Big Mook, and Mum and Dad sprang into action, Dad pouring her a cocamint with two lumps of sugar. Mum set the table in front of her, linen placemat, napkin and soup spoon. Mookin sipped her cocamint, the cup cradled in both hands, and a warmth spread through her from head to toe, a gentle familiar calm. Home.

Mum placed a large bowl of vegetable curry with fried rice and some pitta bread in front of her daughter, reaching out to stroke her face as she did so.

'Thanks, Mum,' she said, really meaning it, looking up into her mother's eyes and seeing nothing but warmth and love reflected back.

'Bowl's a bit hot,' said Mum, returning to her seat.

Mookin watched the steam curling from her curry and took another sip of cocamint. She picked up the salt grinder, crunching a little salt on to her food, then did the same with the black pepper mill. Mookin was fond of very spicy food. She spooned the first mouthful of curry, blowing on it before putting it in her mouth, and went from hungry to ravenous in an instant. Almost before realising it, she had emptied the bowl.

'Sorry, hungrier than I thought!' she said to the room at large.

Mum came around the table again, sweeping up the used bowl and whispering, 'Saved you some dessert, Betty. Later, okay?'

'Well, Bettymook, better now?' asked Uncle Big Mook.

'Yes, thank you, Uncle,' she replied.

'I expect you're wondering why I'm here, aren't you, my dear?'

'Not really. I thought, because you are here, that maybe it had all fallen through and you wanted to give me the bad news yourself? So, no Learning Tree for me? Oh well, I shan't miss what I never –'

'No, no,' UBM interrupted, something he *often* did. 'Not that. Not that at all, Betty. Just the opposite, in fact.' He paused, looking left and right at mum and dad. 'I have discussed the broad outlines of the mission with your parents – it isn't, after all top secret – and I have assured them of the low danger aspect of it. It is, however, crucial that we have a

Mookout of your age in order to carry it out. Contact with Bigfolk will be minimal. We need you to start training full time. Immediately. We have about a month to prepare you.'

Mookin stared in utter disbelief, certain her chance had slipped away from her like a fragment of a dream.

'I... uh...' was all she could manage. She looked at her family for support, Mum and Dad were just smiling, Djinny was smiling and nodding, and Kikkit gave her a gap-toothed grin and a double thumbs-up.

Mookin's feet were pounding hard along the dirt track through the Ringwood. Her heavy rucksack was starting to rub, so she cinched the straps tighter, shifting the weight further up her back. She was glad she had chosen the hiking boots and not pumps or trainers. Although heavier to run in, they were much more suited to the rough ground, supporting her ankles and feet.

Over halfway now, she thought, *although the last part was going to be tough.* She had been gone only half a day, but already it seemed a world away. She was glad to have met Dora, though. One tough old lady, Dora. In her mind, she replayed the morning's events:

Mookin finished dressing in black jeans tucked into calf-length hiking boots. They were old, but fitted like a glove, were moulded to her feet and would not cause any blisters. She also wore a long-sleeved yellow t-shirt with a picture of a baby grumpalump on the front, hand painted by Djinny, and a black gilet which would offer protection but leave her arms free. She packed a few essentials into her spare rucksack (the other one was still mud spattered) and pinned her plaited hair up under a yellow, knitted peaked hat. She went quietly down the back stairs, trying hard not to wake anyone else, and turned the brass handle to the kitchen door, closing it behind her with barely a click.

'Morning, Mookin Bettymook.'

'Dad! What are you doing sitting in the dark? I nearly had a kitten,' said Mookin, sure her heart had skipped a couple of beats. She moved to the dresser and switched on a lamp.

'Sorry, poppet. Just enjoying the quiet. Like some coffee?' he asked, pouring her a mug without waiting for a reply.

'Thanks, Poppa.' She remembered how she used to call her dad Poppa when she was tiny, and he would call her poppet. Poppa and poppet. Dad and daughter. She added milk and sugar, and, stirring, flopped into the chair next to him.

'You're up early. Excited?' he asked.

'Yeah. I slept well, just woke up too early. Anyway, you can talk. Why are you up and about?'

'Me? Oh, I've been milking the chickens,' Dad replied, smiling into his cup.

Mookin peered into the milk jug, a look of concern on her face. She didn't say anything, just stared at him with raised eyebrows, waiting for the explanation she knew would come. He took a long sip before going on, 'Yes, they quite like milk. Bit of a treat for them. I mix it with their feed. Good for their digestion, bit of a boost. They've got a big race next week.'

'Aw Dad, you and those chickens, you really crack me up.'

Mookin had said her farewells to Mum, Dad and Djinny early that morning after a quick breakfast. Kikkit had been snoring gently, but she'd crept into his room and kissed him on the forehead. He just rolled over to face the wall muttering something about school. She smiled and left him to his dreams.

She made her way into the village and down to the small port without meeting anyone. The jetties were filled with a variety of craft, including six fishing boats in brightly painted colours, all biobattery powered now, with mast and sails stowed as a back-up. There was the usual assortment of sailing boats and rowing boats of every size and colour, all bobbing and knocking gently against the jetty and each other.

And there was the ferry.

The ferry sailed between Mookinsouth, Mookinwest and Mookinorth making occasional stops at Zooplex, the island in Starshine Lake that was home to some of Mookination's more exotic creatures. Mookin's dad had arranged a lift with Dora, aboard the ferry Tigerlily. Colourfully painted in orange and black, Tigerlily had been sailing the waters of Starshine Lake for longer than anyone cared to remember. Originally a sail craft, she had been refitted with biobatteries and paddle wheels by Mrs Dorabelle's late husband, the Captain, sometime in the 1700s. The Captain had been killed in a freak accident while climbing the mast. He had been fitting a new masthead light, replacing the old oil lamp. He had had the cable clamped in his teeth when the mast was struck by lightning. The mast was shattered to splinters and the Captain was no more.

Mrs Dorabelle, Dora to everyone, had stopped what she was doing and insisted on taking over from her husband, stating simply that, 'It's what he would have wanted. The ferry must run.'

Except for Kitedays and occasional holidays, she never missed a trip. The round trip took about six hours, depending on passengers and cargo, and sailed twice a day. The dawn run from Mookinsouth rarely had passengers, and today Mookin was the only one.

She helped Dora to cast off, unplug from the charging unit and retract the gangplank. Less than two minutes later, Tigerlily reversed from the jetty, turned on a penny and headed out into the lake, paddle wheels silently churning the black water to silver froth.

From pointed bow to square stern she was thirty-five metres long and eight across the beam. She was flat bottomed with a retractable keel, rarely used now that she was powered. The paddle wheels were added amidships and were three metres in diameter and operated independently or worked in conjunction with the rudder. Turning starboard slowed the right-side paddle and speeded up the left, making her very nimble. She had an orange and white candy-striped canvas awning covering the upper seating deck. The lower deck was open-sided too, but with tables and chairs and a small galley from which refreshments were often served.

Small cargo holds below deck enabled her to carry trade goods around the lake. The aft deck could accommodate livestock or, indeed, two horses and carts side by side if required. The tiny wheelhouse was at the front of the upper deck, accessed from a ladder either side. Dora had kept the front and rear masts, the canvas furled tightly against the timber, but she had not replaced the central mast that had been shattered by lightning.

Mookin heard Dora calling her from the bridge and turned to see her beckoning for her to come up. She swung onto the ladder and climbed in three easy steps up to the little walkway around the bridge. Sliding the door open, she stepped inside.

'Hi, Dora. Did you want something?' she said.

'Well,' said Dora, in a gravelly sort of voice, 'some company would be nice. Pull up a chair, honey.'

Dora's hair was unusual: dark blue and black stripes, cut very short, and tucked under a black and white peaked cap with an anchor and crown in the centre. It was faded, worn and quite grubby. She had a gold pin on her dark blue jacket that read HMS Thunderbolt. She was also wearing khaki cargo pants tucked into short rubber deck boots.

Dora was seated in a padded leather swivel chair with wooden arms in the centre of the bridge. She had both feet on a large brass spoked wheel and was steering Tigerlily with her feet.

The bridge was dark except for a very dim light just above and behind Dora's head. She was sipping noisily from a chipped china mug. Mookin looked for another chair but could see only an old oil drum with a grubby cushion on top. I guess that's it, *she thought and dragged it over to the front of the bridge to sit on.*

'Do you like cocamint, honey?' asked Dora, just as Mookin was about to sit down.

'Oh, yes, it's my favourite.'

'Cupboard behind me, flask and mugs.' Dora pointed with her head. Mookin helped herself to a steaming mug from the flask and perched on the oil drum, looking out through the windscreen into the pre-dawn darkness.

'Dora, how do you know where to steer in the dark?' asked Mookin, genuinely curious.

'Ha! Always asks me that, they do. Usually say I know the lake like the back o' me hand.' She pondered for a moment. 'Come here, honey, stand next to Dora.' Mookin did as she was asked and stood shoulder to shoulder. Seated, she was the same height as Mookin, but standing, Dora's head only came up to Mookin's elbow. 'Now, tell me what you can see, hon.'

Mookin peered through the windscreen but could still see nothing in the blackness. Then she noticed a narrow slot in the glass at about head height. It was actually a little window, cut into the larger pane, which flipped out and up. When Mookin lined her eyes up with the slot, she could just make out a very dim red light against the black.

'Is that Mookinwest?' she asked.

'Heh, heh. Spotted it did you, honey? Clever girl. Yes, that's Mookinwest. Red light on top of the town hall, inside a reflector pointing towards the lake. Mookinorth has a blue light on their town hall and we have an orange one.'

'I've never seen them,' said Mookin.

'No, you can only see them from the lake at night. Close up, at ground level, nothing to see.'

They both enjoyed the quiet for a moment, each deep in their own thoughts, which sipping cocamint was apt to do sometimes.

'So where are you off to so early, honey? Usually just me

and the post this time of day.'

'I'm off to the Learning Tree, Mookout training,' answered Mookin.

Dora sprayed her cocamint, nearly choking. Mookin had to slap her back, hard, several times before she managed to stop coughing.

'Really? Aren't you a little young, honey? I mean, I can see you're tall. Did they drop the entrance age or something?'

Dora wiped at her streaming eyes with a handkerchief. Mookin was concerned now. Did Dora know something she didn't?

'Um, no, I don't think so.'

Dora was silent for a while, then when she spoke again, her voice was softer, full of concern. 'What's your name, sweetheart, what should old Dora call you?'

'My family call me Betty.'

'Well Miss Betty, Mookout training. Do you know much about it? Have they told you anything at all?' Mookin shook her head by way of reply and Dora continued, 'Well, it's different for everyone, of course, tailored to the individual, but one thing it has in common, sweetie, it's damn hard. You have to keep your wits about you, keep pushing yourself. They'll push you past what you think your limits are, to a new level. But you can do it, sweetie. They wouldn't have picked you otherwise.'

'How?' was all Mookin could say.

'How do I know all this? That bit's simple. I'm a Mookout too. Well, was. Used to be. Although you never really retire, still help out when I can.'

For the rest of the trip, Dora chatted non-stop, giving Mookin some valuable tips that she said would help her through her basic training. She also had some stories about Firestarta, which made him seem a little less daunting.

Mookin had only met him a few times, at parties and public events and didn't really know anything about him apart from some of the legends that had grown up around him. It was supposed to be Firestarta who had discovered the Learning Tree, for instance, but as far as Mookin knew, its origin was ancient, lost in the mists of time, thousands of years back. She was positive, though, that she would find out everything she needed to over the next few weeks, so was resolved to not worry over things beyond her control.

As a parting gift, Dora had told Mookin to stay on the Tigerlily at Mookinwest and she would drop her further around the lake, cutting ten kilometres off her journey. Dora knew of a little natural rock jetty that jutted out into the lake, and this was where they bade farewell.

'You keep in touch, Betty. Stop by or send a postcard. "Dora, Tigerlily" will get to me. And remember what I've told you, especially about Firestarta Spekalmook. Give him a hug from me, tell him it's been too long.' She gave Mookin a big hug as she left, and Mookin was sure she saw a tear in the corner of her eye.

Crikey. That was only a few hours ago. Talk about in at the deep end! Jumping a small stream, she turned left and decided to follow it downhill. Sure enough, the stream soon tumbled into a crystal-clear pool a few paces across. She had a tube running from the water bottle in her pack and clipped to the strap of her rucksack. The free end was next to her mouth so that she could sip as she ran, but the last time she had sucked air through the tube, and now she needed to replenish her bottle. She would need plenty of water for the homeward part of her run.

Dropping her pack beside the pool, she knelt down and plunged the bottle into the cool water. Inside the open end was a mesh so fine it could screen out bacteria and other harmful contaminants, not that there were many on Mookination; the water was fresh and cold. She drank over half a litre before refilling and repacking the bottle.

Mookin also took the opportunity to remove her t-shirt and wash it in the pool. Using it as a flannel, she washed the grime from her face and sweat from her neck and torso. She rinsed it again before wringing it out and putting it back on wet. It would soon dry, and although it might chafe a bit, it would keep her cooler for longer, as she knew she would soon be out of the Ringwood and back out in the noonday sun.

She had followed the path for almost five kilometres through the wood. It was wide and well used as Uncle Firestarta had said it would be. It formed a big arc, curving up from the edge of the Pan, up and around through the forest almost to the edge of the jungle. Mookin had come off the path to follow the stream but was confident of finding the path again where it left the Ringwood. The Pan was a depression in the floor the caldera, the only area that wasn't lush, verdant and teeming with plants and trees. The ancient site of a salt lake, it was dry and sparse.

She re-slung her rucksack, to which Firestarta had added two clay bricks weighing, she guessed, about five kilos each, and set off downhill, following the stream. She hadn't gone two hundred metres when she came to another pool. This one, though, was artificial; the stream had been dammed and a small pool dug into the hillside. The overflow from the pool led off to the right, but instead of a stream bed, a clay-lined trench had been dug along the slope. It headed off westwards, gradually descending as it went. Mookin was puzzled and made a mental note to ask Firestarta when she got back to the Learning Tree if he had any idea what was going on with the stream. *Curious,* she thought, skipping over the trench, heading down and slightly to the right. She jogged lightly over the gentle slope of the forest floor, enjoying the coolness of the dappled shadows while she could. It would not last long. She rejoined the path just as the trees were starting to thin out and she emerged on to a grassy plain that stretched between the edge of the Ringwood and the Pan.

The Pan surrounded a small salt lake simply called the Flash, which was shaped like a large lightning bolt running roughly east to west.

Mookin had already crossed the narrow, eastern part of the Flash on the outward part of her journey and was now about to cross the widest part. There was a slight embankment down to the Pan, where the grass fizzled out, and baked earth began. Mookin half slid, half jumped down the embankment, checked her bearings and set off at an easy lope.

The ground was barren, baked to crazy-paving patterns and dotted only with rocks, clumps of feathery grasses and tiny, low-growing shrubs adapted to the heat and salt. She kept a careful eye on the cracked, rock-strew landscape, mindful of sprained ankles. Numerous pot holes and worse, flat-cat colonies were the biggest danger. Their colonies were large and they were territorial, excavating large warrens just below the surface. The ground would subside without warning, up to a metre down, and you could find yourself surrounded by hissing, scratching, biting white fur balls, just as surprised as you, but now also homeless and angry. The only tell-tale sign was to keep an eye out as they scurried for their burrow, a white flash against the pale grey earth.

Mookin reached the Flash incident free, and put on a burst of speed, wanting to spend as little time as possible on the white expanse. The salt was crunchy underfoot, but very hard; she left no footprints to mark her passage. She could see some shimmering surface puddles from the noonday rain, but these were quickly evaporating in the heat.

She crossed the Flash without incident; there was, after all, nothing there but a flat expanse of hot, baking salt. She did have a close call with a family of flat-cats, having run right through them on the last part of the Pan just a few paces from the embankment. For a moment she thought she was in for a fall, but soon realised the flat-cats were all away from their burrow and were stretched out, lying flat in the sunshine like furry towels. They were feeding on sunlight, as they normally do during the hottest part of the day, converting it to energy to digest the coarse plants they ate. The flat-cats had scattered in all directions, hissing at Mookin, but she was through and past them almost before they realised what was happening.

It had been a long, hard slog, especially after the previous day's exertions. Mookin was nearly ready to drop. Since leaving the Pan, the humidity had risen steadily, and now in the woods surrounding the Learning Tree, it had reached the point where the sweat from her body was no longer evaporating, but was soaking into her clothes, which were now a soggy, clinging mess.

She slowed to a walk and started down the incline towards the Tree. She shucked off her rucksack and, carrying it one handed, drank the last of her water, still fresh and cool in the flask. The Tree did its thing again, messing with perspective, and she thought back to this morning – *only this morning!* – and her first shocked encounter. While running, she had been thinking that if the Trevale was five hundred metres deep, and the Learning Tree reached fifty metres or so above the surrounding trees, which were twenty to thirty metres high, that would mean the Tree was around five hundred and eighty metres high. If the Trevale was two kilometres across and the base of the Tree took up about half that, it must be a kilometre in diameter and over three in circumference. Mookin was amazed all over again, but this time was too tired to react.

Mookin had never seen it up close. She, like every other Mook, was told not to go near the Tree from a very young age. Also, like all Mooks, she never questioned the reasons, confident that if she needed to know, her parents or teachers would tell her. She knew it was big. You could see it for kilometres around, and its upper branches towered over every other tree in the vicinity. What she wasn't prepared for was the scale.

She had been following the road Dora had directed her to and was on the main road from Mookinwest to Mookinorth. Shortly, she came to a left turning which ran almost straight to the Learning Tree. She saw the tips of the upper branches from some way off and was feeling quite nervous on the final stretch of road. It climbed gently up and through thick forest until Mookin realised she was climbing up a hill. No wonder the Tree seemed so big, it's on a hill, she thought. But the Learning Tree wasn't on a hill. Quite the opposite, in fact.

As Mookin came to the highest point of the road, she could see there were no more trees between her and the Learning Tree. Mimicking the Ringwood, the forest grew in a circle around the top of the hill, and the Learning Tree sat at the bottom of a bowl-shaped depression, looking, for a second, like a bonsai in a dish.

That was when the scale of what she was seeing kicked in. The bowl was at least two kilometres across and probably a half kilometre deep from where she was standing, and there was the Tree growing in the middle. Just as the size had crawled inside her mind and found a place, the scale lurched again when she saw there were people inside it, walking along the branches, climbing stairways, going into – lurch – doorways, and, oh my goodness, there were houses carved into it too, windows and a crane lifting things up. Up and up and up and more and more people.

Mookin sat down heavily, mouth hanging open in shock. She took off her rucksack and reached in for her flask, took a big gulp of water into a suddenly dry mouth, then splashed some on her face.

'Gets ye like that, don't it, lassie?'

Mookin, already in shock, leapt into the air, turning as she did so, and came down in a crouch on the balls of her feet, arms raised in a defensive posture. Facing her was a huge red moustache. Behind the moustache was an equally huge grin with a gap between the two front teeth, set in a round face with a red nose. Above that were the most piercing dark green eyes Mookin had ever seen. Uncle Firestarta was quite short for a Mook but he had the most enormous chest, arms and hands. A tiny waist and powerful legs made him look top heavy, but he moved towards Mookin with the grace of a panther.

Today he was wearing a black t-shirt with a glyph in gold over the left breast, a ginko tree inside a diamond shape that Mookin realised were two interlocking triangles, one the right way up, one upside down. He had on black cargo shorts too, but was barefoot, with red hair growing on his feet. He had no hair on his head, but Mookin could see that he shaved it as it was covered with red and yellow stubble with tinges of grey around his ear tufts.

He stood appraising her, his hairy arms at rest, fists clenched and resting on his hips.

'Fine reactions, young lady. Come in handy, they will.'

'I... I didn't hear you. I...'

'No, you didn't. You weren't supposed to. Just one of the many things I'll be teaching you. Well, me and the Tree, I mean.'

Just for a second, Mookin had forgotten all about the Tree. She relaxed her pose and turned back to face it again and was once more overwhelmed by its immense size. She turned her head back towards Firestarta and, pointing, said, 'The, um, the Tree.'

Firestarta walked up beside her and reached up to put his right arm around her shoulders. 'I know, I know. Takes your breath away, doesn't it? Still gives me the screaming jib-jabs every day. Well, we'll introduce you to each other later. In the meantime, let's find somewhere to stash your things.'

'Introduce me?' was all Mookin could manage.

'Yes, lassie. You're about to get a new best friend. Besides me, of course. Now, how do you feel about running?'

She wasn't sure how far she had run, or even what time it was. Firestarta had only given her five minutes to prepare, telling her to take water and food for a 'little run in the woods' as he called it. She'd only just managed to change into shorts and re-tie her boots when he had knocked on her door.

It was past lunchtime now, judging from the position of the sun, and apart from the fruit and granola bars she had packed, Mookin hadn't eaten since breakfast and was, once again, starving. She passed into the shade of the Tree, which pretty much covered the whole of the Trevale depression, and started down the incline.

Firestarta had told her it wasn't a crater in the sense that it was not volcanic, but was caused by the weight of the Tree as the roots consumed the rock and soil beneath it.

He was standing in his familiar pose, fists on hips, feet apart, in between two huge thrusting roots, themselves more massive than any normal tree. Behind him was a carved archway leading into the Tree. He was smiling his gap-toothed smile as he stepped forward and took Mookin's bag. He turned and put his arm around her shoulder and began walking her into the depths of the Tree. Without looking as if he was, Firestarta was helping support Mookin whose legs were now shaking uncontrollably.

'Well done, lassie, that was quite a performance.'

Mookin could only mutter a barely heard 'thank you'.

'Quite a performance. You have smashed my personal best by over an hour and we think you've taken forty minutes off the all-time record. We're checking into that. You've done a fair bit of running, have you?'

'Running? No, not really. Just jogging back from the village to home, that sort of thing. I, um, cycle a bit. Was this some sort of race?'

'Hee, hee, hee. Not a race, Bettymook. More of a test. But you've surprised me and one or two others as well. Let's just say, if it were a race, you'd be collecting your medal about now!'

Mookin, who couldn't feel her legs anymore, allowed Firestarta to lead her down the corridor to her room, where earlier she'd emptied her clothes and personal possessions into a heap on the bed. The walls and floor were polished to a wonderful soft caramel colour that caught and reflected the light from above, and at the top of the arched ceiling, electric lights beamed down on them.

Mookin's door was one of dozens set into both sides of the corridor, each with a carved number over it. Her room was number 18, and the door opposite was number 19, so she supposed even numbers were on the right, odd numbers on the left. She didn't know how far the numbers went.

'Does it harm the Tree, carving into it like this?' she asked.

'Eh? Oh, no, lassie. The wood of a tree is dead, only the bark is alive. We're very careful about where we carve, too. We don't harm the structural strength of the Tree, it's immensely strong. In all the time we've been here, living with the Tree, we've carved out less than a fraction of a percent of its mass and we use all the timber in furniture and construction. Originally, the first excavations were just to remove damaged parts or fungi and pests, but now we have a small village in here. Several kilometres of tunnels and, of course, the university is at the centre.'

'I don't understand – university?'

'Och. Just my sense of humour. It's a, um, room, a chamber, at the heart of the Tree. It's our centre of learning, you see. Get it? No? Oh well, never mind.'

Mookin was too tired to pursue it.

'Now then, away with you into your room. Have a bath, have a shower, whatever you need. You've time for a wee nap – no more than an hour, mind. Then down to the canteen, have whatever you want, at least five thousand calories. Sugar is fine, not too much starch. Plenty of fluids, you may not feel thirsty, but you'll be dehydrated. I will meet you in the Commons about half an hour after deepdark. Okay?'

'Um, how will I know when it's deepdark?' Mookin asked, thinking through the fatigue.

'Ah yes, you're new here. I keep forgetting. The lights will dim a little at deepdark, then an hour later, every other light will go off and it's officially night time.'

'And the canteen and the Commons?'

'Och, aye. This corridor is a spoke of a wheel. Thataway is "in" and thataway is "out". Go in, turn left at the end and you're in the Hoop, which goes in a big circle back to where you started. Spokes lead off all the way around. If you're going clockwise, spokes on the left are A, B, C, D etcetera and lead outwards, spokes on the right are 1, 2, 3, 4 and lead in. There are twenty-two spokes on the outside, and eleven on the inside. Follow your nose, you'll find the food. Commons is next door to the canteen. Clear?' Mookin nodded. 'Any more questions?'

'Just one. What's a lassie?'

10. Light at the End of a Tunnel

<u>**Sparkalin/Sparkalin Water**</u>:
Of the family rapeseed (Brassica Napus) with only minor plasmic distortion. Grows wild in marshland around Starshine Lake, has dark green flowers and produces seeds which, when pressed, release a thick, dark oil which can be used for lubrication but has a pungent smell reminiscent of burning rubber. Instead, the oil is air dried and allowed to crystallise. The crystals are added to plain water and stored for six to nine months in darkness. When ready to drink, the bottle looks like plain water with some sediment. But, when shaken and opened, it transforms into a truly delightful emerald-green carbonated brew with green glitter fizzing about inside. Said to be refreshing if a trifle 'peppery' like a cross between cream soda and ginger beer, it is an acquired taste. An alcoholic version can be made by adding sugar and yeast at the bottling stage. Not as popular as it once was, production is limited to only one or two farms.

Mookipedia

Mookin's room was larger than her bedroom at home. There was a separate bedroom with bathroom attached, a sitting room with comfy furniture, a hand-carved desk that looked too big to fit through the door and bookshelves crammed with books. Several landscapes, scenes from the island, hung in spaces around the room, trying to make up for the lack of windows. A tiny kitchen led off the hallway, with sink, stove, kettle and a tiny fridge. On the opposite side of the hallway was a small cloakroom with toilet and sink.

Even the bath was solid wood and looked as if it had grown right out of the floor and walls as there were no seams between them. All of the plumbing, including the toilet, was made from copper and brass and polished to a soft gleam. As you would expect, floor and walls in every part were varnished wood in subtly different shades, but the depth of the lacquer suggested a thousand coats had been applied, which wouldn't have surprised Mookin; this place was old enough.

Growing up, she'd had no idea, and neither did her friends. She didn't think her parents were fully aware either. She had thought the Learning Tree was just a name, a place you went to after you left school to continue learning, like Snake Pass College or Plant Charming School.

She thought she had known all about Mookination, but now she was unsure. Two days, two big secrets. Her whole world was topsy-turvy right now. And there was more to come.

Mookin came awake with a start; water had got into her nose. She had been soaking in the bath, up to her chin in bubbles, and had just closed her eyes for a second. The bubbles were gone and the water was now tepid. She scrambled from the bath, water splashing everywhere, and reaching for a towel, she dried herself as quickly as possible. Her hair was a tangled mess but it would have to do. It was still plaited, so she pinned it up in a swirl on top of her head.

She was out in the corridor less than a minute later, still damp and hopping on one foot as she slipped her other pump on. She had dived into grey jogging pants and an old, faded black sweatshirt with the number 11 on the back.

Mookin wasn't as late as she'd feared, and the lights were still burning brightly in the corridors. She turned left into the Hoop as instructed and could instantly smell the wonderful aromas emanating from the canteen. Uncle Firestarta was right when he said to follow her nose.

Her room had been in corridor E, so she guessed she was in room 18E. Directly opposite her corridor, on the other side of the Hoop, was another arched corridor with a large 'III' carved above it, the next one around, clockwise, should be 'IV': three and four. She looked back at her own archway and sure enough, there was the letter E. The Hoop was easily three times the width and twice as high as the spokes and again had an arched profile. She had seen no one else inside the Tree since arriving and wondered how many people actually lived here.

Heading clockwise, she passed corridor 'IV', and loads of doors leading off both sides of the Hoop, with darkened spaces beyond; she was tempted to peek but resisted. At the next junction, between 'V' and 'VI' she found the canteen. Double half-glazed doors with a sign above that said, 'TINSTAAFL'.* *Sounds Swedish,* she thought.

Mookin pushed through the doors into the canteen, which surprised her by its size. It was big enough to seat fifty or sixty Mooks at tables all around the walls. The seating was divided into cubicles with padded benches fixed to the walls and two free-standing padded chairs. Each cubicle would seat four. The centre part was all tables and chairs in fours, sixes and eights.

Steam was curling from covered metal trays on a heated buffet into an overhead extractor hood, behind which was a walkway and a serving hatch into the kitchen. Next to the serving hatch was a door with a round window set at head height. There was no one else in the canteen, but Mookin could hear and see movement through the serving hatch. She grabbed a tray from a stack next to the right-hand end of the buffet. It was a bit like the cafeteria at school, with a rail in front of the buffet to rest your tray on while taking your food.

She selected fork, knife and spoon from their trays but was unable to find any plates in the plate warmer. She had a quick

---

TINSTAAFL or TANSTAAFL, literally, There Is No Such Thing As A Free Lunch. Attributed to Robert A. Heinlein/Larry Niven.

look in the cupboards underneath the back of the buffet, but still no plates, so she pushed open the door to the kitchen, popped her head in and said quietly, 'Hello, anyone there?'

'Hello, dear. Made me jump, you did. Thought everyone was finished for tonight. But you're new, aren't you? You must be Mookin?'

'Um. Yes. Mookin Bettymook. And you are?'

'Oh, look at me forgetting my manners. Clearwater Mobiusmook. Call me Mo. Or Clearwater, but no one calls me that. To most, I'm just Auntie Mo. Now, what can I help you with Ms Mookin?'

'Um, well, sorry to disturb you, ah, Auntie Mo, but I couldn't find any plates.'

Auntie Mo rummaged in a nearby cupboard and produced a shiny white plate with blue circles on it. 'There you are, dear, in this cupboard if ever you need one again. Feel free to come into the kitchen, except when we're cooking. Or washing up. Actually, best to shout from the hatch. I expect you're famished, aren't you? Firestarta send you on the Jelly Legs, did he?'

'Jelly Legs?'

'The run, dear. Been on the run? They call it the Jelly Legs on account of... well, I expect you know why now. Bit of a tradition around here. For newbies anyway. Puts you in the right frame of mind for what's coming next, if you know what I mean.'

Mookin, who had no idea what Auntie Mo was talking about, thought it best to just smile.

'How did you get on, dear, any problems?'

'Uh, no, it was all fine,' Mookin replied, now moving along the outside of the buffet, her plate and cutlery on the tray, Auntie Mo keeping pace on the inside and smiling every time Mookin lifted a copper lid in a cloud of steam and examined the contents of each serving dish.

She supposed this was what was left over, but there was

still plenty of food. Each lid revealed a separate dish: porkchops, sliced roastbeef, three different types of burgers, and a big bubbling lambstew with plumperlings and a tray of fishyfingas. Mookin went for the stew, ladling it into a bowl Auntie Mo produced as if from nowhere, and managed to find four plumperlings hiding in there. She added two porkchops to her plate and also grabbed a slice of pizza from a hot plate, taking a large bite before adding it to the porkchops. For dessert she chose grapple crumble. The crumble was in portions in dishes under a clear plastic cover. She added custard from a jug bubbling sleepily away on a small, round hot plate of its own. It was very thick, and glooped from the jug over the crumble. She was lucky though, none of the skin escaped.

'Healthy appetite? Good. What would you like to drink, dear? No, no. I'll get it, you sit down and tuck in.'

'Oh, just water please, Auntie Mo, or sparkalin if you have any?'

Auntie Mo disappeared through the swinging door into the kitchen. She was back before Mookin reached her seat, glass in one hand, jug of iced water in the other. She set the glass down beside Mookin and poured, filling it almost to the top. One ice cube escaped from the jug and plopped into the glass, splattering water over the table.

'Sorry dear. No sparkalin. Not much call for it. I could get some in for you, though, couple of days?' she said, lifting the glass and wiping the table with her apron.

'It's okay, don't go to any trouble.'

'No trouble, dear. I happen to like sparkalin as well.'

'You do? I was beginning to think it was just me.'

As with all Mooks, it was hard to tell Auntie Mo's age. She seemed as if she were part of the kitchen, had been there forever, but there was a spring in her step and a sparkle in her eyes that said otherwise. She was quite tall, as tall as Tammy but shorter than Mookin. She was wearing chequered chef's trousers and whites, but with a bright blue apron with a picture of an owl on the front and the words 'wit-a-woo' underneath. Her hair was quite short, tucked under a white cook's hat and looked to be light blue with blonde or silver stripes. Her blues eyes flashed with silver specks.

'So, how *did* your Jelly Legs go, dear? How far did you get? Pass the halfway mark, did you?'

Mookin was a little confused and was busy dipping porkchop into her stew and biting chunks out, but eventually replied, 'Um, well, back here. Back to the Tree, I mean. Uncle Firestarta said I'd taken forty minutes off the record, and I didn't even know I was racing!' Mookin was halfway through her stew and had only one plumperling left.

It was Auntie Mo's turn to look confused. 'You got back here, dear? All the way on your own?' Mouth full, Mookin just nodded.

'Well, I'm surprised, Mookin. That record was never meant to be broken. It was a test, a trial, to see how far... It's stood for over fifteen hundred years.' Auntie Mo's voice was altogether more serious now, more like a concerned parent or a teacher. She leaned close in to whisper, 'They have to go out and fetch most of the Jelly Legs. Some of them don't even get past the Pan.'

'I didn't know any of that. I just sort of paced myself. Didn't know there was a record or anything. Did I mess up? Should I not have tried so hard?' It was all so confusing.

'No, sweetie, no. You've done nothing wrong. You may just have shaken things up a little, that's all. Maybe it's about time. Been a bit... dull lately.'

Mookin was just delving into her grapple crumble when the lights flickered slightly and grew a little dimmer. *An hour to go,* she thought.

'Would you like anything else, Mookin?' asked Auntie Mo, voice now back to normal, all motherly and concerned.

'Is there any ice cream?' asked Mookin.

She left the canteen munching a large cookie Auntie Mo had given her after a bowl of vanilla ice cream and walked next door into the Commons. Another large room about the same size as the canteen behind another set of double doors, but with chairs, desks, work tables, coffee tables, armchairs and sofas scattered randomly around, and bookshelves against any spare wall space. There was no pattern to it as far as Mookin could see. Seats were singles or doubles, groups of three, five or even an eleven clustered around tables of all shapes and sizes. Again, fifty or so people could be in here without it feeling overcrowded.

There were twenty people in here now, scattered about, mostly reading, but a few were in groups, chatting quietly. Some looked up in casual curiosity when she walked in, but just smiled or waved and went back to what they were doing. Sitting at desks against the wall, three people were doing a curious thing that Mookin had never seen before; they were hunched over, looking at large screens. Under their hands they had large keyboards and over their ears, headphones. The keys had letters and numbers in Bigfolk script and they were typing and regarding the screens. One of the screens had just text scrolling up and down on it, the other two, moving pictures. *Computers,* thought Mookin. She had never seen one, never used one, but knew they were for accessing stored information. She also knew that they had recently become a big part of the Bigfolk world, which was undergoing something of a technology and communications spurt. There was a spare desk, and she desperately wanted to have a go, but was just a bit too shy.

It was like the first day of school, except she didn't know anyone. Instead, she walked over to a bookcase and began to examine the book spines. Some were Bigfolk books: economics, politics, history, science, geography, mathematics, all subjects she was familiar with from school, but which she had no in-depth knowledge of. Most were definitely Mookwritten: *Mookination – A History, Basic Plant-Charming, A Guide to Bigfolk, Travels in the Bigfolk World, An Introduction to Masquerade Spells.*

There was a whole section on dragons: *Advanced Dragon Wrangling, The Incubation and Care of Liberated Dragon Eggs, Enter the Dragon – Power Tools in Dissection and Autopsy, A Year with a Dragon (Dragon Bonding – Truth or Myth)?*

Mookin pulled out a particularly slim volume entitled *The Learning Tree Companion by C. Mobiusmook* and a glyph with those two interlocking triangles again but with crossed knives in the centre. *Was that Auntie Mo?* she wondered. She carried it over to an armchair, kicked off her pumps and was about to sit down when someone said, 'You look a bit out of sorts. Do you need any help?'

Mookin turned, and in a big squishy armchair, a boy had looked up from his book and was regarding her with a friendly expression. He had one eyebrow cocked and was obviously awaiting an answer.

'Um, no, I'm good, thanks. Waiting for someone.'

He ran his fingers through his black hair and Mookin noticed his stripes were silver and took the form of lightning bolts running front to back. He ruffled his hair and the illusion was gone. Just black and silver stripes.

'Are you sure you're in the right place? Only Mookouts use this room.' His words weren't condescending as such. Mookin thought he was just puzzled at her presence, so decided to be friendly. She smiled her best smile.

'Quite sure thanks. Uncle Firestarta will be here soon.'

'*Uncle* Firestarta? We tend to refer to him as Sir or Commander Firestarta; *Uncle* is usually for more informal occasions, away from the Tree,' he said.

'Really? He's never mentioned it. And you?'

'Me? Oh, how rude.' He stood up and extended his right hand. 'I am called Boosayya Cleongamook, my friends call

158

me Cleo. I assume you are new? Welcome to the Ellti.' He shook her hand and bowed slightly from the waist.

'New? Yes, I'm new. What's the Ellti?' she asked.

'Why, *the L-T*, the Learning Tree, of course.' He had a look in his hazel eyes, curiosity mixed with disbelief, and he still had hold of her hand.

'Mookin,' she said, a little too forcefully. 'Mookin Bettymook.'

'Mookin? Interesting. Isn't that's a village?' He let go of her hand and sat back down.

'Yes, Mookinsouth, that's where I live, *and* it's my name.'

'Well, as I said, welcome Mookin Bettymook.'

He smiled and went back to his book, *The Principles of Plasmagication*.

She turned back to her armchair, tucked up her feet and opened the book to the first page. Underneath the title and author was Tammy's family glyph, a quill and bottle of ink with a papyrus plant and the words *Piccolo Press* underneath. There was a dedication on the next page which read:

> *To My Beloved Husband,*
> *Who Started*
> *A Fire in My Heart*
> *That Time Cannot Quench*

The door burst open and in strode Firestarta, eyes scanning the room until he spotted Mookin. She noticed that everyone had raised their heads at his entrance and were looking expectantly in his direction. Firestarta seemed not to notice, instead cutting a winding path through the sofa maze to get to her, flopping down in the chair next to hers and cocking a leg over the arm. 'Feeling better now, lassie?'

Mookin now knew that a lassie was a young, unmarried girl and that Firestarta had spent 'quite some time' in

Scotland. She wasn't sure why he hung on to the accent and expressions; perhaps when she knew him a little better, it would be okay to ask.

'Yes, thank you. My legs are still aching, but a bath and food have helped.'

'Tired though, eh?'

'I could sleep for a week, I think.'

'Good, good. That's just how we need you. It won't be a week, Ms Mookin, but it may well be a day or two.'

Mookin had noticed that since she had introduced herself to Cleo, several whispered conversations and covert glances had sprung up around the room. Firestarta leaned in close and whispered to her, 'Take no notice, sweetheart. I decide who goes to meet with the Tree. Come on. Time to go.'

She was worried now. She hadn't realised they were talking about her. She stood, praying her jelly legs wouldn't let her down, and followed Firestarta back through the sofas and out into the Hoop, where they turned right. They had passed a few doors when he stopped, pointed and said, 'Bathroom through there, Mookin.'

'Uncle, I don't...'

'Best to, my dear. Last chance for a while. You'll feel, ah, more comfortable.'

Mookin didn't reply, just pushed through the door that he had indicated. Inside were two doors facing each other with the signs for boy and girl on the wall facing her and an arrow underneath each. Girls were to the left, so she went in. There was a row of six cubicles, all with the doors open and the usual plumbing inside in brass. Four sinks carved in solid wood stood out from the opposite wall with mirrors above; further in, she could see through an arched doorway where there were shower stalls, lockers and changing rooms. Another door lay at the far end with the word 'gym' beside it and an arrow pointing straight up.

She looked at herself in the mirrors. She had never felt so

out of control in her life. Not only did she not have a clue what was going on or what was expected of her, she wasn't even sure if she was ready for this. She would just have to tell him straight out that he'd made a mistake. She walked into the end cubicle, shut the door much too hard and bolted it with a snap.

Firestarta waited patiently in the corridor. He removed a small dagger from his belt and proceeded to clean his already immaculately clean fingernails. He waited a full five minutes before putting his knife away and walking into the girls' toilets, shouting, 'Coming through!' as he entered.

Mookin was still in the cubicle, so he rapped lightly on the door. 'Time to go, lassie.' He heard Mookin give a big sniff before she opened the door. He could see she had been crying and just stood facing her and opened his arms. She rushed forward and wrapped her arms around him, burying her face in his shoulder. Fortunately, no one was there to see Firestarta on tiptoes, his head back as far as it would go, and Mookin bending almost in half sobbing, with Firestarta's giant arms straining to reach around to pat her back.

Mookin was in full sob now, but Firestarta, who knew how these things went, just let her carry on until she was done. After a minute, the sobbing stopped and she let out a huge sigh.

'I'm okay now,' she said into his shoulder.

'Good. My neck is starting to ache.'

Mookin gave a half-hearted laugh. 'I'm sorry, but I don't think I'm ready for this. Maybe you and UBM have made a mistake?'

'Sweetheart, I've been training and sending Mookouts into the Bigfolk world for a long, long time now. You are more ready than you know. If I wasn't happy with you, I wouldn't send you.'

'But Uncle, I feel so out of my depth. No one has explained anything to me, everything is happening so fast.

And I've always thought us Mooks were so open and truthful and all I've found in the last few days are secrets. Big secrets too.'

Firestarta thought hard about this, looking up into Mookin's face and her big, brown eyes. A minute, two minutes, passed and finally he, too, let out a big sigh.

'You're right, Mookin. Too much secrecy. It's not healthy, and it's time it stopped. As a member of the Eldron Council I give you my –'

'You're an Eldron?' Mookin interrupted.

'Why, yes, lassie. I assumed you would know.'

'But how would I? How would I know unless you or someone else told me? This is just the kind of thing I'm talking about.'

Firestarta, slightly flustered, said, 'Yes, yes. I see what you mean. As I was saying, I think it's time for some changes. You're right. Far too many secrets in Mook-life. It's time we Eldron opened the way for younger blood. Fresher thinking, new ideas. Listen, I can't change anything overnight, but will you accept my word that Mookination is in for some big changes?'

Oh flup, thought Mookin, *what have I done?* 'Yes, of course, but...'

'No. No buts. I can see now that we've kept hidden far too much for far too long. It's been done with the very best of intentions, of course, but that in itself is an error of thinking. Mooks, and especially Mooks like you, are more than able to deal with all the facts. Thank you, Mookin.'

We've been over-protective, thought Firestarta, *we sought to give these kids an idyllic, tranquil life such as we had hoped for. It's time they knew the real reason we fled the Fringe. Yes, it was, by now, uninhabitable. But we left some horrors behind that we didn't want to deal with. We ran away rather than face our mistakes. We left them trapped in the inner systems hoping they would destroy themselves or the radiation would get them. Possibly, just possibly, they were still out there, and Mookin's generation would have to deal with them. A million years? A twinkling in the eye of the galaxy. And enough time for a sub-lightspeed species to migrate out from the core. If UBM was right, losing contact with the Million Keyways could be the indication that they were getting near. The Mooks needed a leader, and Mookin was now their best hope.*

Mookin gave a weak smile before Firestarta went on, 'Now, do you feel up to the next phase of your education? I assure you it will be the best thing you have ever done and you will have no regrets.'

'Really?'

'Absolutely none.'

'Will it change me? Will I still be Mookin Bettymook?'

'Oh, Mookin, you will still be you. But you will also be so much more. So much more you will wonder how you ever managed up to now. Ready?'

'Um, well, yes. Definitely. But I didn't use the, um, I still need to go to... you know.'

'Oh, for flup's sake. Hurry up, we're way past late now!' he said, stomping out.

Mookin rejoined Firestarta and headed off down the Hoop until they came to inner spoke 'I' (one), and which, for some reason, was wider and higher than all the other inner spokes.

Every other light went out along the tunnel, and the circle of brightness from each overhead light was now isolated by shadows between each one, like a string of islands; Mookin could see right to the end of the spoke, where there was a pair of open doors, a warm bright light coming from inside.

Just to take her mind off what lay ahead, Mookin asked, 'So, how old are you? Do you have to be a certain age to be an Eldron?'

He looked at her, a little uncomfortably. 'The truth,

Mookin?'

'Of course.'

'Well, truthfully, I am 150 –'

'Oh, I thought... 150 isn't that old for a Mook, is it? I thought you'd be, like, over a thousand or something.'

'Mookin.' He stopped and faced her. 'You didn't let me finish. I'm not 150, or even 1,500. I'm 150,000 – 150,063 to be precise. We all are. All of the Eldron and Eldrex are about the same age, many others too. And that doesn't allow for the time we all spent in the Big Sleep. We all came here together over a million years ago. I know you all call us Aunt and Uncle, Mookin, but our relationship goes back much further than that. We are closer to great great grandparents than anything.'

11. Mother's Day

Mookin was in a place. It was a new place. New to her. She had never been here before, but it felt like home. It felt warm and comfortable, safe. Bread baking in the oven, coffee brewing on the stove, the warm glow of Mum and Dad. She couldn't feel her body, she realised. Although, she remembered lying down after… after… Firestarta took her into the big room.

It had seemed dark in there, even though she had seen light pouring from the open door. When they got there, it was dark. Except for the light, a bright pinpoint, shining down from above, illuminating just a raised platform in the middle of the big room. On the platform, a bed or a couch. The room had been circular; she could feel it faintly all around. Did that mean it was a dome? She couldn't tell because the light from above had been so bright.

Firestarta had said she was to lie on the couch, so she had.

She couldn't see anything then, only the light. She'd heard the door click shut and realised she was alone. She had closed her eyes against the brightness. Just for a second. But fatigue had swept over her like sinking into a warm bath.

She supposed she was asleep, but this didn't feel like dreaming. Now she remembered sinking down. Through the couch. Through the platform and the floor, which was solid. This was crazy, wasn't it? But then she realised she could see through the floor and the platform and the couch and she could see herself still lying there. How was that possible? She had left her body behind. But she needed her body, didn't she?

Mookin could still feel herself sinking and then she was here, in this new, safe place. She tried to look around, which was silly because if she had no body, she had no eyes. But she was seeing, she was certain. It was just there was nothing to see. She was looking at... empty. Lack of. Nothingness. Boring. *Where the flup am I?* she thought.

Welcome Mookin Bettymook. You are with me. You are at the heart of me. Be not afraid.

Mookin, who hadn't been the least bit afraid, was now a little worried.

Who are you and where is this and what does 'at the heart of you' mean? I don't understand.

I am sorry for your confusion. I seek to remedy that. I am the Tree; I am the plasmic; I am the core. I am the teacher. You are my student. Together, we will grow. Together, we will learn.

Um, yeah. Still confused here. Does it get any clearer?

A feeling of such love and warmth washed over Mookin that she nearly cried out. Were it not for the lack of vocal cords and a mouth, she probably would have.

I like you Mookin Bettymook. You are... refreshing.

Does that mean you don't like everyone who comes through here?

Some are… in awe. Wrongly so. Some do not accept. Some are not wholly… suitable. Most are an asset. All are cherished.

Well that's good, isn't it? What's next, where do we go from here? And what do I call you?

Most call me Mother, although I have no gender. Most feel I come closest to the feelings for a mother. You may call me what you wish, however. I have no name. I am not a soul or entity. I am an embodiment.

Mookin felt these things and knew that there was truth in the words. Could tell that Mother wanted only Good, with a capital G, and to prevent Bad. It wasn't love, exactly. It was a motivation. An outward thrusting force of kindness and appreciation, a desire to balance the books in favour of hope and goodness. Cruelty, suffering, spite, misery, jealousy, desire, despair. These were the enemy. Mother was the driving force, Mookouts the warriors.

Mother is good, I suppose. And next?

You are hungry for knowledge, Mookin Bettymook.

Was that a question?

And a statement.

Well, yes, I am. I want answers. There are too many secrets. If there is a reason for not telling me something, tell me the reason. Don't hide stuff away from me. Don't keep me in the dark. I'll understand. How can I put the jigsaw together if half the pieces are missing? If I have all the pieces, even if I'm not allowed to look at some of them, at least I can see what the picture's going to be like. There may be some gaps, but I'll know that one day I can finish it.

Good analogy. Why do you think you are here, Mookin Bettymook?

I don't really know.

I am to gift you.

Gift me? What does that mean?

A part of me, us, we, will reside in you.

Wow. Do I get a say in this? Do I have a choice?

Of course. There is always choice. Choice is fundamental to our way. Would you reject this gift, Mookin Bettymook?

Flup, no. Just making sure it was up to me. Gift away, Mum!

This will... not be... entirely... unpleasant.

Mookin felt an intrusion – intrusion was the only word she could think of – into her mind. A spark of sorts, that she could almost feel reaching out to touch her, sending out tendrils, tiny, reaching, grasping filaments, into her mind. Not her brain. Her brain was still in her body way up there above her. This was her mind, her thoughts, her essence. It was her, Mookin.

The filaments touched and probed and each time they touched they would split into ten, twenty, a hundred, a thousand more threads, all questing, expanding, adding, absorbing, micro-changing, enhancing, completing, repairing. Making whole.

There was fear and trepidation, but these quickly passed. And a point where Mookin could start to understand what was being done to her, even joining in and making suggestions, adding layers and depth and being in awe at what she might become. There was no sensation of time, but she was aware when the process ended. She was also aware there was so much more to follow.

Mookin's mind slapped back into her body like a wad of wet tissue hitting a window. She inhaled like she was bursting from water after staying down much too long, her back arching off the couch, the air tasting so good. She tingled all over as if the blood had been stuck in her veins, waiting for her to return. She lay there for a few seconds, eyes closed. The light had gone but the dome – it *was* a dome – was softly illuminated; she could sense it around her. There were no lights, but the whole dome was aglow. She was alone but could sense Firestarta coming down the tunnel.

How was she *doing* that?

She sat up, put her feet on the floor and slowly opened her eyes and was shocked to discover that the light was coming from her. Her whole body was lit up and radiating a cool, white light which, even as she watched, diminished until there was just a faint glow under her skin, coming through the pores and hair follicles.

Firestarta crashed through the door and ran over to Mookin. He knelt beside her and looked into her eyes. 'Back with us are you, lassie?'

'Have I missed breakfast?' she replied.

'Mookin, you've missed more than breakfast. You've been gone for four and a half days.'

B.J. PAGE

12. The Cutting Edge

Plasmagication:

The employment of plasmic energy (PE), short form: magic. It is important to understand that the use of magic does not contravene the laws of the physical universe. Use is the embodiment of the wielder's will on energy and matter but matter and energy CANNOT be created or destroyed. To the uninitiated, the non-user, it may appear that this is the case, but Mooks make use of an abundant source of power that can push, pull, lift, change, alter. It can displace objects almost instantaneously and open D-ways across vast distances, but it is the mind of the Mook that makes this possible. In the Bigfolk world, many have a belief in magic that bears no relation to the art of plasmagication. Unfortunately, it may be us who are responsible for this belief. It is entirely possible that Bigfolk have seen wielders making use of PE and misunderstood what was, in fact, taking place. To the non-user this would probably look a lot like magic.

Mookipedia

Again please,' said Firestarta. Mookin closed her eyes and concentrated until she felt her awareness slip quietly from her body. In a second, she had a three-sixty image forming in her mind – her new, fabulous, super-charged mind – of everything around her.

She had her back to Firestarta. They were in the gym in the Tree. The Tree which she could now feel, although 'feel' was an inadequate way to describe what she now sensed. She was now a part of it, and it was a part of her.

They were running through the basic senses of magic. In her now enhanced state, she was able to extend her senses outside her body, and she was making excellent progress. On the table in front of Firestarta were a dozen or so objects which he kept adding to, taking from or rearranging. Mookin had to tell him which object he was touching. It was an exercise in depth and control. So far, she hadn't got one wrong in over three hours.

The picture that formed in her mind was complete, like a radar sweep, and each sweep of her senses built up detail around her. The trick was not to overdo the detail. You could be swamped with too much information. She was honing focus and finesse and was getting better and better.

She had a broad picture of her general surroundings – the gym walls, benches stacked at the sides, wall bars, cupboards full of sports equipment, and further away, changing rooms, the Tree on all sides, the canteen and Commons – and at the very edge of her present perception, she could feel the beating hearts of all the Mooks in the Trevale. Working, sleeping, relaxing, playing, all going about their daily lives.

And underlying all of that was Mother.

Firestarta had his hand on a pot plant. Mookin could feel its tiny spark of life like a star in the blackness.

'What colour is this, Mookin?' He had been getting her to work on focusing in on specifics for the last hour.

'Ooh. Tricky one,' she replied.

Firestarta thought maybe they had found her limit at last. She was sailing through basic training; everything he threw at her, she managed with ease. He didn't want her getting too confident too quickly.

'Really? Well, try your best, that's all we ask.'

'Yes. A bit tricky. The pot is dark blue, the leaves are dark green and the flowers are yellow. It's a primrose isn't it? Very pretty.'

'Humph. You are doing well, young lady, but let's keep it under control, shall we? Overconfidence is a killer out in the BFW.'

Mookin turned to face him to see if he was being serious, but it was hard to tell. 'BFW?' she asked.

'Bigfolk World. Okay, that's enough for this morning. Go get some lunch and tell Mo I'll have the usual. I'll be along in ten minutes.'

'Yes, Uncle. What have you got planned for me this afternoon?'

'Hee hee. It's time you met your combat instructor. She's been dying to meet you.'

Mookin knew better than to try and wheedle anything out of Firestarta, he could out-stubborn a mule and seemed to be immune to her persuasive powers. Mookin had tried her sweetest, sickliest smile that even worked on her dad. And failed.

She had chosen a salad for lunch, a particularly sweet and crunchy Waldorf with two slices of Mo's soda bread. The canteen was busy, but she sat alone after giving Auntie Mo the message from Firestarta. It had been over two weeks since she had woken up from her meeting with Mother. It had been hectic, and everyone here seemed so busy; she hadn't had any time to make new friends. They were all friendly enough, of course – Mooks just were – but she missed Tammy and Debs, her family, even school.

From her talks with Firestarta, she had learned she wouldn't be going back to school. The Tree was now her source of education and would provide her with any information she wanted or needed. Now, even sleep was not the same. She needed less time physically asleep, but always awoke feeling totally refreshed and bursting with a new-found vitality. Mother was there too, in her dreams, in her sleep. Mother would come and they would talk and learn and explore together. These times with Mother could seem like hours or days or even weeks, but next morning, only a night had passed.

Mother explained how Mookin's body was changing to enable her mind to make use of magic, and how that when this transition was complete, there would, theoretically, be almost no limits to what Mookin would be able to do. Magic was like a great, broad, slow-flowing river, her body a channel or conduit through which the river could be directed at will to create an unstoppable torrent, her mind like the nozzle on a fire-hose: powerful, able to direct and concentrate that torrent down to a pinpoint if required. Finesse was the key.

Mookin had already opened her first D-way. In the gym, under the guidance of Firestarta, she had reached inside herself for the knowledge of displacement and movement. It was contained in a glyph gifted by Firestarta. She had felt the tingle start behind her bellybutton, grow gently, travel up through her chest and into her shoulder, down along her left arm. As she clasped together her thumb and little finger, the sensation moved along into her wrist and hand. She could feel the floodgate she was holding shut as a slightly ominous presence. So much force! Touching the fingers together was not essential, but it acted as a trigger mechanism, a final hold before unleashing the power of plasmic energy.

Spreading her thumb and finger wide apart, a shining blue spider's thread connected them. A blue beam shot from the centre of the thread, carving the shape of a door a few paces in front of her. Her first attempt had blasted a chunk of the gym floor into smoking charcoal. Picturing a door-sized portal was, at first, essential. The rift she was initiating in the fabric of space must be entirely controlled by Mookin, so, start small. The edges of the rift were jagged, like cloth cut with blunt shears and tinged in blue, surrounding utter blackness. She stepped confidently through and came out at the other end of the gym. Exactly where she had been aiming.

Firestarta was clapping as she stepped out, pleased that she had conquered one of the more tricky skills. It was not unheard of for novices to accidentally open D-ways at the South Pole, which had led to some surprised penguins and frost-bitten students.

Out of curiosity, she turned and looked back through the D-way and but could see only blackness, then the edges of the doorway just kind of zipped back together with a faint crackle.

'Why did it close? What if I'd only been halfway through?'

'It closed because you no longer required it. A lot of what we do is automatic. Although we teach you control, you won't need to be in charge of every tiny aspect. You just have to create the circumstance and your mind will take over and complete the action. It becomes second nature, like brushing your teeth or riding a bike. These things become familiar.'

And so they did.

Mo came over to Mookin's table just then, placing a large bowl of chilli and rice down together with a mound of freshly baked bread and a spoon. She slid into the seat opposite Mookin.

'Finished, dear?' she said, sweeping away Mookin's salad bowl and wiping the table with a cloth in one deft motion. She put the plate on the table behind her and passed Mookin a glass of emerald-green liquid. It was sparkalin water. Mookin's eyes lit up and she mouthed 'thank you'.

Mo looked like she had finished in the kitchen, as she wasn't wearing her apron. Mookin raised her eyebrows at the bowl of chilli and Mo explained, 'It's for Firestarta, dear. It is Choosday and my husband is very fond of his chilli.'

'Husband? Firestarta is your husband?' Mookin said in surprise.

Mo looked puzzled. 'Why, yes dear, didn't you know? Oh, it's the glyph, I expect.' She pointed to the left breast pocket of her chef's whites. The double triangles again, except Mo's had crossed knives in the centre. Wait! She had seen that glyph somewhere else. Why hadn't she noticed it before on Mo? *Because Mo usually wore an apron which covered it.*

'All of us here at the Tree have the same basic glyph,' she explained, tracing the outline of the triangles with her finger. 'The bottom one represents Mookination, the volcano, the upside-down one represents magic and knowledge flowing from the volcano, the two forever interlocked. Then we have our own personal logo in the centre, representing our chosen profession. We don't combine glyphs when we marry, though. Indicative of a lifetime devotion to the Tree and education.'

'So you chose knives to represent... the kitchen?' queried Mookin.

Mo sniggered and stared at Mookin, thinking it might be a joke. She was soon laughing so hard, everyone in the canteen was looking over to see what was going on. She slapped the table so hard that the salt and pepper pots jumped. 'Oh, that's a good one! Knives, kitchen. I get it.'

Just then, Firestarta appeared, slipped into the seat next to Mookin, grabbed his bowl of chilli and dipped a large chunk of bread into it. 'Something funny?' he asked Mo. Mo explained about the glyph and Firestarta nearly choked on his bread. He needed to cough several times before he could speak again, even then, it was in a slightly squeaky voice.

'Humph. Excuse me, Mookin. I wasn't laughing at you. Just at the... absurdity of your, ah, misunderstanding. It's entirely possible that in our rush to get you settled in, we may have omitted some of the, ah, finer points of life here at the Tree. We all, obligations permitting, take turns at what you might call the "service" jobs. This month, my charming and ever lovely wife, Clearwater Mobiusmook, is our designated chef. Last month it was me, and very good I was too. If you were to stay for more than six months, you would have to take a turn. Or it might be in the laundry, or maintenance or recycling or any of a dozen others.'

Firestarta was wilting under Mo's gaze, and it took him an extra second to realise why. 'Of course, my own cooking ability is very limited, just a few plain simple dishes, not a patch on my dear wife's skill.'

Mookin couldn't help smiling. 'Nice save.'

'Thank you, Betty. I thought so too.'

'So, if the crossed knives don't refer to cooking...?' asked Mookin, pointing at Mo's glyph.

Mo looked from Mookin to Firestarta and back again before answering. 'Those are swords, dear. I'm your combat instructor.'

It was fair to say that Mookin was just a bit gobsmacked.

'I... I saw your book *The Learning Tree Companion* in the Commons. That was you, wasn't it?' said Mookin, remembering now where she had seen the glyph before.

'Yes, dear. You didn't get to the combat section then? Most of those are mine, although for some I used a pseudonym. Spekal here, also has many. I write some fiction, too, from time to time. You need lots of hobbies when you're as old as us.'

'Does this mean you're an Eldron too? As well as the combat instructor?'

Mo smiled at Mookin. 'Yes. Full of surprises at the Learning Tree, aren't we?'

'Phew! You're not kidding,' said Mookin, unsure how many more surprises she could take.

Firestarta finished his chilli, wiping the bowl clean with the last of his bread, before answering. He took a big gulp of Mookin's sparkalin water, pulled a weird face at the taste and wiped his moustache on his sleeve. 'You will be spending a few days with Mo now, Mookin. We can't send you out into the BFW unarmed, as it were. Mo is going to prepare you for any situation you might find yourself in. So. Have fun. Don't hurt each other too much.'

Firestarta stood, bent and kissed Mo on the top of her head and, grinning at Mookin, walked out of the canteen.

They sat quietly for a few moments, brown eyes regarding blue as Mookin re-evaluated Mo and she swore to herself that she would never again make assumptions. In those blue, silver-speckled depths she could now see an edge she hadn't noticed before. She knew Mo was aware of it too, had been observing her and evaluating her over the past few weeks. Mo was serene, a hint of a smile playing across her mouth.

'When do we start?' asked Mookin.

'I believe we already have, Betty.'

13. The Way of Fist and Foot

Gifting:

Glyphs, as you know, are required to perform acts of plasmagic. In the mind, these take the form of a three-dimensional shape reminiscent of a 'snowflake' but with uncountably more points, sides, layers and branchings. The glyph is a shortcut to initiate an act without further preparation or thought. Most of you will have been 'gifted' with glyphs by parents and teachers at various stages throughout your lives for performing basic plasmagic acts. These glyphs have been learned over many, many generations and are entirely safe to use in normal circumstances. The glyphs you will be gifted with at the Learning Tree are of a far more advanced and serious nature and require a delicate hand, a cool mind and a sure knowledge of their effect. Gifting is the means by which we impart these glyphs, usually in the form of a one-to-one Mindlynk. They require practice in a controlled environment before *use in the field.*

Mookout Handbook

Next morning, dressed in tracksuit trousers, t-shirt and trainers, Mookin set off to find the training hall, the 'dojang' as Mo called it.

The dojang, like Masquerade and the gym, was located in one of the outer Tree segments, so Mookin set off round the Hoop to find it. A few minutes later, she came to a set of double doors and walked through into a deserted outer office that held four chairs and a table, a desk with a computer on it and, against one wall, a low table on which sat a Japanese maple bonsai in a rectangular pot with a spotlight above. The maple was growing sideways, its roots clinging to a large rock like the fingers of a gnarled hand. Its branches draped with smooth elegance below the rim of the pot, almost touching the table, the delicate foliage a riot of reds and purples. Without having to think about it, Mookin grasped the metaphor: we all need something solid to hold on to from time to time, especially when it feels like we are standing on the edge of a cliff.

Mookin went through the only other door where she found a transformed Auntie Mo. She was wearing a black V-neck top and trousers made of thick cotton fabric but washed so many times it was bordering on dark grey and looked soft and comfortable. The top was worn over the trousers, not tucked in, and came down to mid-thigh. It was cinched at the waist with a wide black belt, wrapped twice around the middle and tied in a double knot at the front, loose ends hanging. It, too, looked old, worn and faded. Mookin could just make out yellow embroidered lettering on the belt, but it was too faded to read.

Auntie Mo was barefooted and kneeling at the far end of the hall, which was as large as the gym, but devoid of any furniture, except for what looked like built-in cupboards along the one wall. The floor was covered in a rubbery foam material in red and black squares. Mookin instinctively removed her trainers, leaving them at the side of the door, and approached Auntie Mo, whose eyes were closed, hands enfolded in her lap. She was breathing slowly, in through her nose, out through her mouth. Mookin knelt also, at a respectful arms-length distance, as quiet as possible, not speaking. Auntie Mo's eyes flicked open so unexpectedly, Mookin nearly jumped. When she spoke, it was but a whisper, but Mookin heard every word, every inflection.

'Welcome, Mookin. In here you will call me Mo or Teacher. Nothing else. This is my domain; I make the rules. You comply. No questions. I will never ask you to do anything without a sound and valid reason. Everything you learn here is designed with only one purpose: to keep you from harm. We abhor violence in any form but accept its necessity for self-defence. We detest causing harm or suffering, even in those who would relish causing it to us or others. We seek always the path of least harm. Do you understand?'

'Yes, Teacher.'

'Good. Then we can begin.'

They spent the rest of that day and all of the next four performing sets of strange exercises and movements that baffled Mookin entirely. Nothing they did seemed remotely connected with what Mookin thought might be self-defence.

She performed each movement, each task, exactly as requested, to the best of her ability, regardless of how bizarre it might seem. On the fourth day, she was left alone in the room for forty-five minutes, performing a tripod headstand. Mo was genuinely surprised to see her still in the same position as when she left, but didn't comment, just said, 'Enough.'

Mo taught Mookin how to control her breathing, her heart rate and blood flow, and how to slow her heart and respiration down to conserve oxygen. She explained there were levels, degrees, of meditation that could slow the heart almost to nothing or to states of near hibernation. All it took was time and practice. She taught her how to increase blood flow to specific parts of the body to speed up injury recovery or away from wounds to prevent blood loss. Above all, she taught her where to find and how to tap into hidden reserves of power and energy in a crisis.

At the end of the five-day session, Mo informed Mookin that she had been undergoing a series of tests and assessments to determine her level of readiness. Fitness and flexibility she had in abundance; she was young and strong and had exceptional reflexes, even for a Mook. This last had been the final stage. Mookin was ready.

As had happened most nights since she had received her gift, Mookin spent time with Mother. Sometimes this would seem like only minutes, other times it was as if whole days had passed. Always, when she woke, she found that just one night had gone by and she felt awake and refreshed.

The night after Mo told her she was ready was different. That night, Mo was there too. That night, Mo had a gift too. A gift of knowledge, experience, power. Mookin was like a sponge. She sank into the gift and became part of it. It became a part of her. This night lasted for days, weeks, months, years.

Mookin awoke as normal. She felt refreshed, happy and vital but when she stood up to go into the bathroom she knew at once that there was a change. Her mind felt detached, part of her body but separate. There was a physical change too. She wasn't just walking across the floor, she was feeling it, assessing it, using it. She could feel every grain of dust under her feet and the grooves in the grain of the wood floor, buried under dozens of coats of varnish and wax, felt like the grooves in a ploughed field. She could sense the walls and the ceiling, every object in the room by the movement of air and the echoes of her own heartbeat, every muscle and tendon in her body poised and ready.

Wow! Too much. This was sensory overload. She didn't think she could cope with this. It was just too much information. Even as these thoughts ran through her head, she felt her mind go 'snick', and everything slotted neatly away like a cat's claws retracting. Still there, but close at hand. Ready.

As she showered, she realised what Mo's gift had been. A lifetime of training and experience of martial arts, analysed, tested, distilled, trimmed, honed and perfected. She couldn't wait to see her again.

After a large but hurried breakfast in the canteen, Mookin rushed off to the dojang again. Mo called the hall a dojang which Mookin now knew was a reference to the Korean word for training hall. She bowed respectfully on entering, removed her shoes and moved on to the training floor.

Mo was waiting in the centre of the room, standing with her arms behind her back. Mookin approached to within two paces, stopped and bowed, holding the bow for five long seconds. Mo bowed in return and they both straightened up together. Mo was smiling broadly and Mookin stepped forward to hug her with as much love and affection as she could manage. Mookin whispered, 'Thank you, Teacher.'

As they parted, Mo held on to Mookin's shoulders and looked into her eyes. 'It worked. I can tell just by the way you move, by the way you breathe, by the look in your eyes.'

'Yes! It worked. I know tae kwon-do!'

Mo smiled again. 'A bit more than tae kwon-do, I hope? We weren't sure if it was possible to pass on physical abilities along with knowledge, but Mother said it was, for the right candidate. We've discussed it for years and had partial successes, but last night you were the first.'

'The first? Doesn't every Mookout get, um, this?'

'No dear. We have been waiting for... someone like you for a long time. Someone with the right combination of attributes. Young, bright, keen, physically capable. Over the past few weeks, you have proved yourself in every department.'

'Mo, I feel so different today. Is this what it's like for you? I feel like a panther balanced on the edge of a razor, balanced on the edge of the finest sword. With coils of steel inside me ready to unleash... something!'

'Oh Mookin,' Mo laughed. 'There's only one cure for that. Would you like to spar?'

'Would I? Just try and stop me!'

In the changing room, Mo presented Mookin with a package, carefully wrapped in hand-made paper and tied with red twine. Mookin looked questioningly at Mo. 'Open it. It's for you.'

Mookin pulled the twine bow and unfolded the cream-coloured paper. Inside was a black dobuk, a tae kwon-do training suit of the highest quality. Soft and supple but very tough.

'Oh, it's beautiful. But I...'

'You only get the suit and a white belt. If you've earned it, we'll see about the black belt later. Put it on!'

Mookin needed no more prompting and changed into the suit. It was a perfect fit and felt familiar and comfortable. She looked at herself in the mirror and tied on her white belt.

'Thank you, Mo. It's wonderful.'

'I washed it a few times to get the stiffness out. Right. Sparring, I think.'

They went to the lockers, put on the rest of their kit: shin pads, feet and hand protectors, head guards and gum shields, and returned to the centre of the floor.

Facing up, Mo gave the traditional Korean start to mock combat, '*Charyot* (attention), *Kyung-nae* (bow), *Chun-bi* (ready position), *Sei-jak* (go).'

Mo, the more experienced fighter, despite Mookin's gift, unleashed a terrifying onslaught of high section kicks, all aimed at Mookin's face, the last one just clipping her nose as Mo's reverse-turning kick whooshed past her face. Mookin retreated several paces, rubbing her nose, and felt a 'snick' in her mind. Her eyes flashed and narrowed, and she advanced on Mo, delivering a flurry of punches and a wicked step-in side kick that both surprised and winded her mentor. Mo rubbed at the spot on her ribs with the back of her glove. She smiled at Mookin, nodded her pleasure at her pupil's skill, then *her* eyes narrowed and she let out an animal roar that would have frozen the nervous system of any lesser opponent.

What followed was over an hour of martial arts sparring unlike anything the world had ever seen. Two opponents with such grace, speed and controlled power it became something new, something in its own right. It became a dance, a ballet. It was a machine and a symphony, the finely honed parts moving as one. Each could feel the heart of the other beating in their chests, taking up the rhythm and becoming a matched pair. So closely matched in knowledge, ability, technique and application that there was nothing between them. Neither had the desire to harm the other, but each wished to test themselves, find their limits and test boundaries with the only other living person against which it was possible.

Finally, bodies and suits soaked in perspiration, even though it was not a contest, an overall victor started to emerge: Mookin had a tiny edge over Mo. Each had mentally kept score the whole time they had been sparring, Mookin built up a lead, a fraction of a point here, a tiny particle of a point there, until at last Mo was forced to concede. She finally stepped away, removed her gum shield, held up her arms and said, 'Enough. You win.'

Mookin's tiny advantage had been her height and reach. Just fractionally enough, all other things being equal, it was the divider. In real combat, it would probably not have been as much of an advantage. For one thing, Mo's body was hardened and toughened from centuries of training. Mookin would not have been able to withstand even one fully delivered technique. Mookin still had some catching up to do, the kind that would only come with time. They faced up and bowed to each other.

'Kneel,' said Mo pointing at the floor in front of Mookin, and then trotted off to the changing room. On her return, she knelt opposite Mookin and brought her hands around in front of her, holding out a neatly folded black belt. Tears rolled down Mookin's cheeks as Mo placed the belt on the floor in front of her, put her hands on the floor face down and bowed to Mookin, her forehead touching the belt briefly.

Mookin sniffed and wiped her face on her soggy sleeve before copying Mo's actions, touching her forehead to the belt. She sat upright and picked up the belt, hugging it to her chest. Too choked for words, she smiled and mouthed 'thank you' once more.

In the changing rooms, Mookin shouted to Mo through the steam in the next cubicle, 'Why tae kwon-do?'

'You mean why is my style mostly based on TKD?'

'Yes.'

'Ah, well. Long story. I have something of a soft spot for Korea. I spent a long time there in its very early years. Some nice volcanoes in Korea, if you know what I mean. Anyway, regardless of the claims of any other martial art, Korea is where it all started, it's the one true source, the sun source, if you like, of all the world's martial arts.'

They were sitting on the benches in the changing room, reluctant to leave or break the mood.

'How can you be so certain?'

'Because it was me. I started it all. That's where I started teaching.'

Mookin was shocked. 'What, Bigfolk?'

'Yes, Bigfolk. The Koreans were nice people, Mookin, early developers of civilisation. I know, it was all a bit bloodthirsty and barbaric back then, but ultimately, the Koreans just wanted to be left alone, just wanted to get along with everybody peacefully. They had a society founded on Confucian principles, which they adopted early on, but they kept getting pushed around, bullied by their bigger, more powerful neighbours, China and Japan, dragged into conflicts that had nothing to do with them. We hoped we could start something there, a beginning. Tinka had ideas of the same thing in Japan.

'I just wanted to help them a bit, give them an edge. So I began training warriors. High ranking officials and their families, princes, lords and noblemen. They all came to me. Of course, I had to bust a few heads before they accepted a woman as a teacher, but they came, or I went to them. It didn't even have a name, then. So they called it after me. Subak, that was the name I was using. Later it became known as taekyon or taekkyeon; it means, uh, "empty hands". These people taught it to others and soon we had armies of trained, skilful warriors. It worked for a while too. Then the Mongols came. Ruined everything, overran the whole continent. Took years to sort that one out.

'Anyway, I'm going off topic a bit. Martial arts spread all over the Far East, as far as Japan and down into India. Each time a master trained a student, off the student would go and start teaching somewhere else and claim he'd invented some new style. The style – my style – got diluted, but retained the essence, I suppose. Little old Subak, that survived for two thousand-odd years, largely unchanged. Sure, it wasn't mine any more, but it had the heart and soul, the spirit.'

'And that's where tae kwon-do came from?'

'Nope. After the Japanese occupation of Korea, there was an attempt to resurrect the old Korean styles. Subak and taekkyeon were amongst them. But instead, they formed a committee who couldn't agree on anything. They deliberated for years and finally announced a new martial art to the world called "tae kwon-do", the "way of fist and foot". Nearly taekyon. Near enough, anyway. The core is still there. Maybe in time it will evolve. You see, Betty, martial arts evolve and change all the time; it's the practitioners that are important. You'll come to realise that. Martial arts are about people. Anyway, must be lunchtime by now, do you think? I'm famished!'

B.J. PAGE

14. Mookout's Rock

Mookout's Rock:

ACCESS RESTRICTED – Snake's Head Quarry is located in the north west of Mookination's caldera. It is the site of an up-thrusting promontory called Giant's Henge of interlocking hexagonal basalt columns which protrude six to 10 metres above the surrounding terrain and are thought to extend 30 to 40 metres below ground. Quarried since early times for building materials, they were cutusing explosives. Mookout's Rock, as it is now called, was first discovered at the heart of the formation during routine blasting. Comprised of six columns fused around a seventh, it has the appearance of midnight-blue glass shot through with gossamer gold marbling. It is over a metre across and four high and is quite imposing. Quarrying continued around the rock, so that it now stands in a U-shaped area within the promontory. It was unaffected by all early attempts to remove it and even today, its surface is smooth, unmarked and defies testing. How far it extends below ground is unknown, but it is without doubt connected to Mookination's fourth plasmic, which goes some way towards explaining its unique properties. These properties were first discovered by Security Director Mobiusmook while live testing Bigfolk shoulder-launched weapons into the disused quarry. The rock is reported to hum on occasion and certainly rings like a bell when struck by a mallet. Some have reported light dancing along the gold threads within, but this is unsubstantiated.

Mookout's Handbook

They followed a well-worn path from the western end of the Trevale which took them west then north towards a rock outcropping or promontory. It didn't tower over the landscape, but just sat there, part of it, a dark grey line amongst the green. It was still early, sparkling drops of dew still glistening in the shadows.

After an hour, the path joined a single-track road which led straight to the promontory, and they turned left to follow it. Behind them, the road led back to the road Mookin had taken from Starshine Lake to the Tree. The road was compacted stones from years of wagons trundling up and down. In the centre was a grass strip that was once kept trim by the passage of the wagons; now it was overgrown and starting to reclaim the road too.

It ran between waist-high hedges and drystone walls, and they watched as the promontory gradually grew in front of them. Mo had not said anything about where they were going or why, so Mookin was deliberately not asking any questions. She knew her curiosity would eventually get the better of her but was determined to hang on as long as possible.

As they got closer, the farmland petered out into tall grasses and the road led into a fenced-off yard with an industrial feel to it; only one building was on the site, a large stone barn, about twice the size of a normal barn. There was a sign hanging on the side of it which read, in peeling white-painted letters, *Snake's Head Quarry*.

Mo had brought her to a quarry.

They ignored the building and carried on towards the promontory which, as they approached, resolved into hexagonal columns or pillars which rose up above the surrounding area. Mookin could also see that the columns had been quite extensively quarried, as there were pieces of column lying all over the site. Next to the barn she could see some pallets that had been stacked with pieces of column cut into slices. *Bricks!* she thought. *This was the brickworks.* Most of Mookination's older buildings were constructed from hexagonal bricks. Today they used mainly land-based coral, developed in conjunction with the Merfolk, but occasionally, these bricks were still used.

'Worked it out have you, Mookin?' Mookin just smiled and nodded. 'They still take some stone away from here, which is why the road is still open, but no one comes here anymore unless they are heading for Snake Pass, which, if you follow the outside of the rock face, you will come to eventually. But there are easier ways to get to the college.'

Mookin couldn't hold it any longer. 'So why are we here?'

'Ah, follow me.'

Mo set off into the quarry proper. It was spooky and unnatural, walking over the uneven, roughly hexagonal shapes; they had been snapped off, but not always cleanly. It was like a badly tiled floor. It was quite alien, with the columns all around in various shades of grey and mottled blue, even some rust-red browns, but Mookin followed closely behind, not afraid, just curious.

As they approached the middle of the quarry, Mookin could see something out of place. Something that didn't quite fit its surroundings, didn't blend in. Mo had stopped, dropped her backpack on the floor and was waiting, smiling slightly at Mookin.

She was standing next to a column unlike any of the others. It was much larger, to start with, and it rose up from the floor of the quarry to a height of about two metres above their heads. It looked as if it was made of dark blue glass with fine gold beading running throughout. Mo was still smiling and beckoned for Mookin to join her.

She slipped off her pack, walked over to join Mo and stepped into a... tingling, a presence, like walking into freezing cold mist on a hot day. 'You can sense it, can't you, Mookin?'

'What... what is it?'

'Mookin, welcome to Mookout's Rock!' Mo said, quite dramatically. She held out her left hand which Mookin grasped as she cautiously stepped up until her nose was almost touching the surface. 'Can I touch it?'

'Oh yes, that's the whole reason we came.'

Together, they both placed their fingers on the mirror-smooth surface. There was nothing at first, then there was a sensation like being drawn, sucked into the column. Her mind floated free and entered the mindspace.

It was an introduction, really. In this place, she was shown the whole Mookout network. She acquired a kind of link to every other Mookout, and they to her. From now on, if she wished, she could link at any time to any other Mookout. They could talk, exchange information, call for help, assist each other, find each other. It was a way of keeping in touch, of not feeling isolated and alone when on a mission. She shyly said hello, and every Mookout said 'hi' back. It was a warming, comforting experience. She could stay here forever. It was so cosy and snug amidst the warmth of friendly feelings. She felt Mo's hand in hers, squeezing gently, and with a snap, she was back again. She staggered slightly and Mo caught her elbow, steadying her as she let go of the rock.

They returned to the mill, sat on a stack of pallets and sipped coffee from Mo's flask in tin cups. It tasted wonderful. As most things did these days.

'How you feeling?' asked Mo.

'Fab. Still dizzy. A bit like these columns though.'

'Sorry?'

'Completely blown away!'

They returned to the Learning Tree using the same roads and paths. Hardly a word was spoken or needed to be. Mookin felt closer to Mo than ever, but sensed the mood had changed. Instead of the joy they had shared earlier, the closer they got to home, the more solemn she felt.

Soon, the Trevale was in sight, the now familiar Tree towering above them. As they walked down the slope to the base, Mo stopped before entering and turned to face Mookin.

'Well, sweetheart. That was the last of your training with me. For now, anyway. You are as ready as I can make you for this mission.'

Mookin swallowed in a dry mouth. 'Oh Mo. I don't know what to say. This past week has been...'

'No need to say anything, Betty. It has been as special for me as it has been for you.'

They embraced for a few short moments, bathed in each other's warmth, until Mookin, as they parted, was able to ask, 'What now?'

'I promised Firestarta I'd have you back by teatime. He has a treat for you.'

'Home?' asked Mookin, 'Really?'

'Yes, really. Just a flying visit, mind. Um, not literally flying, of course, you haven't passed your test yet, but we'll be staying tonight, then back tomorrow morning. You've earned a wee break.' said Firestarta.

'Before we go, do I have time for a haircut? It's been bugging me for ages.'

'Haircut? I'm not sure we have enough...'

'Spekal, take the young lady to see Bood,' said Mo.

'Well, if you think so, but...'

'I do think so. Hair is important to us girls.' Mo winked at Mookin, and Mookin gave her a thumbs-up and again mouthed, 'Thanks.'

It turned out there was a whole department of the Tree devoted to haircuts. And more. Much, much more. Bood and her son Persi between them ran Masquerade, the department responsible for preparing Mookouts for the BFW. They provided clothes, make-up, disguises, documentation, technology and any one of a thousand things a Mookout could require, up to and including vehicles and currency.

Bood and Persi looked enough alike to be twins: same height, same yellow and brown striped hair in similar close-cropped style, same grey-green flecked eyes. Same clothes as well: black shoes, dark blue cargo pants, light blue baggy polo shirts. Bood's glyph sported scissors and comb, Persi's was crossed needles over a bobbin of thread.

Masquerade took up a space as large as the gym and was accessed from the Hoop. The front office was a workshop, with Persi hunched over a sewing machine when Mookin walked in with Firestarta. He looked up and smiled at her, nodded to Firestarta and returned to his task.

Bood was standing behind a high work table with a number of fake heads in front of her, each adorned with a wig in different hairstyles and in various Bigfolk colours and shades. She was brushing them and fussing over them with a brush and comb. She came out from behind her work table, hugging Firestarta and kissing both cheeks before turning to face Mookin.

'Hello Mookin, been hearing lots about you. All good too. What can we do for you today?'

'Hi Mrs Boodera, I, um, just wanted to get my hair cut short; it keeps getting in the way and I don't seem to have the time to look after it anymore.' She gave Firestarta a sideways glance when saying this, but he didn't notice as he was busy trying on wigs.

'Call me Bood, Mookin. What did you have in mind? Is it personal or is it for a mission? Firestarta, does Mookin have any hair requirements for a mission?'

She turned to look at Firestarta just as he had donned a long blonde wig that covered most of his face and was down past his waist. He was parting the wig with his fingers to see himself in the mirror. Even Persi had paused from his sewing to see what was happening. Firestarta realised it had gone quiet and was peering out from under the wig, grinning sheepishly at Bood.

'Oh, for goodness' sake. Firestarta Spekalmook, don't you ever grow up?'

He tried to remove the now uncooperative wig, which had somehow become entangled in his moustache and ear tufts. Bood strode over to him shaking her head. 'Hold still, will you? You're just making it worse.'

He did as he was told, standing with his arms straight down by his sides as Bood untangled him from the wig. As it came free, he just looked at the floor, embarrassed, and, especially in his short trousers, appeared just like a naughty schoolboy.

Mookin would never forget this moment: big, tough Firestarta being told off by Bood. She had thought him invincible, infallible, tough as old boots. This showed him in a different light. More Mook, less super-Mook. It was hard not to love him.

Twenty-five minutes later, a smiling Mookin almost skipped out of Masquerade, her striking purple hair cut short, tight to her head, a slightly chagrined Firestarta tagging along behind. Bood had also trimmed her ear tufts, as she would be going to BFW soon, and given her some cream that would stop them growing back.

'Right, get your bag, Mookin, and meet me in the gym in twenty minutes. Go!'

Phew, it didn't take him long to get back to his old self, thought Mookin as she tore off down the Hoop to her room.

She collected a few essentials in her rucksack and had time for a quick shower, as she was feeling a bit itchy from her haircut, and a change of clothes. She was back at the gym with three minutes to spare. She paused for less than a second to check her new hair in the changing-room mirror, giving it a quick flick.

Firestarta was already waiting and had changed into clean but identical black cargo shorts and t-shirt with his glyph, together with black leather running sandals. He had on his back a large, faded black cloth bag, bulging with who-knew-what, that looked similar to the gym bags Mookin's mum used to make from old curtains. It was draped across one shoulder, bandolier-style.

'Ready, lassie?'

'Yes, Uncle. Are we catching the ferry?'

'No dear. Pleasant as that would be as I've not seen Dora for several years, we don't have time. Instead, you are going to cut us a D-way.'

'Me? But I've only done it in the gym! It's way too far, isn't it? Am I even allowed to? What if I mess it up?'

'Mookin!'

'Yes. Sorry.'

'Look at me. Do I look worried? No. I have every confidence in you. It's important that you realise there is no difference between D-ways you have opened here in the gym, and between here and anywhere else. Between them, there is no distance. We call it side-stepping because you effectively turn at right angles to this space, like slipping between the bars of a cage. We are using a kink in the fabric of space, a flaw in the design we are able to utilise. Doorway, keyway, portal, whatever we call it, it is a tool to help your mind visualise the required steps. We picture a door because it makes it easier to conjure. Understand?'

'Yes, Uncle.'

'Good. I want you to relax and find us a secluded spot near Mookinsouth, somewhere you know very well but that is isolated, safe. It's almost impossible to side-step to somewhere you haven't been before, so somewhere familiar is preferable. Safety is paramount, not halfway up a cliff, for example. Somewhere flat, open, quiet. Okay?'

'Is my parents' farm okay, or did you want to be closer to the village?' asked Mookin, suddenly very business-like.

15. The Heart of the Matter

Grapples:

Grandmaster plant-charmer Stormchasa Slidamook is renowned for his innovation and skill in developing new food plants, and among his many successes is the grapple. A hybrid apple/grape variety, the vine was planted over 450 years ago. The main trunk or stem is now over two metres in diameter and grows outwards in a large rectangular spiral. Originally trained over poles and wires, much like a grape vine, it is now self-supporting, with downward-sprouting roots every 20 metres or so. The branches, leaves and fruit grow two metres overhead, but as the grapple bunches grow, the branches bend downwards, when they reach ripeness and are at the perfect height to be picked. Colours, varieties and flavours are spread out along the vine with every colour from bright yellow and green to glossy, sumptuous red, and all mixtures in between. Mr Stormchasa reports that there are now in excess of 1,000 types of grapple on the vine, and that many were rescued from extinction from Herefordshire and Kent in the British Isles, and he will shortly be producing several new types of cider. Such is his dedication to his art.

Mookipedia

Pangs of hunger drove the predator onward through the undergrowth. He was in stalking mode now and nothing would deter him from his prey. His olfactory senses were amongst the largest in relation to body size for any animal on the planet and he knew instinctively that he was nearly invisible, perfectly camouflaged for his environment.

His prey was not far away now. He could tell which direction to follow just by the increasing strength of the scent trail: more molecules that way, less molecules this. The scent trail did not rely on the wind but clung to every surface like the morning dew. The scent trail was strong now. He began to tremble in anticipation; it wasn't just the hunger, it was the hunt, the stalk, the leap, the utter shock and surprise of his chosen quarry.

Without being aware of it, he had circled his target until the faint breeze was blowing straight towards his face, so that his own scent would not betray him. Black nose twitching, black eyes sparkling, he kept low, he kept to the shadows. Ears swivelled and twisted in every direction, building a mental map of his surroundings. His eyes, though sharp enough, were useless over distance but exceptional in the final micro-seconds of a kill, enabling him to execute his leap to perfection. His superbly muscled body could be wound like a coiled spring for explosive reactions, triggered in the tiniest fraction of a heartbeat and with such agility, he could change direction mid-leap.

Close to starvation, hunger was a constant companion, the price paid for occupying the top of the food chain, and it had been hours since he last gorged himself on sweet flesh. He must eat now or starve. He pushed his snout forward between two stalks and the scent nearly overwhelmed him. There! Right there! His eyes came into play now, shutting down his sense of smell which had triggered a flood of saliva into his mouth, drooling from his lips and dripping from his needle-sharp fangs.

Finally, there was his intended victim. Resting, sleeping or injured, he didn't care. Unmoving was always best, safer, easier, but he sometimes hankered for the chase. His ears flattened against his head in final preparation, adrenaline was fed into his system, priming his body and... The trajectory was perfection itself. Razor-like claws snicked into place, mouth open, fangs glistening, and he could already taste the sweetness in his mouth when... No!

Mid-leap, there was a terrible sound like ripping paper, a momentary flash of brightness and a faint tang of ozone in the air. Landing in a crumpled heap, he was stunned as something huge and black descended onto his prey, crushing it.

Mookin looked all around as she and Firestarta stepped through the D-way from the gym. They were in a small grassy clearing in the middle of the grapple orchard on Rosadale-Dell.

Mookin turned to Firestarta. 'Can you hear that?' Since the slight crackling noise of the D-way had zipped shut, Mookin could hear a high-pitched squealing noise, so faint she wasn't sure if it was some sort of after-effect of side-stepping.

'Aye, I can just about hear it. It's coming from your direction.'

'Me?' Mookin froze on the spot and carefully began scanning the ground around her. There were snakes on the island, but they weren't especially dangerous, only mildly venomous, but could still give you a nasty bite. She chuckled when she looked down at her right foot which had squashed an over-ripe grapple that had fallen from the vine. Scratching and biting – with no effect whatsoever – at her trainer, was a small bundle of furious fur.

She stooped and picked him up carefully by the loose fur on the scruff of his neck, holding him up for Firestarta to see. 'Look, it's a tigermouse!' she laughed. 'He's really angry too. I think I stepped on his lunch.' Firestarta leaned in for a closer look and nearly lost the tip of his nose. 'Ooo, careful Uncle, mean little devils, tigermice. Adult male this is. Tend to have ideas way above their size. Pretty though, isn't he?'

Resplendent in his black, gold and orange stripes, he did indeed look like a miniature tiger, and when Mookin tried to scratch his belly, he performed a hissing, spitting, scratching and biting impression of one too.

Mookin held him up in front of her eyes, shouted 'Oi!' and blew into his face. He stopped struggling, fixed Mookin with his angriest stare and let out his mightiest roar, which, to be fair, was so high-pitched it barely registered in Mookin's ears. Satisfied he had defended his honour, he swung silently between her finger and thumb, resigned to the fact that he was now probably going to be eaten live and whole.

'I'm sorry I squashed your lunch, okay? It was an accident.' Mookin looked around, then reached up and picked the reddest, most ripe grapple she could find.

The tigermouse, which was now ignoring Mookin in the belief that if he ignored her hard enough she would vanish into thin air, swivelled his eyes towards the grapple she was holding up. She held it closer and his nose started to twitch until it was pressed up against the fruit. He started drooling again, drawing back his head and opening his mouth to take a bite.

Mookin moved the grapple away, out of reach. His little head swivelled back and forth between grapple and Mookin. He looked at her imploringly. 'Do you want this?' she asked. He glanced at the grapple, back to Mookin and nodded his head vigorously.

Firestarta looked on, amazed. Who else but Mookin would bother about the feelings of such a tiny creature? Most would just say 'Oops' and walk away. She set the grapple down in the shade and plopped the little chap down on top. He waited all of two seconds before taking a big bite, filling both cheek pouches. Within ten seconds, he was buried shoulder deep in his lunch, all thought of Mookin completely gone.

Mookin and Firestarta headed off towards the farmhouse, which they could see through the gaps in the vine. 'So all of this is one plant?' Firestarta asked, having been unaware that grapples grew on a vine, grape-like, in big bunches.

'Yes. We've got a thousand or so varieties now, all on the same vine. We rescued some from extinction, but a lot were cider apples, grapples now, I suppose. You have to graft apples, you see; the seeds or pips don't produce the same fruit as the parent tree, so you can't store seed. Some of the ones we saved were over a thousand years old. Dad thought it would be a shame to lose them entirely.'

'I see. Why were they becoming extinct?'

'Dad says it was just that there was less and less call for cider, more and more imported stuff was being used in the manufacture. Orchards were closing everywhere. Hundreds of years of plant breeding going to waste.'

Making their way down the gently sloping fields towards the house, they crossed several streams which, although they looked natural, were part of a complicated irrigation system that ran throughout the farm and was fed from a reservoir further back in the hills.

Presently, they came to the side of the barn and followed the path around to the courtyard, where Mookin was surprised to once again see the Mayor's carriage parked, this time crookedly, across the front of the house. Fleet had his head buried in Mum's precious flowerbed and was happily munching his way along the border. Mookin rushed over, grabbed his bridle and led him around in a big circle, tying his reins to an iron ring in the stable wall. 'Oh, Fleet. That was not funny.'

He looked at her, shook his head and mane, and said, in his horsey voice, 'NO-d NAWW-Dee?' (*'Not naughty?'*)

'Well, it is a bit naughty.'

'SHAW-RY.' (*'Sorry.'*)

'Okay. I'll tell Mum you're sorry. Promise not to do it again, though, okay?'

'DOH-KAY.' (*'Okay.'*)

Mookin scratched between his eyes. 'I'll see if I can bring you a carrot later.' She rejoined Firestarta, who was waiting by the front door.

'Betty, do you always talk to animals?'

'Uh, some. Mainly the ones that talk back, really. Not all of them do; but you can tell the talkative ones, can't you?'

'Ah Mookin, you never cease to surprise me. To my ears, all I heard was a horse making horsey noises, I tell you, I've never actually heard of *anyone* who talks to animals. Well, not anyone who was sober, or expected a reply.'

'Oh. I thought... You mean it's just me, then?'

'It's not an ability I've heard about. Perhaps no one's ever really tried before. How long have you been, you know, talking to them?'

'Since I was little, I guess. When Mum and Dad used to take us on the ferry to Zooplex for the day. I always thought it was a bit strange they never seemed to speak when other people were around. It's hard to understand them sometimes. A lot don't even have vocal cords like us. My school friends used to laugh at me, so I kind of stopped mentioning it after a while. Is it a bit weird?'

Firestarta chuckled but looked up into Mookin's eyes.

'What you have there is a rare gift. But keep it to yourself for now. It could come in very handy one day.'

As Mookin pushed the kitchen door open, she just had time to see that everyone was there again before she was smothered by Tammy and Debs, leaping at her and enfolding her in a major hug. There was squeaking and squealing and the hug quickly escalated into crying, laughing, back slapping and more hugging. They kept pointing at her hair and saying, 'Your hair!' and off they would go again. Finally, after a warning 'Hurrumph' from UBM, the girls fell silent, back in the room with everyone else, and Mookin finally managed to hug her mum and dad, sister and little brother, and, of course, Uncle Big Mook. Then followed the usual raft of questions.

Mum: 'You look thin. Have you been eating? What have you done to your hair?'

Dad: 'Have you been behaving? Have you been getting to bed on time? Is your hair different?'

Djinny: 'What's it like? Your hair!'

Kikkit: 'Have you done magic yet? How big is the Tree? Have you been on a secret mission yet? Is it really cool?'

She answered as best she could, with frequent glances at Firestarta for approval, and eventually everyone seemed satisfied and Mookin and her friends were able to retreat to a corner of the kitchen to catch up.

Firestarta was shaking hands all round, careful not to omit Kikkit, who got a very grown-up handshake, but who was speechless at the sight of Firestarta's huge red moustache which he seemed unable to take his eyes off. Djinny got a handshake and a peck on the cheek, Mum a 'Lora!' and a resounding kiss on both cheeks and a hug. Dad received a 'Slida, been a while,' punctuated with a slap on the shoulder that knocked him half a step to his left, and he would have gone further if Firestarta's firm handshake hadn't held him in place.

Uncle Big Mook was last, and he received a mock curtsy, Firestarta bowing his head low and saying, 'Your Bigness,' before grabbing him in a bear hug and kissing him soundly on both cheeks. When he put him down, they were both smiling and red faced.

'Spekal, always a pleasure!'

'Likewise, Freddi.'

Mum and Dad had opted for a barbecue, as the dining room table sat only eight and the kitchen only six. The garden extended the full width of the back of the house and was mostly given over to lawn. It was very neat and formal close to the house, with stone paths, borders, low hedges and topiary and a stone-bordered koi pond with central fountain.

A large magnolia stood off to one side of the lawn, and in its shade was a wooden bench. Suspended from its upper branches was a swing that had seen such frequent use in the past that the grass beneath had given up and there was now a strip of bare earth half a metre wide and a metre long, marking where the toes of little shoes had acted as a braking device.

The garden gradually descended into increasing random disarray, becoming a jumble of assorted sheds, workshops and greenhouses interspersed with all manner of garden implements, ladders and dubious-looking machinery. A wood and wire fence ran across the bottom of the garden, with a gate in the corner that opened on to Dad's racing chicken stable. Another shed, really, but Dad called it a stable.

The garden was enclosed on both sides by a tall yew hedge, cut so tight and square it looked like a solid wall of dark green. A pergola ran across the back of the house, covering the patio and providing a cool, shaded area for tables and chairs. Potted palms stood at attention around the edges of the patio.

Dad had fired up the barbecue and pizza oven and was merrily flipping burgers, rolling hot-dog sausages, turning kebabs and trying not to make charcoal out of beefsteaks. Several of Mum and Dad's friends had joined them from neighbouring farms.

Mookin was waiting for Dad to finish cooking her Peking duck pizza, which would be ready any second judging by the smell. 'Dad, pizza,' she reminded him. Dad slipped a thin wooden paddle under the pizza, removed it from the oven and sliced it into pieces. She went to rejoin Debs and Tammy who were sitting under the pergola. Mookin had briefly filled her friends in on what she had been up to over the past few weeks but there hadn't been time for details. Mookin had promised to hi-speak everything to them before they left for the evening.

Savouring the moment, Mookin realised she was incredibly happy, surrounded by her family, friends, and the uncles who she now knew were nothing of the sort. Quite a lot of the questions that had been spinning around her head had now been answered or would be soon. She was embarking on a whole new chapter of her life that promised to be both exhilarating and important. Only one thing was puzzling her now: the complete mystery surrounding the star map and the sealed door with its flooded corridor.

She was talking to Tammy and Debs about this, Tammy

having drawn a complete blank with her research into the strange writing on the doors. 'Betty, I've tried everything I could find without involving my parents. Maybe I should just ask them? I hate this sneaking around, pretending it's homework,' said Tammy. 'It's Old Mook, I'm sure, but it makes no sense. I'm baffled.'

'Tam, I don't know. I haven't had time to do any research at all. Perhaps you're right...'

A glint of sunlight flashed across her face from the other side of the garden. Uncle Big Mook was talking to Dad at the barbecue and was looking at his silver pocket watch, which he had just pulled from his waistcoat pocket. It was sending reflected flashes of sunlight in Mookin's direction.

She had one of those strange mental quirks – her mind performed a back-flip and she was back in the school hall with the others from her year, listening to Uncle Big Mook giving his talk. She remembered him taking out his watch then, too, and noticing the unusual fob he kept attached to the other end of the chain. Then she was back in the garden, but it was her sixth or seventh birthday.

UBM had been pushing her on the swing under the magnolia and she had insisted she could jump off when it reached its maximum height. He had insisted on catching her in case it all went wrong. They both ended up in a heap on the lawn and she had seen something glinting in the grass. UBM's watch fob, fallen from its chain. Its sparkling facets had fascinated her. It seemed lit from within by rainbows to her little eyes, a thing of magic. She asked, of course, and he had replied, 'No, not magic. Well, maybe a little. I will tell you the story one day.'

'Hang on, I really need to talk to UBM about something. I think today might just be the day.'

Tammy and Debs were surprised to see Mookin walk straight up to Uncle Big Mook, who was still talking to her dad at the barbecue. There was no mistaking that Mookin had changed since they had parted after their last adventure. She had always been the leader of their group, always the instigator of so many of their adventures. But, Tammy was thinking, she had a certain way about her now. So much more confident, capable.

'Excuse me, Dad. Uncle, I need to talk to you, please.'

'Certainly Betty, what can I do for you?'

'Um, in private, if that's okay? Sorry Dad, Mookout stuff.'

Dad and Uncle Big Mook were a little taken aback, but UBM said, 'Hurrumph. Ahh, very well, Betty. Sorry about this, Slida, please excuse us.'

'Yes, of course, Uncle, looks like I've got work to do anyway. I think everyone is ready for seconds.'

Uncle Big Mook and Mookin strolled off down the lawn, making small talk on the way, until they reached the swing under the tree. Mookin promptly sat on the faded wooden board and said, 'Push me, Nunky!' as she used to when she was little.

'Mookin Bettymook, I don't think...'

'Please, Uncle?'

Reluctant, and a little curious, Uncle Big Mook walked around and began pushing her, hands on the wood of the seat. After just a few swings, Mookin said, 'Uncle, do you remember my seventh birthday?'

'I'm not sure, Betty. There have been so many birthdays. Is it significant?'

'Yes. Yes, it is. It only sticks in my mind because of one thing.'

UBM walked around to face Mookin, who had stopped swinging now and had planted her feet either side of the mud strip.

'Is this leading somewhere? Do you want to ask me something?'

'Yes, I really do. And I'm so sorry I have to.'

'Sorry? What on earth would you have to be sorry about?'

'On my sixth birthday, or it may have been my seventh, I'm not sure, you were pushing me on the swing, and I wanted to jump off because I'd seen Mikki and Jaci do it, so you insisted on catching me. We ended up on the lawn and somehow your fob came off your watch chain. I saw it there in the grass and picked it up. I was mesmerised by it, the way it sparkled in the sun. I asked you where you got it from, and you said –'

'I said, 'I'll tell you the story one day.' I remember. Uh, seventh, I believe. On your sixth I was rather late and didn't have time to wrap your present properly. A book on caving.'

'I think it's time. I need to know.'

'Well, I'm not sure...'

'I've seen it. I've seen the star map, the sealed door, the flooded corridor. I've seen it all. At the Love Pool, on Giant's Stairway. Tammy and Debs too. Your fob is the key that unlocks the star chamber, isn't it, Uncle?'

Uncle Big Mook couldn't conceal his shock. 'But... but how? It was sealed, hidden, how did... when did you...?'

Mookin had never seen anyone, particularly her Uncle Big Mook, look quite so flustered. He took a big breath in, loosened his bow tie and undid his collar button. He even unbuttoned his waistcoat, then exhaled slowly. He walked over to the bench and sat down. Mookin regarded him from the swing, waiting for him to compose himself. 'Tell me, Betty. Tell me how you found my star chamber, please.'

Mookin gave him a brief description of her recent adventure with her friends, how they'd intended to explore the Plunge but got sidetracked by finding a cave behind Wysend, Spyda Falls, Mud Monster Cavern, the Shimney, Crystal Flute Cave and how, when looking for an exit, they'd found the star map.

'So the salt-water barrier had leaked out?'

'Yes, the roof was quite badly damaged, and there was no

way to tell how long the water had been gone. But we flooded it afterwards, so it should be all right, shouldn't it?'

'Mmm, possibly. Well, thank you for that. We may have to make some repairs. If it leaked out once, it may well do again. Have you given any thought to what might lie beyond the sealed door?'

'Well, I'm not sure. Bit of a guess, but I would say that it leads to, or is in some way connected to, a plasmic?'

'Very good. How did you come to that conclusion?'

'The salt water really. We were taught in school that fresh water causes a plasmic to explode violently, so the water wasn't just to seal the corridor shut, it had to be protection as well. I'm guessing something about salt water makes it safe to come into contact with a plasmic?'

'Quite correct. And the star map?'

Mookin had been thinking long and hard about this. 'We're not from here, are we? We somehow use the plasmic to jump between stars, don't we?'

UBM smiled at her from his seat on the grass. 'You really are a very bright Mook, my dear. Can I ask you one favour though? We intend, the other Eldron and I, to make all this information freely available to all Mooks. Largely, this has been prompted by you and your time at the Learning Tree. Big changes are underway, and I would ask you to allow us to pass this knowledge to our people in our own way. It has been our error, so it's for us to put right.'

'You want me to keep your secret?'

'Only for a short while.'

'Okay, but not from Tammy and Debs. They've earned the right to know now.'

He nodded his assent. 'Crystal Flute Cavern, eh? I like the sound of that. It was just a dry and dusty hole last time I was in there.'

'You were in there?'

'Yes, of course. When we first came here, I had to make

sure the star chamber was safe, There was no Plunge then; the river formed a lake on the plateau below Wysend and flowed straight over the top of Giant's Stairway. Crystal Flute, as you call it, was dark and empty. I explored the Shimny but the bottom was blocked by a rockfall, so I thought that was it. When the Plunge fell through, we had to seal the star chamber behind airtight doors. The salt water was an added protection in case of flooding.'

'So why did we come here? Where are we from?'

'Mookin, the story is a long one, and I would need to do it justice. For now, I will just say there was an exodus from the core suns. Closer in, the galaxy is no longer suitable for any form of life. We had to leave, so we left in small groups. Ours came here.'

'The Big Secret?'

'Yes. A rather Big Secret. But not the only one, Betty. Not all life forms are like us. There are those who would misuse the gift of PE; they would seek to subjugate and control where we would nurture and assist. We chose to abandon them rather than confront the threat. We left them to their fate. We each left by a different route, different keyways. Our goal was to spread the word through the inner galaxy of the danger to all life forms. Fortunately, the very thing that was rendering our home star uninhabitable proved to be our salvation. The plasmic energy, magic itself, had increased a million-fold, enabling us to build the Million Keyways, a network of routes from star to star, allowing us to travel freely. There were over a million links in the network, a million groups of Mooks. We called it, rather grandly, the Million Keyways. A network of highways out from the core.'

'There's something else, Uncle. What are you *not* telling me?'

He took a deep breath before answering, ran his fingers through his ear tufts and scratched his nose. 'Only Eldrons are aware of this, Betty. This goes no further. Understand?'

His voice had lost the softness of her uncle. There was a sharp edge to it that she couldn't ignore. This was her leader, her commander-in-chief speaking. 'Yes, sir. I understand.'

'Very well.' He held up the heart-shaped fob, he had been holding it in his fist all this time. It glittered as it twirled, throwing rainbows across his face. 'As you quite rightly surmised, this is indeed the key that opens the star chamber, but also the means of its destruction.'

'What?' Mookin was horrified.

'Patience, young lady. The keyways are an incredible thing, obviously, but we have never shared their secret with anyone, and probably never will. We have never disclosed the secret of opening D-ways and G-ways. Can you think why?'

Her head was spinning with this new information. She ran through the parameters of this ability she had only just learned. It was a good thing, surely? Then, like a shot from the dark, it hit her. 'Weapon. It could be used as a weapon. It could be used against us, couldn't it?'

'Precisely. A weapon. Imagine for a second the havoc and devastation of opening one end of a D-way inside a sun and the other against the surface of your enemy's planet? It does not bear thinking about, Betty.' He held up the heart jewel again. 'This is to stop a keyway falling into the wrong hands. Each of the Eldron has one, and we are sworn to protect the Million Keyways.'

They both sat quietly, each regarding the other, letting the silence build. 'Now, that's enough for today. We will continue this another time.'

'Just one more thing. What does the writing on the doors say? Tammy has been looking for weeks, but hasn't found any reference to it.'

'Writing? On the doors? Oh. Oh yes. Old, Old Mook. I remember...'

Mookin was chuckling as she walked back to Tammy and Debs; she sat back down and looked at her two friends.

'Well?' they both asked.

'Well what?' said Mookin.

'Mookin! What did you need to see UBM for? And why were you laughing all the way back?'

'I'm not sure I should tell you, really.' she replied.

Debs glared, grabbing the ketchup bottle from the table. 'Mookin Bettymook, spill it! Or this,' she shook the bottle at her, 'is going up your nose.'

'You wouldn't...' Debs stood up from the table, and Mookin looked to Tammy for help but she just shrugged as if to say, 'Sorry mate, you're own your own.'

'Mmm. Yes, you would. Okay. Sit back down. I'll tell you. But first, let me hi-speak you up to date. I've so much to tell you.'

'Promise?' said Debs, sternly.

'Of course. I tell you everything, don't I?' *Well, maybe not quite everything, this time,* she corrected herself. 'Eventually.'

She held their hands, squeezed them gently and looked into their eyes. It started with a low hum from Mookin's throat, the carrier wave to which Tammy and Debs locked on. Then began a warbling, like a hundred small birds twittering in a tree top, the data-stream, containing layer upon layer of information: sounds, vision, emotion, touch, smell and impressions. Everything that Mookin had experienced since she had been away. Weeks and weeks distilled and compressed into twelve seconds of hi-speak. Like a zip-file for her friends to take away and unravel in their own time.

Tammy and Debs felt dizzy. That was by far the largest hi-speak they had ever undertaken. Mookin left briefly and returned with three glasses of sparkalin water. Her friends were not partial to it, but in their befuddled state, they sipped without thinking. Debs pulled a face at the flavour of the green liquid, but then smiled as she swallowed. 'Hey. That really helps. It's clearing my head already,' she said.

Tammy too seemed to have a new appreciation for the

unusual brew. Her eyes refocused and she turned to Mookin. 'So, why were you laughing, Betty? Going to share the joke?'

'Yes, of course.'

She told them what she and Uncle Big Mook had been talking about.

'Sorry Mookin, I'm getting a bit lost here. What was it about UBM's watch that got you so excited?' asked Tammy.

'No, not the watch, the fob. The fob on the other end of his watch chain is a faceted diamond in the shape of a heart. It's a diamond that's actually a very special key for a very special door.'

'Oh, I get it,' Debs chipped in. 'It's all hearts, isn't it? At the Love Pool, there were hearts on the rock face marking the entrance. There were hearts on both doors of the corridor too, and the sealed one had a heart-shaped recess in the middle of the other heart. And now, a heart-shaped key!'

'And you were laughing because?' added Tammy.

'I'm almost too embarrassed to tell you,' Mookin replied.

'Pass the ketchup, Debs...'

'Okay, okay, but you won't like it. Uncle Big Mook told me what the writing on the doors said.'

'What? He did? What did he say?' Tammy was very excited; she had spent all her spare time since that day pouring over books, looking for clues.

'Well, it's Old Mook, but much older than the version we know. It dates back to before Mookination. They borrowed the doors from a Mook mothership.'

'Mookin! What does it say on the doors?' snapped Tammy.

'Okay. The first door says, "Caution: wet floor ahead".'

'What? You are joking!' they said in unison.

'I'm not. And the second door says, "Danger: plasmic ahead. Tinted goggles must be worn".'

'Crick on a stick, Betty. Do you know how much time I've spent pouring over books and manuscripts and... and...?' said Tammy incredulously.

'Yes,' added Debs. 'Tammy has been... wait a second. What did you say?'

Mookin had been waiting, a smile just curling her lips as they both realised what she had said.

'Mothership?' they exclaimed together.

B.J. PAGE

16. The Eye of the World

Bigfolk:

ACCESS RESTRICTED – Bigfolk is the colloquial term for the Transplanted Emergent Species (TES) of Fringe system A-519-S3-0072-LS, which is 72 light years anti-spinward of Homestar. The term first came into use prior to the Big Sleep, as many of the original hominids were large-boned and massively muscled compared to Mooks. Cross breeding and evolutionary pressures inherent in the development of any species has served to reduce the overall bulk and stature of the Bigfolk, apparently in a trade-off for a more erect posture and increased brain size. It had been hoped that all of the TES hominids might emerge during the Big Sleep, but alas, it was not to be, and several suffered extinction or were incorporated by cross breeding while we were in hibernation. The Toba Lake catastrophe may have also had an effect (approx. 75,000 years ago), although the rest of the primates, of the same origin as the hominids, managed to adapt and survive. Sadly, apart from the Bigfolk, only five or six others are thought to have survived. Principle amongst these are the Bigfeet, the forest-dwelling giants, the diminutive Dwarfolk and Floresfolk, the Eldridge and isolated reports of the Kangadmi, the high-altitude dwellers.
The Troglodytae have not been seen for over 2,000 years and may also have disappeared into extinction.

Mookout Handbook

Firestarta and Mookin made an early start next morning, long before the sun peeked over the horizon. The previous evening had been wonderful, and it was great to sleep in her own bed again but, no matter how much she loved her family and friends, she was keen to get back to her training.

She felt a new closeness to Firestarta, just like with Mo, a feeling of camaraderie she had never known before. What had it been, four weeks? But he had become both friend and mentor, confidant and inspiration. His knowledge of magic and his skill as a wielder were phenomenal. Almost every second spent with him was priceless; she was acquiring new skills and applications all the time.

He never stopped teaching. Everything was a lesson, and there was a lesson in everything, even something as mundane and natural as walking. He taught her how to walk silently, how to move without putting pressure on the things she stepped on. Over dry leaves and twigs she made no sound; in sand she left no footprints. Now she could blend with the darkness and shadows, the wind and the mist. She was sure, if she attempted it, she could run on water and made a mental note to ask Firestarta if he'd tried it.

Tammy and Debs had left the previous evening looking a little fuzzy from the hi-speak. Mookin was missing them already. Uncle Big Mook had set off in his carriage with Fleet looking pleased after Mookin had given him the promised carrot. Don't break a promise to a horse; they would never let you forget it! Mum hadn't noticed half her flowers were missing from one side of the door, so Mookin thought it better not to mention it. They would, after all, grow back.

Only Dad had been awake when they'd set off, and he'd promised to give her love to everyone. She felt a bit guilty: she had left Mum a pile of washing which she had intended to put in the washing machine before bed but had just forgotten. She'd taken all her remaining clean clothes from her room; everything she was likely to need was folded neatly in her rucksack. They had also raided the pantry but hadn't taken much as they intended to be back at the LT by mid-morning.

They retraced their steps back to the grapple vine, as Firestarta said it was a good spot for side-stepping and that she should use it as a 'haven'. These were safe places that Mookouts could retreat to if in danger, and it was important, he said, to have two or three such places.

When they reached the clearing, Mookin went to the centre

while Firestarta held back at the edge, and she closed her eyes, allowing her senses to reach out, memorising the spot in some detail. Her mind took a snapshot and now this was Haven 1. She could return here almost without conscious thought, her mind need only form around the words Haven 1 and a D-way would happen automatically, even if she were injured or only partially awake.

'Are you done, Betty?'

'Och, aye.' Mookin said, in imitation of Firestarta's accent. He eyed her suspiciously but made no comment.

'Now, the more you use this location, the faster and easier it will become to make the side-step. We'll find you a couple more places, and you'll be set. The gym is no good, you never know what's going on in there, you could step straight into a plasmic bolt. Theoretically, you could open a D-Way between you and any other spot, but it's much safer if you've been there before. You don't want to be zipping into mid-air or halfway through a wall that wasn't there last time you looked. It's messy and it hurts. It won't kill you, but you'll wish it had. It's not to be advised, okay?'

'Okay. Where are we off to this morning, somewhere nice?'

'Erm. Yes. Quite nice. I like it. You may need a jacket though, bit nippy this early.' He rummaged in his bag and came out with a creased black leather jacket with a fur collar. He was still wearing shorts and sandals though, so Mookin wasn't too worried. She also opened her pack and removed a wool jacket with a hood.

Firestarta opened the D-way with a quick movement of his left hand and stepped through, Mookin close behind. The temperature dropped suddenly, like standing in front of a fridge on a hot summer's day. All the heat was sucked from your clothes in a second.

There was rock underfoot, but it was still dark and windy. Mookin got the impression they were high up.

'Watch the edge there, about a metre and a half to your right.'

There were patches of ice. They were on a rock shelf, a cave entrance behind them, quite narrow, but widening further in. Firestarta snapped the fingers of his left hand, showing Mookin how to conjure a spryte, a tiny point of blue light that almost seemed alive. They had several uses, and Firestarta was using this one just as a light. They seemed almost to be able to second guess what you wanted them to do. For example, this one was lighting their path from slightly above, but without getting in the way and dazzling them.

Using the correct summons, which involved flicking her left index finger and thumb, Mookin's spryte popped out of thin air just in front of her, whizzed around her head twice and zoomed off into the cave. It came back out and checked Mookin again, then Firestarta and his spryte, which seemed to upset it a little, and finally settled down above Mookin's left shoulder.

'Mmm. Think you have a frisky one there, Betty.'

'Do they come in "frisky"?' she asked.

'Not usually. Perhaps because it's new? I've had mine since forever.'

They were in a cave only a little larger than Mookin's room at the Tree, roughly circular, with a domed roof that had a small hole in it. For a cave, it was very comfy: two over-stuffed but threadbare armchairs, a wooden table and chair next to a makeshift fireplace set in a recess in the wall with kindling, a pile of split logs and a hearth of rough stones. The fireplace was black with soot and had two metal arms, one on each side. The left one had a blackened kettle hanging from a hook, the right one a small cooking pot, also black. The arms could be swung into the fireplace to heat either or both. Cut into the back wall were two sleeping spaces with straw-filled mattresses and sleeping bags. A small shelf held half a dozen books as worn as the armchairs. Two chipped mugs, two plates and two sets of cutlery stood on the table. Mookin wondered what the plumbing arrangements were but was afraid to ask.

Firestarta used some kindling and a box of matches and soon smoke was curling lazily up the wall of the cave, disappearing into the hole in the roof. Adding some smaller logs, it wasn't long before a rosy glow started to creep up the wall, changing the whole atmosphere of the place.

'What do you think?'

'Fabulous. Your little "home from home", is it?'

'Aye, just a little retreat. I come here when I need a bit of a break. Sort my head out. Cool down a bit. That sort of thing.'

'I assume we're in the Crown somewhere, not halfway up Everest?'

'Yes dear. The Crown. Thought you might like to see something magical. Magical, I mean, not *plas*magical, for a wee bit of a change?'

Mookin just smiled. She thought she'd guessed what it was, but didn't want to spoil his surprise.

Firestarta left the cave carrying the kettle, his spryte zooming after him, and was back in just a few moments, setting the full kettle on the fire. Leaving their packs in the cave, Firestarta beckoned Mookin and she followed him back out on to the rock shelf. It was quite broad in front of the cave, and she wondered if the ledge went anywhere or just fizzled out.

Sprytes lighting the way, Firestarta led Mookin a short distance to the right and they sat down in a sheltered spot, out of the wind, backs against the cold rock face. They put their sprytes away by the simple act of snapping their fingers again. The only sound was the howling of the wind through the peaks of the Crown, a haunting, lonely sound, but it set the mood perfectly. Stardust sprinkled the sky, and as the black of night gradually gave way to the grey of twilight, Firestarta explained more about the sprytes.

'They've been about as long as Mooks have, but no one knows for sure where they come from or what they are. They are undetectable by any normal means: no mass, no heat, just the blue light. They pass through solid matter at will and are unaffected by energy or magic. You can talk to them and set them simple tasks, to act as a guard, for example, or to warn you if someone approaches. The light, you've seen, is useful, practical, and can be turned up or down by saying "big light" or "small light".'

'Crikey, aren't you curious? It's all a bit of a mystery. Has anyone ever tried to communicate with them?'

'Och, aye. Many times. No response of any kind.'

'But they must be alive, in some sense, mustn't they?'

'Like I said, no one knows. Just treat them as a kind of insubstantial friend, and they will try to help as much as they can. Don't tell me we shouldn't all be grateful for a wee light in the darkness now and again.'

It was light enough now for Mookin to see they were indeed in the Crown, and about as high as it was possible to go. They were on one of the highest peaks, almost directly opposite Giant's Cleave. As the sun rose and the dawn light settled across the island, Mookin could just make out the Cleave as a bright patch against the grey. Inside the bright patch, a pink-tinted diamond exploded into being, shining laser-like straight at them. It was eye-achingly intense and they were forced to look away but their fascination drew them back. They wanted to look. The diamond grew to a thin sliver, then an arc of shining brightness and in moments the whole orange orb of the sun was above the mist and Mookination burst into existence below them.

They were surrounded by golden light reflecting from every surface, the magnificence of the Crown stretching away on both sides of them, jagged peaks like the teeth of some great monster fading into shadow on either side of Giant's Cleave. The interior of the island was now visible in exquisite detail, like a finely drawn map before them. It reached into your heart and grabbed at your soul.

Mookin found tears rolling down her cheeks and glanced at Firestarta. He too had glistening eyes and damp cheeks. From their vantage point, Mookin noted that Starshine Lake from this high up and at this angle looked exactly like an enormous eye. Zooplex Island formed the iris and, in the middle of Zooplex Island, Lake Ness made the pupil. The Pan and the Flash looked eerily like a huge eyebrow. She mentioned it to Firestarta. 'Aye, lassie. The Eye of the World, I call it.'

They had a late breakfast in the cave which was now snug and warm. Firestarta brewed coffee and they took turns making toast over the fire with a long toasting fork. They talked some more about sprytes; Mookin was curious and flicked hers on and off several times while they ate. Firestarta showed her how to use them to send messages by flashing Mook-kode and how you could set them to find things or people.

'Och, enough chit chat, it's time we got going. We haven't even touched on shield charms and plasmic bolts and you'll be on your way in a couple of days!'

B.J. PAGE

17. The Spanish Queen Awaits

Three days later, Mookin was with Mo and Firestarta (he had told her several times to call him Spekal, but she just couldn't) in Masquerade. Mookin was being fussed over by Persi as he made final additions and adjustments to her masque. Mookin had received her mission briefing yesterday and would be leaving this evening. She would be posing as a sixteen- or seventeen-year-old Bigfolk schoolgirl, for which she had needed no major adjustments. To Bigfolk, she already looked of indeterminate ancestry: slightly dark skinned with large, almond-shaped eyes; she could pass easily for many combinations of mixed parentage. At a push, she looked of Mediterranean extraction. She could pass for Greek, Turkish or Egyptian.

Her cover story was to be kept as simple as possible:

mother and father divorced, she lived with the wealthy father. He was something in security, she wasn't sure, didn't know, string of boarding schools, a bit too much money really. Mookin was quite looking forward to it and had been coached by Persi who seemed to know all about how Bigfolk behave.

She was off more than halfway around the world to another volcanic island: the Canary Islands. Her mission, should she choose to accept it (What? Are you nuts? Of course I'm going to accept it), was to retrieve an as-yet unspecified object or artefact, known to have been causing some problems on the west coast of Tenerife, centred around a quite exclusive girls' boarding school. Hence the reason for Mookin's selection to retrieve the item.

It was nearly time to leave and she would be accompanied by her contact from Tenerife who would be here to collect her in the next hour. Her travel documents and passport had all been prepared by Masquerade with meticulous attention to detail and were indistinguishable from the real thing. Her bags were packed: two suitcases filled with everything a modern, young, twenty-first century traveller would need in the Bigfolk world.

Firestarta was just explaining mobile phones to her and had given her something called a Samsung SX. It had two screens, the outer one which functioned as a phone, then it folded outwards to reveal a larger inner screen which became a small tablet. It would work the same as Bigfolk phones but, she had been informed, the inside was not accessible. The inside of hers was Mook-built by the Masquerade tech department, including a case which was a solar cell, so it never needed charging. If anyone attempted to open it, the inside would fizzle and burn. She also had a laptop for school work, and on which were crash courses in Bigfolk music, youth culture, slang, mannerisms and how to fit in; she was bemused but getting used to it. Her hair they had decided could stay its natural purple. Striking as it was, it went with her new persona of being slightly rebellious.

There was so much still to learn, especially about the internet, which she was struggling to understand, but they had run out of time. Firestarta gave her a ten second hi-speak on the subject, which would take care of the basics, he said. She would unzip it later.

Her new mobile chirped with an incoming text. 'I thought these things didn't work here because of PE?' asked Mookin.

'They don't normally. Yours is Mook-made, so that should only be from another Mookout,' explained Firestarta.

Tapping the inbox icon revealed a single new message.

'Who in the world is Ziggy when he's at home?'

'Ah, that will be your contact in the Canaries, runs the Tenerife office. Young but very capable. In fact, he put together this whole mission, so pay attention to him, Betty. What does he say?'

'ETA ten minutes,' quoted Mookin.

Persi stepped back saying, 'Okay Mookin, you're as ready as I can make you. Just relax and you'll fit right in.' He took a last look at his creation: faded black designer jeans with ankle boots which only had a slight heel as Mookin was quite tall, purple scoop-necked sweater, studded leather belt with large buckle, black leather bolero jacket with studded lapels and a sequinned beret. She was also sporting numerous rings on her fingers and a dozen silver bangles on each wrist. Her nails had been manicured and painted with clear nail varnish. Bood had trimmed and washed her hair earlier, but it was essentially unchanged, just waxed and spiked in a random style. She wasn't comfortable, but would get used to it, she was sure.

'I think you're ready,' said Firestarta, looking at her reflection in the full-length mirror.

'Yes, I think you're right.' She hugged each of them in turn, Persi, Bood, Firestarta. She saved Mo for last.

After the trip to Mookout's Rock, they had grown closer still, if that were possible. They now shared so much, they were almost like twins, despite the enormous age difference.

'Time to go, Mookin,' said Mo.

Mookin, Mo and Firestarta made their way to the gym, which was often used as a jumping-off point, as all Mookouts knew it so well. Mookin was carrying a shoulder bag in black leather which contained her laptop in its case – she hadn't even switched it on yet. Her mobile was zipped into her jacket pocket. Firestarta was pulling a suitcase on wheels and carrying a slightly smaller one. He stopped just inside the gym, took Mookin's face in his hands and looked up into her eyes.

'Take care. No pressure. If you can't get it done for any reason, get the hell out; we'll regroup and try something else. Clear?'

'Crystal.'

The familiar ripping sound that announced the opening of a D-way came from the centre of the gym, accompanied by a brief flash of blue light. Silhouetted in the D-way was a tall figure who stepped through without hesitation. The D-way closed behind him.

'Evening, Mo. Commander.' And turning to Mookin, 'And you must be our new recruit?'

'Evening, Ziggy,' they replied together.

'Mookin, may I introduce Zenovia Ziggymook? Ziggy, this is Mookin Bettymook.'

'Hiya, Mookin. I said hello at Mookout's Rock, but I was just one of the many, so you probably didn't notice.'

'Um, no. Sorry,' said Mookin, who was suddenly uncharacteristically shy.

'So, what name have you been stuck with for this trip? I got Ziggy Stardust, would you believe.' Ziggy, too, was acting a little strangely, Mo noticed. Very hyped-up and unusually talkative. He glanced at his wristwatch.

'Yikes, is that the time? We'd best be off.' He grabbed Mookin's cases and turned towards the doorway, which was, of course, not there. He looked over his shoulder, grinning. 'Did that close? I meant to leave it open. Would you mind, Commander?'

'Back of the shop?' he asked. Ziggy nodded, Firestarta opened a D-way with the merest flick of his left hand and Ziggy stepped through.

Mookin turned her back on the D-way, facing Mo, and said, around a big cheesy grin and so quietly only she could hear, 'Where have you been hiding him?'

Mo beamed back, whispering, 'No romance until *after* the job is done.' She kissed Mookin on her bright red cheek. 'Go on, be off with you.' Mookin turned and ran, pausing only to kiss Firestarta firmly on the cheek, and side-stepped into her future.

The D-way zipped shut, but Firestarta stayed, looking at the place where it had been. Mo came and stood next to him, putting her hand on his folded arm. 'She'll be fine. She's the best we've ever turned out.'

'I know, I know. I just want to be there, keeping an eye on them. Keeping them safe.'

'You know full well we can't leave the island for any length of time. Not enough to be useful. Otherwise we'd both be out there saving the planet again, fighting the good fight, like the old days. It's their turn now.'

'Yes, dearest. If only these bloody Bigfolk would sort themselves out. All the models predicted they would be ready by now. I don't understand it.'

'Tinka says we are getting old and maudlin. Perhaps he's right. Come on, I think it's curry for tea tonight.'

Mookin stepped out into, well, quite a cramped space, she had to admit, quite unexpectedly. She didn't know *what* she had been expecting, though. It was a storeroom of some kind, or a pantry. There seemed to be shelves and boxes everywhere. There were sacks of flour on a rack, a row of floor-to-ceiling fridges on one wall and a stack of yellow buckets. Ziggy's back was towards her. He'd put her cases down and was peeking through a sliver of open door. He closed it again, turned to Mookin and said, 'Okay, coast is clear.'

'Pardon?'

'Coast is clear, oh, I see. It um, means there's no one outside, it's clear. We can proceed.'

'Why are we still here, then?' *Gosh, why am I being so sharp with him?* she thought.

'Erm, quite.' He picked up her bags again, struggled to open the door and went through into the next room, which was almost identical, but not as cramped.

'Ziggy, where are we?'

'Tell you all in a sec. What do I call you by the way? Your cover?'

'Oh, yeah, sorry, Lyzabeth. Lyzabeth Farre. Betty for short.'

'Okay Betty, or Ms Farre. Give me two minutes and I'll be back. We can get you out of here and on with your briefing, okay?'

Ziggy vanished before Mookin had had time to reply. She sat on the chair. *Phew, tense*, she thought. *Gosh, this was silly. He's not the only boy you've known. He is flupping gorgeous, though.* Slightly taller than Mookin, deeply tanned, dimple in his chin, thick, wavy black hair – dyed, of course. Very muscular – was that part of his masque she wondered? *Red polo shirt, brown baggy shorts, flip flops. Oh, pack it in, Mookin!*

Mookin jumped when the door opened again. Ziggy grabbed her bags and said, 'Okey dokey, then.' She followed him into a fully equipped industrial kitchen in stainless steel, all function, no form, and through into a darkened restaurant. He put her bags down yet again, waving at a booth with padded bench seats.

'Have a seat, Betty. Can I get you anything?'

'Um, coffee would be nice, thanks.' Mookin pronounced it 'kawfee'.

'Ah, only got coffee I'm afraid. Not quite the same. Bigfolk drink. Not bad, but not as good as ours. You do get used to it though. The Columbian is good, have that if you can get it. I don't have any here, though. I'm babbling, aren't I?'

'Just water then, please.'

He returned moments later with two clear plastic bottles of water with blue labels with the word *Firgas* on them. He unscrewed both tops, gave one to Mookin. The bottle quickly misted up on the outside and it was as cold as mountain spring water. It tasted fine.

'You have to go through immigration first,' he told her. 'There has to be a record of you arriving on the island. You are booked on a flight from Birmingham, ticket stub and boarding pass are here,' he slid them over the table. 'It lands in about...' glancing at his expensive-looking watch again, 'thirty minutes. Don't worry about who was on the plane in your place, that's all taken care of. Even the cabin crew, if questioned, will swear they remember you. *Purple hair? Yes, she was on our flight.* I've just got to insert you into the arrivals hall at the right moment.' Ziggy produced printed luggage tags and threaded them through the handles of her cases.

'Ziggy, where are we? It's some kind of restaurant, isn't it?'

'What? Oh, yes. You probably won't know. They always leave this bit out. This is what the Bigfolk call Pizza House. It's part of a big chain. Hundreds of them, all over the world, every city has one, pretty much. Larger cities can have several. This one is located at Tenerife Airport, *Sur Reina Sofia,* named after Queen Sofia, or was. They call it Tenerife South now. Preferred the old name myself.' Mookin just stared.

'Was I babbling again? Sorry. So, I've closed the restaurant early, no more departures today anyway. It's all part of the cover we use out among the Bigfolk. Not such Bigfolk compared to us mind, eh? More sort of your average folk, I'd say.'

This last part threw Mookin for a second, then she realised what he was on about. 'What do you mean? I've never actually met any Bigfolk, only seen pictures.'

'Oh, of course. Sorry, keep forgetting, you're new. Well, you and I, we fit right in. Most Bigfolk are about our size, a little bigger boned, certainly, but not any taller.'

'I didn't know that. I always thought they were huge.'

'No, far from it. You *can* get some big ones, but few and far between.'

'Well, that's a relief. How does closing the restaurant work? Are you the manager?'

'Um, kind of. They just haven't told you, have they? Back at the Tree?'

'Told me what?'

'Betty, we own Pizza House, lock, stock and most of the barrels too.'

'I don't understand this. How can we own it? Wouldn't that cost a lot of Bigfolk money?'

'Mookin, we have more money than most countries. We own the internet too, well a large part of it. We own big chunks of Goggle and Bookface, quite a bit of Sicromoft and others too. It all started with Goggle. When they came out with GoggleEarth, we had to do something, couldn't risk Mookination being seen by satellites and aerial photos. We've infiltrated dozens, possibly hundreds of companies and organisations, all to protect Mookination.'

'But how? Where does the money come from? It must have cost a huge amount.'

'Mookin, what do you think happens to all the decayed plasmics? We've got more gold than all the governments on Earth put together. We have so much, we don't know what to do with it.'

'I don't know what to say; that's incredible.'

He handed her an envelope containing a large quantity of euros. 'Pocket money. You'll soon get the hang of it. You also have credit cards in your wallet, but remember, you can't take anything home with you.'

For the next twenty minutes, Ziggy briefed her on the mission. Handing over a micro SD card that held all the information she would need: maps, plans, alarm systems, CCTV cameras etc. It would fit her phone or her laptop. Briefing over, he then led her through a back door into a service corridor, and from there, down some metal stairs to another door. He paused. 'Well, good luck, Betty. Any queries, just text me. If you're in trouble send me 999 and I'll come running. If you're in serious trouble,' he tapped his forehead, 'use the MuRM and we'll all come running.'

They hadn't had time to test that out, so she stopped him from opening the door. 'Wait.' She closed her eyes, reached inwards, found the place, dived in. It was like swimming in crystal clear water with a tinge of blue all around. There were sparks, bright points in the water. She reached out, pinged the nearest, the brightest, which was, of course, Ziggy.

'Hi,' he said.

'Hi,' she replied. That was where it all started, really.

As before, he cracked the door open a tiny sliver and peeked through. 'Okay – now!' Mookin slipped through, unnoticed, in a CCTV blind spot, into the baggage claim area of Tenerife South airport, following the general stream of people moving towards immigration, and was soon queuing with everyone else. They slowly moved forward towards the customs officer in his glass cubicle, bored but vigilant, opening, looking, checking, stamping. Repeat.

Finally, it was Mookin's turn. She pulled her cases forward, stopped, passed her documents under the glass and across the counter. The officer looked at her and she smiled back nervously. He examined her passport and fed it into a scanner which beeped its acceptance.

'Negocios o placer, señorita?'

'Pardon? Perdóname?'

'Your trip, is it for business or pleasure, señorita?'

'Ni el señor, yo voy a la escuela en la isla.'

'Ah si, I understand. You are to attend *escuela*, school?'

'Yes sir, school.'

He again checked her face against the passport, then with a flourish and a stamp, her passport was sliding back to her across the counter.

'Disfrutar de su estancia, la bienvenida a Tenerife Señorita Lyzabeth Farre. *Enjoy your stay, welcome to Tenerife, Ms Lyzabeth Farre.*'

Mookin put her passport and travel documents into her shoulder bag and hitched it further up her shoulder. Grabbing the extending handles of her suitcases, one in each hand she smiled at him.

'Gracias señor. Estoy seguro de que lo hará. A lo grande. *Thank you, sir. I'm sure I will. Big time.*'

The End

Epilogue

Return of the Mutineer

Tenerife:

Tenerife is, with its area of 2,034km² (785 sq mi), the most extensive island of the Canaries. In addition, with 904,713 inhabitants, it is the most populated island of the archipelago and Spain. Two of the island's principal cities are located in the north: The capital, Santa Cruz de Tenerife and San Cristóbal de La Laguna (a World Heritage site). San Cristóbal de La Laguna, the second city of the island, is home to the oldest university in the Canaries, the University of La Laguna. El Teide (no English translation) reaches 3,718 metres (12,198ft) above sea level, making it the highest peak in Spain and also a World Heritage site. It is also the third tallest volcano on Earth on a volcanic ocean island*. The municipality of Icod de los Vinos in the north east of Tenerife is home to the Cueva del Viento-Sobrado caves. This is Europe's largest lava tube and is considered to be the fifth largest in the world after four of Hawaii's volcanic wonders. Its underground passageways form tunnels spanning over 17km (10 miles).

Wikipedia

* fourth, see Mookipedia.

He checked his watch for the fourth time in ten minutes: 7.30 p.m. Too early to go to bed. He could go into town, grab a meal and a few beers? Pop in to see Jake? He felt restless. He wanted to *do* something. He needed something physical to occupy his hands and take his thoughts away. He had come here for some peace and quiet, it was true, but he was coming to the conclusion that he just wasn't cut out for the quiet life.

Tenerife.

He had been here only once before, lifetimes ago.

233

Something had drawn him back. Three years now, he'd been here. Hiding from his past, from the nightmares that all too frequently permeated his slumber. But it was better now that he had the 'object'.

Two years now since he had found it. Discovered it in the deep darkness of the Tenerife cave system. Pure accident, but fate, surely? Why else had he been drawn here? Why else had circumstances and events led him right to the place where it was entombed?

He was close; he could feel it. Two years he'd been chipping away at the surrounding rock where it was embedded and soon he would pry it from the living mountain where it had rested for untold millennia. It was fate. It was destiny. What else could it be? He visited it whenever he could, sometimes two or three times a week. It was like a drug now. He needed it. Needed to be in its presence. He always felt complete, powerful, refreshed and elated when he was down there and he wanted that feeling whenever he chose, not just after a two-hour climb down a shaft that was barely wider than his shoulders. One, maybe two more visits and it would be his forever. He had excavated all around it until there could be nothing holding it in place apart from a tiny space at the back that he couldn't see. He had a pry-bar ready for his next visit, 1.2 metres of solid steel that should finally finish the job.

And the book. Jake had loaned him the book. And the place. He had the place ready, primed, and it *felt* right. On an impulse, he stood from his desk in the tiny cramped office that had been assigned to him, grabbed his torch from the desk drawer and turned to face the wall. He pulled the bookcase away from the wall, enough that he could squeeze behind it, and turned the knob of the door that had been boarded up, but which he'd uncovered to reveal a rickety staircase. With extreme care, in the beam of his torch, he made his way down to the cellar and opened a second door leading into the ancient vaulted basement. A vast space, as big as the huge building above. There was no sound, no scurrying of rats nor leathery flap of bats' wings, it was bone dry with a faint smell of dust.

He strode confidently halfway down and then turned right to face floor-to-ceiling wine racks. He'd done this several times already and now noticed his footprints in the dust. He would have to take care of that; he wanted no sign of his presence here. There were perhaps now only a dozen wine bottles in racks that could hold thousands, remnants of a previous era of opulence. One of them was fake.

He grasped the neck of the bottle, pulled and twisted until a section of wine rack swung towards him. Behind, a short tunnel led to a stairway that wound down into the rock. At the bottom he shone his torch around into a vast natural cavern, empty apart from a few dilapidated barrels and broken packing crates. *Smugglers*, he thought. There was another exit at the far end leading downwards at a steep angle. It smelled of seaweed and ocean. He had not yet explored it. This cave had been cleared of rubble and flattened, you could tell from the chisel marks, which were everywhere. Whatever its former use, now it was his, to do with as he pleased. In the centre, perhaps ten paces across, there was an area that had been smoothed and polished.

It was this that had given him the idea. Carved into the black stone, a hexagram, a six-pointed star set in a circle. He'd always thought witches used a five-pointed star, but some research told him that the hexagram pre-dated the pentacle by thousands of years. He had no idea how long this had been here, no idea if it helped, or if there was any credence in their use for what people called 'magic', but it told him that someone had used this place before for their experiments into the mystical realm. It was all coming together. He'd need a table, could probably get one from the piles of junk in the basement above, and candles. Lots of candles. And chalk.

He returned to his office, shoved the bookcase to its normal position and put the torch back in his desk drawer. He looked at his watch. It was 8.45 p.m. Still early.

He left the office, locking the door behind him and walked through the deserted corridors to the side entrance and back to his cabin, just inside the woods. He showered, shaved and dressed, running his hands through his thick, black hair. *Time for a haircut*, he thought. He grabbed his car keys from the dresser and his leather jacket from the hook on the back of the front door which revealed, hanging there, a battered satchel blackened with age which no one in their right mind would hang on to. He turned and regarded himself in the mirror on the adjacent wall.

He unbuttoned and opened his shirt and looked at the reflection of the sun-burst tattoo on his left breast. He had to, now and again, just to remind himself. He looked into his own eyes and, in all truth, did not mind what he saw there. *You are not a bad person*, he thought.

He spoke out loud. 'Not bad, Fletcher Christian. Not bad for a bloke in his 260s. I wonder how much time we have left?' *Christian Fletcher,* he reminded himself. That was the name on his passport. He smiled, re-buttoned his shirt and put on his jacket against the evening chill. His watch said 9.30 p.m. Los Christianos would be waking up for the evening.

Mookin will return in:

TENERIFEAN TANGLE
THE POWER OF THE RED

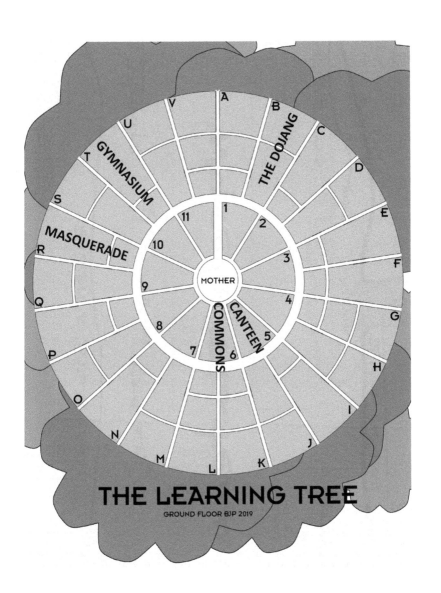

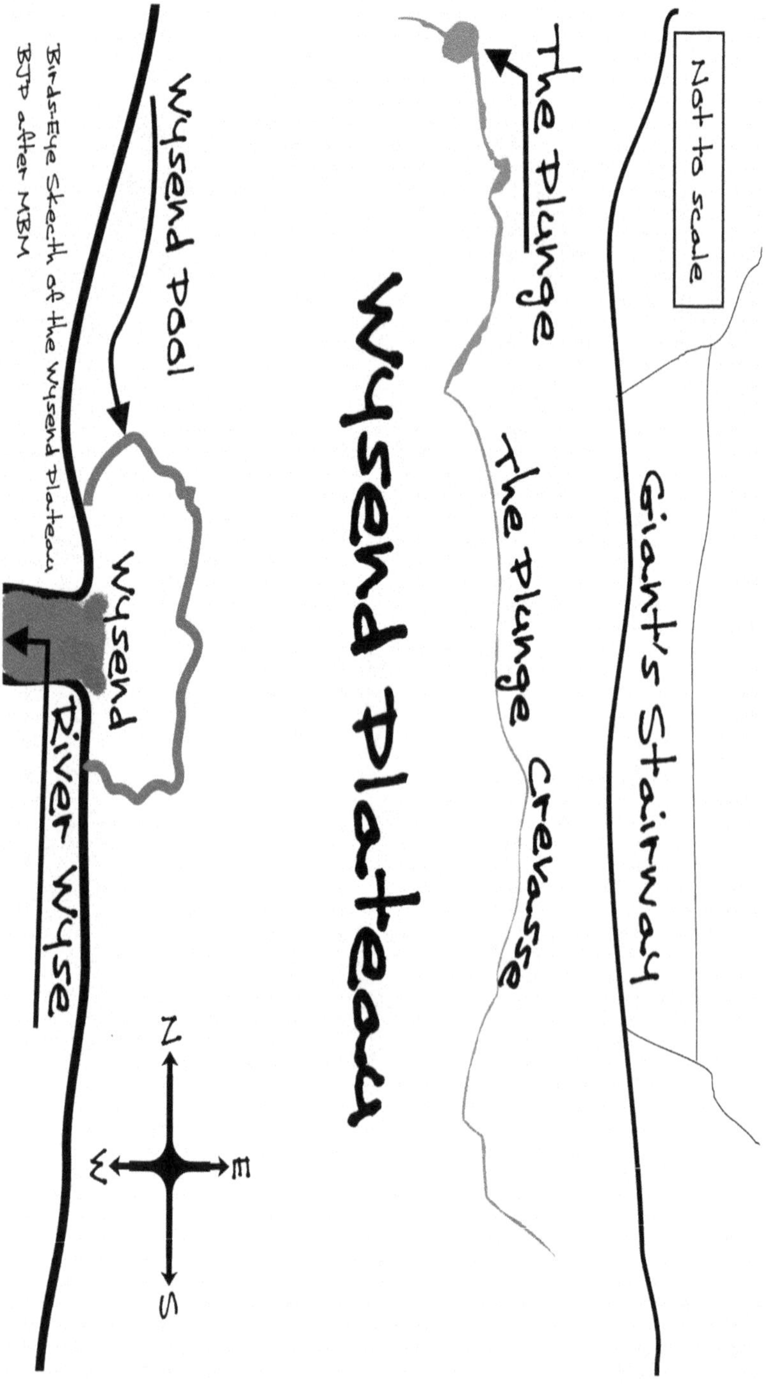

ii.

Not to scale

The Plunge

Giant's Stairway

The Plunge Crevasse

Wysend Plateau

Wysend Pool

Wysend

River Wyse

Birds-Eye Sketch of the Wysend Plateau
BJP after MBM

N
W — E
S

Please note:

Following maps contain
SPOILERS!

iii.

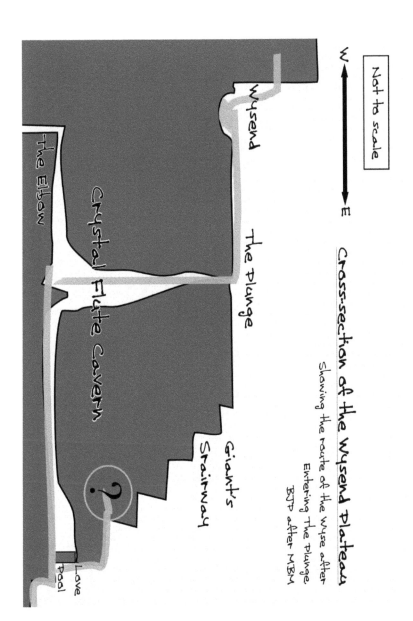

Cross-section of the Wysend Plateau

Showing the route of the Wyse after
Entering The Plunge.
BJP after MBM

W ⟷ E

Not to scale

Wysend

The Plunge

Crystal Flute Cavern

Giant's Stairway

The Elbow

Love Pool

?

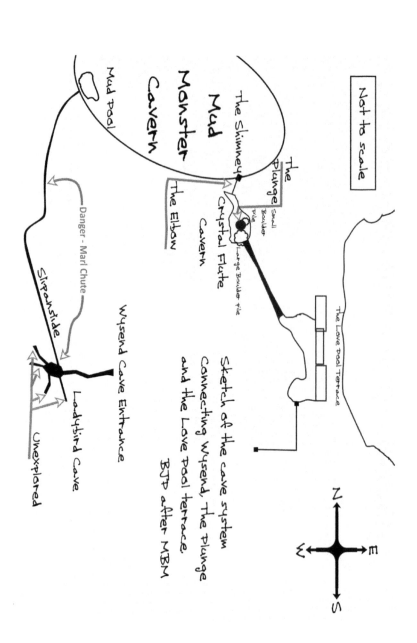

Not to scale

The Plunge

Mud Monster Cavern

The Shimmey

The Elbow

Crystal Flute Cavern

Mud Pool

Danger - Marl Chute

Sliporslide

Wysend Cave Entrance

Ladybird Cave

Unexplored

Small Boulder Pile

Large Boulder Pile

The Love Pool Terrace

Sketch of the cave system connecting Wysend, The Plunge and the Love Pool terrace.

BJP after MBM

N
W — E
S

PICCOLO PRESS

In association with

GRANDDADMADETHIS & KICKIN' DESIGN / GRAPHICS

Lightning Source UK Ltd.
Milton Keynes UK
UKHW020659040320
359750UK00011B/936